QUEST OF STONE

THE TRANSFUSION SAGA
BOOK 14

STEPHANIE HUDSON

Quest of Stone
The Transfusion Saga #14
Copyright © 2023 Stephanie Hudson
Published by Hudson Indie Ink
www.hudsonindieink.com

This book is licensed for your personal enjoyment only.
This book may not be re-sold or given away to other people. If you would like to share this book with another person, please purchase an additional copy for each recipient. If you're reading this book and did not purchase it, or it wasn't purchased for your use only, then please return to your favourite book retailer and purchase your own copy. Thank you for respecting the hard work of this author.
All rights reserved.
This is a work of fiction. Names, characters, places, brands, media, and incidents are either the product of the authors imagination or are used fictitiously. The author acknowledges the trademark status and trademark owners of various products referred to in this work of fiction, which have been used without permission. The publication/use of these trademarks is not authorised, associated with, or sponsored by the trademark owners.

Quest of Stone/Stephanie Hudson – 1st ed.
ISBN-13 - 978-1-916562-38-7

I would like to dedicate this last book to all my fans who have followed me through this journey and trusted me to tell this story the way it was always meant to be told.

As always, my heart aches at the end as I hate saying goodbye to characters I have spent years writing about. Which is most likely why we will see lots more of Lucius and Amelia in the future, making cameo appearances in other books.

As always, It has been an honour writing every word for so many amazing kind souls and I wanted you to know that I appreciate every single one of you. You bring me comfort and strength on the days I find it hard to find the right words, knowing you deserve nothing less than my very best. You drive me forward and keep me going just by knowing you are there at the ready for the story, waiting with bated breath for these characters to show themselves. That means the world to me. So please know that you have my heart on each and every page.

Thank you for supporting every word.
All my love
Eternally, yours,
Stephanie. x

I would also like to thank all those at Muncaster Castle, for

the beauty I found there inspired a writer's love of history and became the most perfect backdrop for this story to be told. If you ever get the chance to visit this wonderful place then you will not be disappointed by the beauty and historical adventure you find there.
I would also like to personally thank Claire Boyle for taking this journey with me, for she has played an integral part in discovering this story and helped me every step of the way with her honest guidance.

'A true friend is not the friend who always tells you what you want to hear but always tells you what you need to hear.'

Thank you always,
My dear friend.

PROLOGUE
AMELIA

Thunder in my heart.

That was what this felt like.

Yet even as I thought it, I still knew deep down that it was so much more than that. It felt as if I was running along wet sand and trying to catch up with the footsteps ahead of me. Trying to catch up with them before they sank away to the memories that no longer had the power to hold them to this world. As if someone had already made this journey once before and I was merely the unseen shadow that lagged behind.

Because I knew, in that moment, I wasn't the first to experience this deep-rooted fear.

The fear of that threat against my neck.

The fear of who's hand now held my life tightly in their grasp.

The fear of the love I knew he might no longer feel for me, not after I had broken his trust.

For I may have been the Keeper of his heart in my future…

But right now, I was his prey.
And he was my hunter in my…

Quest of Stone.

CHAPTER 1
LIA EARHART STRIKES AGAIN

The very last sight I ever thought I would cruelly be forced to witness was what faced me now. What was his past now became my painful present, as across the room there he was.

There was my Chosen One.

There was my Vampire King.

And he was kissing someone else.

The moment I saw this, two things happened simultaneously, the first was that it felt like my heart had just been shattered into a million pieces. And the second was when I turned quickly, only to bang my tray into a marble bust of none other than the image of my father. Thankfully it only wobbled slightly. However, what drew everyone's attention to me was the echoing sound of the single glass falling from my tray and shattering on the floor. It was one that someone must have placed on my tray when I had been transfixed for a moment on the sight of Lucius kissing another woman. But for seconds I couldn't help but stare at all that glittering glass in pieces on the floor, feeling that the symbolic sight now mirrored that of my heart.

I managed to keep hold of the tray at least, but party goers gave me a wide berth and scowled at me as if what I had done had been a crime. I don't know why, but I quickly looked back at Lucius, and the horror of what I had just done by drawing attention to myself must have played on my face. He found me in the sea of people, lifting his head up from where he'd been kissing the mystery woman's neck.

His gaze seemed to burn into mine and soon I saw that questioning frown frame steel blue eyes, making me instantly internally panic. I also knew that, most likely, over fifty percent of the guests in this room could hear my erratic heartbeat. It was the one good thing in my favour as that was a natural reaction after just dropping a wine glass and smashing it.

However, what no one knew was that the heart hammering in my chest was not down to broken glass at all, but from seeing my husband with his arms around another woman. Of course, no matter how much I tried to rationalize this as not being a betrayal, especially, considering Lucius didn't even know I existed (and technically, I didn't in this time), it didn't mean my heart survived the sight without taking a hit.

The last I saw of Lucius was him whispering something in the woman's ear, making me turn away quickly before I found myself faced with who looked like the butler furiously scowling down at me. He was an older man, with a mostly bald head, beady brown eyes made even smaller due to frowning, thin lips and a beak like nose giving him an air of arrogance. Naturally, he was dressed immaculately, in a black suit with tales at the back of his double-breasted jacket.

"Pick it all up and do it quietly, girl!" he ordered through the grit of his teeth before ushering another maid through the

door to come and take my place offering fresh refreshments. This then granted me some peace as he walked away scowling, leaving me to clear the mess I had made, thankfully leading partygoers' eyes away from me on my knees picking up pieces of glass and putting them on the tray.

"Good job... Perfect, just perfect, clumsy hands," I muttered, chastising myself and resisting the urge to swear just in time. Especially when suddenly as I was about to stand, I found a hand come into my peripheral vision. But it wasn't just any hand... no, *it was one I would have known anywhere.* One that had strong, thick pale fingers that had more often than not been entwined with my own. Or in contrast had been felt collaring my throat in a possessive hold of ownership I adored in the bedroom.

It was of course...
Lucius's hand.

"Then please allow me to help you to your perfect feet," he said, mocking what he had obviously heard me muttering to myself. Of course, hearing his voice and having him now standing next to where I was still crouched down, made my heart hammer even faster in my chest. I started to shake my head refusing to look up at him, telling him in a quiet voice,

"That's quite alright, kind sir. I can manage." I heard him scoff before telling me,

"It's been quite some time since I've been referred to as a kind anything, the sentiment is most certainly novel and despite the many that would disagree with your assumption of me, I must insist... *now take my hand, girl."* I swallowed the hard lump at the stern order given at the end, one that had been a stark contrast to the amusing tone before it. I also knew that I would only end up drawing more attention to myself should I refuse again. So, because I had no other choice, I placed my hand in his, holding the rim of the silver tray sturdy with my other before I allowed him to help me to my feet.

However, the moment I did place my hand in his, he tensed his fingers around my own, making me wonder if I wasn't the only one that felt the connection between us. It was like an unspoken, sexually charged static that didn't sting and bite at our skin, but instead just made it tingle with a comforting heat.

I tried to act like this didn't affect me as I rose to my feet with his help. Although, I still refused to look at him, keeping my gaze lowered, not knowing what I would do if I was forced to take in his grey-blue eyes up close. Eyes that I had, more often than not, gladly found myself lost in. Eyes that if I was forced to look in now, my own would no doubt produce tears.

"Thank you, Sir," I said, this time keeping out the kind part of that statement, making him chuckle.

"I see you're a fast learner. What is your name, girl?" I closed my eyes for a few seconds too long before answering, and what I deemed was the only way I was going to get out of this without giving him my name.

"I'm a person of little consequence, if you please, I must get back to my work," I said and then because I forgot the pain it would cause, I looked up at him and the second I did, his eyes widened in surprise. It was as if now being able to see all of my face had cast him into some kind of spell. He was certainly affected but then, he wasn't the only one.

Lucius was dressed very similar to my father, and what was obviously considered the known style for a ball. However, whereas my father's jacket was purple, Lucius's was a deep navy colour, bringing out the flecks of blue in his eyes, something that was worn with a shorter ivory waistcoat underneath. It was also one that matched the colour of his breeches that fastened at the knee. His sandy hair was also longer than I was used to seeing and was currently tied back from his face, making him look even more strikingly handsome.

But like I said, I wasn't the only one affected by our encounter. I knew this because the second I snatched my hand out of his own, his reactions clearly hadn't been fast enough, seemingly too distracted by our contact. I could sense his displeasure, and I swear I heard the slightest of growls. A sound that told me that if he had been expecting my quick departure, he would have done something to prevent it. And that hand around mine would have tightened to prevent me from leaving.

But then I knew for this time period it would have looked odd to see a noble man conversing with a servant that was not his own. Which then had to make me wonder why he did so, and so openly in front of others of his rank. Then again, Lucius usually did what he wanted, so why I thought he would be any different in any other time I didn't know.

However, as for now, I quickly bowed a little, thinking this was most likely the right response, and made my escape. Doing so before he could say anything else, meaning that I was now practically running to the kitchen. And with each quickening step I made, I did so with the sound of my heart pounding and the tinkling of glass bouncing on the silver try. I dumped the tray on the nearest surface I could get away with and ran to the first dark corner so I could catch my breath.

"You foolish girl!" the butler snarled at me from behind, making me gasp the second he grabbed my arm and swung me round to face him. Then he practically threw me up against the wall, before stepping into my space.

"Just what do you think you were doing speaking so openly to Lord Septimus?!" the butler snarled at me, his skin turning red in his anger.

"I… he offered me his hand, what was I to do, slap it away?!" I argued back and then got the shock of my life when he reacted.

"Insolent girl! How dare you speak back at me!" He suddenly slapped me, making my head whip to the side, and I gritted my teeth as the hit obviously reopened the cut on my forehead. I knew this as I felt a trickle of blood drip down my cheek from beneath my bonnet.

I took a deep breath, readying myself to put this asshole in his place, when suddenly I felt a whoosh of air and the man that had been in front of me was now gone. I looked to the side to find him now pinned to the wall with a hand around his throat. Oh, and that hand was one that had not long ago been gently offered to me, only now, it was doing it again but in a far more brutal way.

"You dare hit a woman I have chosen to converse with!"

"N-n-no… My Lord, I… I…" The butler stuttered and before this could get even more out of hand and draw the attention of say, my father, well this was my time to react. So, I rushed over to him and despite him now looking furious, and scary with it, I knew he would never hurt me. This was confirmed as soon as I wrapped my hand around his wrist, as it seemed to have enough of an effect on him that it brought him back to his senses. Meaning he dropped the man before he could choke him to death, making him land on the floor in a heap coughing as he tried to gain back his breath.

"I'm… sorry, My Lord, my… my grave apology, My

Lord," the man stammered out, now clutching his sore throat as if he could still feel Lucius's grip there.

"It will be your grave indeed if I see you hit another woman... now go and leave her to me!" At this the butler quickly scrambled back to his feet and ran down the corridor as quickly as he could. I was breathing heavily but it was nothing compared to when I felt my face being lifted to his.

"You're bleeding?" he stated the obvious, make me reach up and do the same by touching my forehead.

"I..." I didn't know what to say, but then I was forced to find some words, and quickly, as his features turned murderous. Especially when he turned his dark foreboding gaze back down the corridor as if he was seconds away from hunting the man down and snapping his neck. I had to question why he was having such a violent reaction to what essentially should have been seeing a nobody maid getting slapped for not doing their job well enough. Yes, it was a harsh punishment for sure but in the era I was in, it was most likely one that happened more often than not.

"It... it wasn't him... I fell, a day ago, for I am clumsy and..."

"You lie, for this is fresh," he stated sternly, cutting me off with his fearsome narrow gaze. I took a deep breath and said,

"It must have reopened, that is all."

"If you think by telling me untruths it will save the cretin from my wrath, you are mistaken, for I saw him strike you," Lucius replied, his voice cutting like a blade.

"He struck me, yes, but I promise, he did not cause this, My Lord." At this he sighed before he pulled a handkerchief from his pocket, and came closer to me, making me take a step back. He didn't like this reaction to him as he frowned and made a sound like he was displeased.

"Be assured, girl, I will not hurt you. Now hold still." He took another step towards me, and my back was suddenly against the wall meaning I had nowhere else to go. Clearly, Lucius had not instantly recognized that I was his Chosen One, making me wonder if Pip was somewhere close by preventing this from happening.

However, I didn't know just how far her powers of persuasion could reach, not when he came this close to my blood. His eyes heated the moment he saw it and I knew he was scenting it in the air. He even licked his lips, despite it being done in a subtle way. I held perfectly still when he reached up, pushing my hair and my cap back, before dabbing the cut and making me wince back from his touch.

"Easy now," he cooed gently before wiping away the blood and holding it to my forehead, now applying enough pressure to try and get the bleeding to stop. Although, soon, another voice was added to the party, and I instantly froze because of it.

"What is this, my second in command has found a broken bird to mend?" The sound of my father's voice made me tense all over. It came from behind Lucius and he looked at me with curious eyes, obviously not missing my reaction. However, he must have read my unease as fear, as once again he was soothing me with a simple sound before comforting words followed,

"Ssshh… now take a breath, little one." I nodded a little, telling him I would and with a brief glance down at my chest, it was clear he was waiting to see the evidence for himself. Only then when he saw it lift as I filled my lungs did he acknowledge my father by taking a step back away from me.

"I believe your butler's hard handedness towards the rest of your staff is unacceptable, My Lord." At this I watched my father frown before stepping closer, now taking Lucius's place. He then took hold of my chin, before lifting my face up making me wince. It was so odd being this close to my father and having to pretend he was nothing more than an employer to me. But then again, it was just as hard trying to pretend Lucius wasn't the love of my life and the man I called my husband.

"Jacobs did this?" My father asked, making me stutter,

"I…"

"Speak, girl, for I have no patience to be away from my betrothed for long," my father demanded in a hard tone.

"She would, should you choose not to crowd her," Lucius said, standing up for me, and my father gave him a curious smirk.

"¿Esta mortal significa algo para ti?" my father asked in Spanish and because I spoke the language, I knew he had just asked him,

'This mortal means something to you?' and Lucius's answer to this was a simple,

"Sí," which of course meant yes in return.

"Ah, then I see I am not the only one afflicted by a beautiful face, for to be sure, she is a pretty little thing, however damaged. Now answer me, did my butler do this to you?" my father asked again, and this time in a significantly gentler tone. I swallowed hard and answered more promptly this time.

"He struck me, yes, but the cut on my head I received from my own clumsiness, My Lord, just as I was telling… uh, My Lord here," I said, bumbling for what I should call either of them, making Lucius smirk and my father raised an amused brow.

"He is your Lord, yet you serve in my household?" he

asked with a raise of his brow and because I knew my father well, I knew he was also teasing.

"I… no… erm, I am here working in your home, My Lord, for the ball and…"

He raised a hand, making me stop talking and Lucius simply stood back and looked amused, despite his arms behind crossed.

"Now that is curious, indeed for perhaps my second, you are willing to take on this broken little bird and offer her a stronger wing, as it is clear she is new here and needs guidance under a different Lord perhaps." I nearly choked hearing this, whereas Lucius simply smirked as I knew now what my father was doing.

"Or are you not in the mind to employ any more staff at present, for am I not right in saying you arrived without a footman?" my father asked with an amused tone, making me internally panic as it was clear now that, strangely, my father was currently playing matchmaker! He then turned to look back at Lucius who hadn't taken his eyes from me this whole time.

"Unless of course there isn't something different about this one?" Again, my father's question would have been confusing to anyone else, but it was clear as day to me. He was asking Lucius if I was something special to him, and perhaps this day was the time for more than one King to find his mortal Chosen One.

"Oh, she is different all right, and like you have so kindly pointed out, my friend, I am in need of a new housemaid and did indeed travel without my footman, so am in need of assistance while I am here… and she will do, *oh so nicely."* I swallowed hard at this and all the hidden sexual overtones in that sentence, as this last part he had almost purred the words!

"Well, girl, what say you? For I release you of any claim I

have on your employment and put you in the hands of my second, who it seems is in great need of you," my father said, making me wonder how the Hell I was going to get out of this one.

"I... well, it is a great honour to be considered but I fear I am vastly unprepared for such a... erm... undertaking." At this my father looked even more amused and after taking a step away from me, he slapped Lucius on the back and said,

"Well now, it looks as if your charms must be slipping... However, I will once more come to your rescue, old friend, and say as such... while you are still under my employment, then I will assign your duties to aid my friend here for the duration that he is a guest staying in my house, for he is foolishly without a footman." I opened my mouth about to speak when my father held up his hand again and continued,

"I know assigning a woman to the job is somewhat unorthodox but where our Lord here originates from, it is quite usual, isn't that so?"

"Indeed," Lucius said with a smirk, clearly loving the fact that he was getting his way and finding himself entertained that I was getting steamrolled into this.

"And this way you can gain knowledge first-hand and discover the truth of his temperament, seeing for yourself if you could live with his brooding countenance." At this Lucius rolled his eyes.

"I thank you for such praise, dear friend," Lucius said sarcastically, making my father laugh again.

"You never know, something may come along that has the ability to make even you smile... but until then, you'll be staying in your usual room, and seeing as he arrived only a short time ago, perhaps you could start your new duties by unpacking his things. If that is acceptable to you as someone who potentially will become her new Lord?" my father said, glancing back at Lucius like this was already decided whether I cared for it or not.

"If it keeps her out of the way of that damned butler of yours, then yes, I would prefer that be the first of her duties," Lucius replied, scowling down the hallway as if the butler was still there hiding.

"You leave that Jacobs to me, for he will be back to being a second footman before long. Why don't you run along and take this opportunity to get yourself cleaned up, my dear," my father said, and I had to wonder if the reason he was being so nice to me now was because he felt guilty that I had been struck under his home? Or was it because of what I clearly meant to Lucius? In fact, I as so stuck on this question I nearly missed Lucius quietly asking my father his own,

"Her name?" I barely caught Lucius whisper this to my father after I bowed and bid them a good evening before trying to walk away.

"Wait… I believe you have yet to give my friend here your name," my father asked, making me sigh before my shoulders slumped. Then I gave them both a name I never thought I would ever hear myself use again.

"But of course, My Lord, my name is, Lia my Lord, Lia Earhart," I said as it was the first name to mind, especially considering I had used it once before when trying to elude Lucius and well, it only seemed fitting.

"Very well, it is a pleasure, Miss Earhart, for I have a feeling I will be seeing you again… and under quite different circumstances," my father said, bowing his head in respect, and I knew then it was most likely he was under the impression I was Lucius's Chosen One.

"Indeed," Lucius agreed, making me blush and suddenly I knew how my mother had felt. Because it wasn't what my father thought that had me worried. No, it was what Lucius

thought I was to him, as this definitely made shit more complicated.

I quickly bowed again and made my exit and the second I was out of sight, I leaned against the nearest wall, placed a hand to my pounding chest, and muttered,

"Now what the Hell do I do?"

CHAPTER 2
RULES OF TIME TRAVEL

"There you are!" Pip said, drawing me out of my inner panic. I grabbed her and pulled her closer until both of us were hidden around the corner.

"We have a big problem," I hissed in hush tones.

"Yeah, I know, that's kind of what we're here for, Sugar," Pip said, jerking her head back towards the ballroom.

"No, what I mean is, now we have an even bigger problem… Lucius is here!" I said after looking around the corner to make sure we were still alone.

"Oh Sasquatch… yeah, you should stay away from him." At this I shook my head a little, trying to gain patience despite the situation quickly draining it from my body.

"Yeah, well, it's a little late for that." I told her, making her raise a brow before asking,

"Just how late is it?"

"It's a train that totally missed the station, in fact it missed every damn station there ever was… *think freight train without the brakes!"* I said this last part after gripping the tops of her arms, making her eyes widen.

"Diddle darn, yeah, that doesn't sound good," she agreed as I was completely losing it, now holding my head and muttering over and over,

"No, no, no, no...."

"Okay, you're gonna have to stop repeating the same word, honey, and give me more of them by leaving out the locomotive here. So, let's go with what makes sense and, yes, I see the irony here considering this sentence just came from out of my mouth."

I had to agree with her on that, but then looking at Pip now and I had to admit it was the most normal I had ever seen her. No piercings, her tattoos were covered and she had no crazy makeup or accessories. Her usual mad hair colour was covered with a dark wig and her clothes were plain like mine. It was like someone had doused out my own personal rainbow and it didn't bring me comfort but only emphasized where we were… or more like, *where we weren't.*

"Okay, so short version, I saw him kissing another woman, I broke a glass, caused a stir, got shouted at to pick it up by some asshole prick, Lucius came over and helped me in front of everybody, which caused an even bigger stir, I ran, got slapped in the face by the same asshole butler, Lucius saw this, he then gallantly intervened, the heroic act conquered my heart, oh and then my father came and found out that Lucius wanted me as his own personal maid, so pretty much gave me to him. Now I am on my way to clean my face and to unpack his clothes… seriously, how does this shit happen to me in the space of being here for not even a day?!" I said, now breathing even harder but when she didn't reply, I hissed her name,

"Pip!"

"Oh, that was an actual question, and you wanted an

answer to it, uh... just unlucky I guess," she said with a shrug of her little shoulders. My mouth dropped before asking,

"Really, that's all you've got?"

"Okay look, I got my mojo working overtime here, our biggest hope is he just fancies you." Her reply made me shake my head a little as if I had just heard her wrong.

"I'm sorry?"

"Or perhaps he just wants a bit of a holiday fling while he's here," she added. My mouth dropped again, making me wonder if I was starting to resemble a fish.

"But it's forbidden," I reminded her in a shocked tone, something that caused her to burst out laughing.

"He's the King of Vampires."

"Yeah, I kinda got that memo before I married him, Pip... what's your point?"

"So, you really think a bit of forbidden candy isn't going to make him lick his lips and open his mouth?" Again, this was another fish moment.

"Okay, we are really going to have to work on your analogies and pick ones where it doesn't make me sound like a tasty treat... besides, why would my father openly be okay with that?" I asked.

"I don't know, because maybe he's just found his own bit of mortal candy that he can't wait to stick his... Okay, I'm stopping before I finish that sentence because I don't want you to wig out even more than you already are." I rolled my eyes at this and muttered,

"Gee, thanks." Naturally my naughty Imp of an aunt smirked at this.

"Look, my point is, he shouldn't know that you're his Chosen One." I thought about this and decided not to tell her what was hinted at between Lucius and my father. Because if Pip was wrong and Lucius did know, then it wasn't like we could do much about it and I didn't want Pip worrying that her mojo was off.

"So, you're telling me he wants me to become his maid slash piece of mortal fluff on the side?" I asked, making her pat my hand before telling me,

"Oh sweetheart, you're way more than mortal fluff, besides you can't have sex with him anyway." This last part was what worried me the most as it was said in a way like I should have known this.

"Okay, so pretending that I haven't taken the course on time travel and it's been a while since I have watched the Back to the Future trilogy, remind me again why I can't sleep with him?" I asked, already wondering how I could manage it so as I was never alone with him.

"Oh, so you wanna sleep with him?" she said in a knowing tone wagging her eyebrows.

"Pip!" I shouted, forgetting myself and now looking around the corner again making sure this mad conversation wasn't being overheard.

"Okay, here it is, time traveling 101…" she paused so she could reel off these pointers on her fingers,

"No seeing your past self. No getting dead."

"Really, no getting dead is one of the rules of time travel?" I asked sarcastically.

"Hey, you wanted the list."

"Yeah, I know, I know… please continue," I replied with a roll of my hand.

"No coming out and saying that you're somebody's Chosen One." I released a sigh and agreed,

"Okay, that I can do, what's the next?"

"No sleeping with your Chosen One," she said, getting to the part I really needed to know.

"Right, now that one, explain that one to me in detail."

"My mojo will only work so far, you sleep with him or feed him your blood or any other... well, you get the picture... he will know that you're his Chosen One... which means..."

"Time traveling game over," I finished for her.

"I mean it's not like we will get sucked back to our own time or anything but yeah, obsession, addiction, caveman behaviour ensures, princess prison tower... you get the picture."

"I'm screwed," I replied, rubbing my forehead and catching my cut making me hiss.

"No, being screwed is precisely the opposite of what we're trying to achieve here," Pip pointed out, making me point out something obvious in return,

"Yeah, big problem with that is, this is Lucius we are talking about."

"Haven't you ever said no to him?" Pip asked and again, I was once more pointing out the obvious.

"Have you ever said no to Adam?"

"Oh I could never resist Adam... right, gotcha," she replied, quickly getting it.

"What am I gonna do?" I asked, letting my head fall back against the stone wall and wincing, forgetting that I was still kind of tender all over my head.

"First things first, let's get you cleaned up, and then unpack his stuff."

"That's not much of a plan," I said with a wince.

"Okay, so unpack his stuff at the speed of light and then get the Hell out of there. I mean, you are a maid, which means you're there to do a job, so he's not going to expect you to be sitting in his room waiting for him." I nodded, thinking this sounded like a better, more comforting plan.

"I could do that... I mean the speed of light unpacking thing, not the waiting in his room like some sex starved puppy."

"Also, something to consider in case he does come back quickly and finds you not speed of lightning the shit out of unpacking his clothes."

"What's that?" I asked, wondering what else I could do to get away from him.

"Most chicks of this era save their virginity for their wedding night. I mean, granted, you are considered an old maid at this age without being married but, still, you look young enough."

"Again, thanks," I muttered wryly.

"My point is, if he turns on his sexual charms, tell him you're a virgin." I narrowed my gaze at this, remembering the first time I had told Lucius I was a virgin, something of course he knew thanks to stalking me for half my life.

"I hate to point this out, but won't that be like waving a bloody red flag to this horny Vampire?"

"There is the potential of it backfiring, I have to admit." I resisted rolling my eyes this time.

"Yeah, I might save that one for never." After this and a moment of clarity thanks to this strange conversation, I asked,

"How's it going on the saving my mum front?"

"You mean from the big bad wolf King... well, Sophia at least convinced your father to leave your mother alone for five minutes, which is when I gather he intervened with your own love life." I sighed at this.

"At least my mum knows that she's no longer alone," I added, thinking right now this was the best we could hope for.

"She also knows to be ready for whatever plan we come

up with, which is going to be soon, otherwise she's going to find herself at another wedding, and seriously, there are only so many times she can marry that man." I couldn't help but chuckle at this.

"So, you and Sophia… you've got this, right?" I asked, knowing that with me having to deal with my own husband issues, I wasn't much help in the breaking my mum out department. She winced at this question, and I didn't take it as a good sign.

"Not exactly, but we're still working on it. But in the meantime, you're going to have to play the dutiful little maid… sorry." Again, I sighed before reminding her,

"This is messed up… like on a grand scale, monumental scale, this is the Tikal in Guatemala, the Parthenon in Greece, the great pyramid of Giza sized scale of messed up."

"I would have gone with Mount Vesuvius but, hey, any time you get to throw one of those archaeological monuments in there," she said this time patting my arm like she knew me all too well.

"Well, I best get to my duties then, my father said he was in the guest room he's usually in, so how do I know which room is Lucius's?" I asked, looking around and having no clue where anything was in this castle.

"Come on, I'll show you," she said, surprising me.

"You've been here before?"

"Not exactly but I'll be able to smell him." I tensed as this only served as a reminder that I was now back to being human and no longer had that same ability.

"Ah, okay, didn't think of that." After this I followed Pip though the grand home and up one of the servant staircases, one that was narrow and definitely not as grand as the stone staircase we passed. As for his room, I took one look at the bed and shivered. It was made of dark, wooden pillars and a roof over the top with carved edging that made it look like an upturned rectangular crown. Every inch of it was decorated in carved pictures, but the candles that Pip had lit with even more magic mojo didn't provide enough light to make each one out.

The room was quite dark with its panelled walls, and only one window with its view of the valley and what could be classed as a road below that ran along the side of the castle. Wooden chairs with spiral spindled high backs were positioned in front of a writing desk, and two around a square table. One that had matching carved spiral legs near the window that was most likely there for if drinks and meals were preferred to be taken inside the room. There were another two positioned either side of the decorative dark wooden fireplace that already had a fire blazing inside the metal grate.

The other pieces of furniture in this room consisted of two large chests of draws, a wardrobe and a carved trunk to the side of the bed.

"You know this lightning speed would go a lot quicker if you helped me," I pointed out as I was folding his shirts and placing them in the shelves inside the wardrobe. I had opened one chest and found it full of armour, so I quickly slammed the lid on that one.

"Most likely, yes, but if I go touching his stuff, then he would know and let's just say that if he found me up here, then trust me, the shit really would really hit that freight train."

"Why is that?" I couldn't help but ask as I folded his tailored jackets and waistcoats.

"Because out of the two of us, there's only one that he

would recognize. He would also wonder what the hell I am doing here considering, right about now, I'm most likely on a mission he sent me on and finding me here without Adam would also be considered as insane." I swallowed hard at that.

"Oh crap, I didn't think of that… Yeah, in that case, you better get gone," I warned, tossing a pair of leather gloves in a draw after taking a minute to feel them in my hands, reminding me of all that times he had worn one constantly.

"Don't worry, we will save your mum and we will get you out of this. I promise," she told me, coming over and before she could give me a hug, she thought better of it, knowing that getting that close might make her scent linger on me.

"Thanks, Auntie Pip," I replied, putting a hand to her shoulder instead and giving it a squeeze.

"Anytime, little bean… oh and there might have been one more thing that I left out of the rules." I tensed at this, knowing it was most likely not something good.

"What's that?"

"My mojo only works as long as I'm working… kapish?" I thought on this and yeah, it certainly made sense.

"Okay, so no sleeping on the job then," I teased, making her give me a salute.

"Yep, pretty much no snoozy for this magician so, FYI, it does also mean our time here is kind of limited." This worried me, as I didn't want Pip over doing it.

"How long can you keep this up for?"

"I guess we're about to find out, last time I pretty much collapsed from exhaustion." I winced knowing this was bad, as we all needed to be top of our game if we were going to make it out of here on the run.

"Then I suggest this plan of yours happens sooner rather than later, or Lucius is going to find out that I'm not a virgin, realise I'm his Chosen One, and I'm going to end up getting locked up here along with my mother," I joked, making her smirk.

"Yeah, that's pretty much worst-case scenario... oh shit." Pip ended this with a panicked tone.

"What?"

"Let's just say it wasn't worst case scenario and this is now worst-case scenario, as Luc is on his way upstairs!" I quickly gripped onto the chest of draws to hold myself steady.

"What... but that gave me hardly any time to do this!?" I complained, now looking at Pip who gave me a pointed look as if to say,

'duh' because of course he wanted me to still be here.

"Damn fiddle fuck sticks!" Pip hissed.

"What? What are you going to do?" I asked, looking around as if we could hide her from Lucius, who would recognize the extra heartbeat.

"I've masked my scent as much as I can but the only thing I can do now is climb out of a damn window *again.*" I ran to the window, pushed the red curtains out of my way and looked out.

"Is that safe?"

"Yeah, why not? Just call me a ninja kitty. Now remember, little bean, you're a virgin fair maiden and you're gonna stay that way, at least not until you're married, so that should buy you some time."

I sighed and quickly shushed her out the window before turning around and ripping open the last trunk I could find. Which meant by the time Lucius opened the door he found me gripping on to one of his jackets to my chest like it was a shield that could protect me against the force of just the sight of him.

Because with just one look it seemed as if Lucius had

finished the party for the night and was in the mood for a very different...

Form of entertainment.

Me.

CHAPTER 3
DESTROYING SHADOWS

As soon as Lucius took one look at me, he smirked to himself before turning around and closing the door. Although, I had to admit that I didn't know how I felt about him locking it as the sound seemed to echo throughout the room, making me shudder. But even *that* he didn't miss,

"I'm sorry, My Lord!" I blurted out, and again it was easy to see the tell-tale signs of when Lucius was amused by my actions.

"Pray tell, for I fail to see what you could be apologizing for?" I looked around the room, focusing on his open trunks before down at the one next to me that was still full of his clothes.

"I didn't get very far in unpacking your things." He too looked around his room as if he had only just noticed this fact before shrugging his shoulders.

"It matters not," he said before tilting his head a little as if trying to read my thoughts.

"You have something more to say?" he guessed when I started to look uncomfortable.

"If I'd have known you were retiring early for the night, I would have perhaps worked a little faster to get the job done sooner, but I think it is probably best I come back and continue this when you're not here," I said hoping this would give me freedom to leave. However, I noticed then that he purposely made a show of putting the key to the door in his pocket, silently telling me he obviously didn't agree.

"You are very uneasy around me, Miss Earhart, any reason for that?" he questioned as he walked further into the room and leaned back casually against a writing desk before folding his arms. It was if he knew to give me space seeing as I was clearly nervous. Gods but it was like skipping back through my own past and finding Lucius standing behind me at the gala once more.

"I do not know you," I said, thinking this was the most obvious answer despite it being the least truthful thing I could have said to him. Although in this time, did I know him? A few hundred years could definitely change a man… *could change anyone.*

"It is curious then, that when you first saw me across the ballroom the look you gave me…" he challenged, making me take in a breath before trying to lie my way through his line of questioning.

"I… I don't know what you mean." Another smirk played at the corner of his lips, one he managed to refrain from turning into a full grin this time. Oh yes, he was certainly enjoying himself.

"Perhaps it was just my imagination, but I could have sworn I saw recognition in your gaze. You even seemed perplexed to find me with another woman," he said, reminding me of my mistakes in the ballroom. But then I remembered what time period this was and recalled all my knowledge from books and TV shows to come up with a viable excuse.

"I would have been perplexed to see any man of wealth and status so openly displaying affection for his wife in front of so many," I said, knowing that I would have to pretend to assume whoever he was with was his wife, if I was to continue to play the naive little servant girl.

"Then you will find yourself shocked even further, for she was not my wife." Despite knowing this, I still acted the way he expected, by taking in a quick breath of surprise.

"Then it is not my business to question you any further," I told him, hoping this was the end of the conversation.

"That is a curious thing considering I'm the one questioning you, for you have yet to ask me anything, even my name which I do find quite odd," he said, making my breath hitch for real this time before trying to hide the obvious flaw. But then, once again, going from what knowledge I did have and thankfully being historian enough to know of at least some etiquette in this time, I answered with what I thought was in the best way.

"Surely it is not expected of you to introduce yourself to all of your staff, and I would not be so presumptuous to expect you to introduce yourself to me, an inferior maid of no rank in a household that you do not own by name." He looked surprised by my answer and also a little annoyed when I called myself inferior.

"Upon my word you speak very well for someone, as you put it, so inferior and so low down the food chain." I frowned at this and pointed out,

"Now you're merely adding words to my lips." At this he finally smiled again.

"I would very much like to add something else to your

lips," he told me inexcusably, shocking me sincerely enough to gasp.

"You should not speak of such things," I whispered, now having proof that clearly even the Lucius of this time period did what he pleased and obviously said what he thought without apology. I knew that when he smirked at my scandalized reaction, something that wouldn't have happened back in my own time as I was certainly used to this side of Lucius.

"According to you, I'm allowed to speak of whatever I please seeing as I am a Lord, one whose name you have still yet to ask." Well, he had me there.

"And one I am now fearful to ask," I replied, and at this he allowed himself to fully grin.

"Then you have good sense, along with a quick wit, one I might add makes for a dangerous combination given your beautiful face... ah and now she blushes. Do not presume I would believe that you have never heard those words said to you before," He said, gifting me with the compliment and one that, yes, did make me blush. It also made me lost for words and I found myself thankful that he still awarded me the space between us.

"I…"

"And now you have nothing to say… although I confess to quite enjoy the ability to render you speechless, although it is not my preferred method." I swallowed hard knowing exactly what he meant by this.

"You're very open with your meaning and the manner in which you speak, although honestly, I would not call it gentlemanly," I said, now showing him that quick wit he clearly admired. At this he scoffed a laugh before placing a hand on his chest and in a teasing tone, told me,

"Upon my word, my lady, you wound me so."

"I doubt that," I replied under my breath, but still loud enough for him to hear. Again, he grinned at my reply as if he was enjoying this conversation far more than he should. But when he suddenly pushed away from the writing desks to walk closer to me, I couldn't help but take a few quick steps back. And upon doing so, only now realizing I still was clutching his jacket to my chest, like this would save me and provide a shield between us.

"Then perhaps there are other things you should not doubt as well."

"Like... like what?" I asked dangerously, now having no choice but to look up at him as he soon was standing that close. Then he leaned a forearm above my head against the carved wardrobe I was backed up against.

"Like the reason you are here and that I feel greatly relieved to have the key to your exit, *firmly in my pocket."* He practically purred this reminder as he had leaned closer to my ear to whisper the quiet threat.

"You would refuse me my will to leave?" I challenged, making him tilt his head slightly to the side as if this was answer enough when thankfully his words followed,

"Your will to leave does not serve my purpose for having you here." Again, I was surprised as much as I wasn't by his honesty.

"And what is my purpose exactly for being here?" I asked, despite knowing once again it was a dangerous question.

"Tell me, little one, how did you feel when you saw me kissing that woman?" He answered my question with a question and one that made me inhale quickly.

"I... I did not feel anything," I lied and his grin told me he knew it too.

"Ah ah ah, it is quite sinful to lie, you know," he said, and

I would have laughed considering I knew what he was and more importantly, his past.

"And how would you know I'm lying?" At this he ran the backs of his fingers down my cheek, along my jawline, and down my neck before tapping twice against my pulse.

"Mmm, I do like how it races for me, how your heart beats quicker at the question." I shook my head a little before telling him,

"No man alive has that ability." He raised a brow at this before giving me more than he should around a mere mortal.

"Then maybe I am more than just a man… now answer the question for I am impatient to hear the answer."

"I gave you my answer," I said, now trying to be adamant in my tone. But this was when he shook his head in return and called my bluff again.

"No, you gave me a lie, now I am waiting for the truth, and I will know it, for I will feel it this time," he said, now collaring my throat and making my eyes go wide in fear. Because despite believing that he wouldn't hurt me, I also had to remember that right in this moment, to him, I wasn't his Chosen One. I was, however, hoping that every impulse inside of him knew that I was something important to him, if not knowing what exactly. And that more than anything, it was enough to keep me safe.

But I also knew that if I hadn't reacted like this was a threat, then that in itself would have been strange. Which was why I did what anyone would do when put in this position, I started to struggle. Which meant I dropped his jacket on the floor and tried to push him off me.

He gripped my neck slightly tighter before putting his hand at my waist and pushing me further against the wardrobe.

"Easy now, little maid, for I have no intention of hurting

you, so do not struggle so." I swallowed hard and it was a lump of fear he felt going down past his palm.

"The intention is clear when a man has his hand around your neck." At this, a tick in his jaw jumped before his eyes turned hard and cold.

"And which man do I need to kill that has ever done this to you before?" My mouth opened in shock, as much as his hand would allow, before telling him,

"You do not question truly being at the mercy of a wolf when in its presence or to know that it is dangerous to have one's jaws at your neck," I replied with logic.

"Hmm perceptive indeed and surprising for one so young," he said looking from the top of my head all the way down to my chin.

"I'm hardly classed as young," I replied irrationally considering I was still at the wolfs mercy, something he continued to look amused by.

"Come now, you can be no more than one and twenty."

"Then I am blessed with a young face for I am older than that," I told him, and his features showed a flicker of surprise before he guessed...

"And yet you are unclaimed by a man."

"I... how would you know that?" I asked in a fearful tone as this was the exact conversation I had been trying to avoid. At this point he dropped even more of his mortal facade and leaned in close. Then I felt his nose to my cheek, at the same time he was turning my face one way with the use of his thumb by my chin. Then he took a deep, purposeful breath, now breathing me in deep. This meant that his next words spoken were brushed across my skin.

"Because I would scent him on you, and you still smell very ripe to me." Another hard swallow was one he felt push

past his hand that he still held firmly to my throat, making him grin before moving back.

"Now I will not ask again... how did you feel when you saw me kissing that woman?"

Damn him for not dropping this question! But knowing that I had no choice but to give him the truth, seeing as he would feel every lie through my lips, I did something I knew I might regret.

I fed the wolf

"I felt jealousy," I admitted quietly.

"Ah but there it is... you see, the truth can be quite beautiful when you are brave enough to let it out," he told me, and before I could stop myself, I replied,

"It can also be quite dangerous when in the wrong hands." At this he pulled back so that he could look directly into my eyes, and the grey-blue in his own were almost like looking up directly into a storm overhead.

"Now why do I feel as if that answer was fear blanketed under a veil that hides a multitude of sinful truths beneath it?"

I decided not to answer this, because I wouldn't have had the first idea what to say, not when I wasn't completely sure what he meant by it. Did he mean he felt that I was keeping secrets from him?

"This jealousy you speak of, where did it stem from if you have never seen me before?" he asked, making me answer the only way I knew how... *vanity.*

"I believe you have a mirror, my Lord." At this he threw his head back and laughed before finally taking pity on me and loosening his hold around my neck. Now stroking it gently along my skin with his fingertips dancing and creating tingles in their path.

"Is that your way of saying that you think me handsome, Miss Earhart?"

I blushed and he stroked the pad of his thumb along the apple of my cheek where my skin was heated the most.

"Hmm, I must say this is a delicious colour on you... and look at that, it deepens further with every compliment I give you." I shook my head a little, making him grin.

"I will confess, once I saw you from across the room, my attention diminished very quickly from the woman in my arms, and soon fixated with having another take her place." I frowned at this.

"Then you chose the wrong girl to take her place, for I am not that weak of character, nor that type of girl," I said with a bite of anger and again, it was a reaction he seemed to enjoy.

"And what type is that, Miss Earhart?" he pushed.

"Not the type to kiss a man she only just met, most certainly not the type to kiss so boldly in front of so many," I stated, now wishing that he would give me more space so as it would make this easy to prove my words and take the temptation away from me.

"Now that is a pity, for life is for living, is it not?" I swear it felt like he was just some big cat playing with a mouse now.

"I do not know what type of life you live, sir, but it is vastly different from mine, I can assure you," I said, once more playing the life of the servant girl and strangely finding it easy to do. Perhaps it was my own insecurities built over years of Lucius's rejection of me. I had always been the girl standing on the sidelines at my father's lavish parties, and now I knew why everyone was too scared to ask me to dance for if they did not fear my father... *no, they had feared Lucius in the shadows.* But I hadn't known that, back then. I hadn't known what I knew now. So, it was easy to slip back into that role of insecurity, despite Lucius being so open with me now and clearly making his intentions known.

"I would be most happy to rectify that, I can assure you in return," was his reply.

"Then you must speak in jest for the very last thing I expected when coming to work here at this grand castle tonight was a proposal of marriage." I knew that this was the right thing to say as he jerked back, clearly taken off guard by my comment.

"Ah so that is what your virtue requires, a proposal of marriage?" he asked making me hope now that this would work enough to get him to back off like Pip thought it might.

"Isn't that what most honourable girls' virtue requires? Like I said, I am not like the woman who kissed you so freely in front of high society," I said, now folding my arms and telling him with not only my words but my stance that I was serious.

"Ah yes, but I do not see any high society here keeping watch," he said, making a show of looking around the room.

"Yes, but my integrity shadows me always." Then he did something very uncharacteristic for Lucius, as he bit his lip as if to look to stop himself from chuckling. Oh yeah, he was enjoying this alright and had clearly never been turned down by a woman in his life!

"Well then, I would just have to see about getting rid of those shadows once and for all." At this a window suddenly opened, making me cry out as the wind blew out every candle in his room and plunged us both into darkness.

But my cry of shock was soon swallowed up, when Lucius took no time at all by leaning in and capturing my lips…

In a kiss from the past.

CHAPTER 4

TEMPTATION

The moment Lucius kissed me, the same thing happened that it always did. However, right now, it was somewhat poetic to feel as if time stood still. Because we could have been any one of our past selves. We could have been anywhere in the world. And the sands of time could have had us both caught in the eye of the storm as it raged around us, and I wouldn't have known.

But more importantly…

I wouldn't have cared.

Not when I was kissing the man I loved, the man I adored and the man in at least one moment in time, *I called my husband.*

However, for Lucius, this was our very first kiss and the passion that raged between us was most definitely not one sided. I could tell he hadn't been expecting it from me. Maybe he had prepared himself for an unsure response or tentative kiss in return. But what he hadn't expected was the heated desperation I had felt when claiming his lips with a fever I wondered if he had ever known the likes of before.

My hands reached up, anchoring him to me as my fingers

found their way in his long hair tied back at the base of his neck. In turn, he growled the moment he felt my nails raked slightly against his scalp as I slanted my lips so as we could deepen the kiss further still.

I yearned for him just like I did in my own time, and there was no way I could have ever managed to hide the passion I had for this man. It was a flaw in my acting, I knew that, but I couldn't find myself to care. Because, for me, kissing Lucius was always going to be about coming home, despite this being about as far from it as I could get.

As for Lucius, his hands found their way into my plain black dress gripping the material so tight, I would never have been able to escape his hold. This despite knowing that I should want to, that I should need to. He seemed like a man possessed and it was most definitely a different kiss than the one he had bestowed upon the girl earlier. This was almost animalistic in its nature. Like the cure to a disease we were both inflicted with, and one that heated our blood and made it thunder in our veins. However, when he picked me up so that he could take my lips with more ease for his height, I knew the moment he stepped towards the bed that I was in trouble.

How could I deny the want I displayed so freely? Not now, after every action I had taken in the last five minutes screamed against it. Yet Pip's words rang in my mind and all her rules rolled over me like a painful mantra. Because Lucius could never know who I was to him.

Which meant we could never have this. Not in this time.

So as much as it pained me to do so, I pulled my lips from his, managing only a breathy plea,

"No... no, we can't... do this."

"You think you can kiss me with that much passion and fool me enough to think you don't want this?" He almost growled the words.

"Please, just put me down?" I asked again, making him look at me incredulously.

"Surely you must jest?" I shook my head, making him narrow his gaze before doing as I asked. I sighed in relief when my feet touched the floor.

"I am sorry, I should not have…"

"I suggest you do not finish that sentence, not when I still have the pleasure of the taste of you against my tongue," he said, making me snap my mouth shut.

"I don't know what came over me," I said after a moment of silence ensued between us. A statement that made him sigh, now losing some of his anger at being denied.

"I know exactly what came over you, little maid of mine, for it is the same need I feel when you are near."

"Then I should leave," I said, making him growl slightly before telling me sternly,

"That is not what I mean."

"No but regardless, it is what I must do," I replied and he narrowed his gaze again.

"Why, because you are afraid of giving yourself to me?" I swallowed hard before telling him,

"This is too much… too fast… please, let me leave, sir." The moment he could hear the panic in my tone he released another sigh before I saw him taking the key out of his pocket.

"This does not change things," he stated and for my heart, it leaped in happiness hearing it but as for my logical mind, well that was in turmoil at what he could mean.

"I don't know…"

"You are still my maid, and you will act as such, which means there is no getting away from me for long. But I will grant you your leave as requested, if only so you do not think of me as a brute with no good intentions for you or your wishes." I nodded at this, and I was thankful as I could see it looked as if it was going against the grain by Lucius letting go of something he obviously wanted. Yet Lucius did have honour and I knew he would have never have held me here against my will when he could see I was distressed. He was not the type to force himself on a woman, despite how much he clearly wanted me.

"I will honour my duty to you, My Lord," I replied to this, making him nod the once before he unlocked the door. However, the second I turned ready to walk out, I felt his hand at my belly. Then he pulled me hard against his chest and spoke in my ear,

"Now ask me of my name, Miss Earhart." I decided to give him what he wanted in return for letting me leave, knowing that me asking this obviously meant something to him. Something symbolic. Something monumental to this first meeting in time.

"What... what is your name, My Lord?" I felt him smile at my ear before granting me a kiss there and telling me softly,

"Lucius Septimus, my name is Lucius Septimus... now I wish to hear you repeat it." I nodded once and did as he asked once more, knowing that I would not escape this room without doing so.

"Lucius Septimus," I said in a breathy way as I would have been lying if I said it didn't affect me when doing so.

"Good girl, now you may mark my words as being that of a vow, for I will hear it said from your lips again and soon, but be warned, my little beauty, for that the next time you do, there will be no key in my hand and no escape out of my door... *do you understand?"* I held my breath at this and nodded again.

"Good, now keep away from that fucking butler or he will

find himself on the end of my blade should I hear he has touched you again. Is that also understood?" The harsh order made me gasp as his tone had flipped now to being furious. As if just thinking about what the butler had done to me earlier was making him murderous.

"Yes… yes, My Lord," I answered him this time in what I knew was a fearful tone, and one that made him sigh before releasing his hold on me.

"Now go, before I change my mind!" he snapped, making me suck in a quick breath before running away quickly and jumping in fright when I heard the door slam behind me.

Once again, I found myself around a corner with my back against a stone wall, trying to calm my heart as I thought about everything he had said. His kiss still lingered on my lips like he had also seared the memory to my skin, branding me with the knowledge of what this man could do to me.

Of course, I knew more than anyone else in the world what he was capable of in the bedroom. But it was more than that. This was my Chosen One in that room behind that door. The man I loved no matter what time in which we lived. So, to walk away from him now was just as hard as it always had been. Half of me hoped my aunts had a plan that would happen tonight, so I wasn't put through the pain of lying to him for longer. So, I wasn't put through the pain of denying myself and my heart of what I wanted.

Which would always be… *Lucius.*

But I knew the longer I stayed, the harder it would become to keep up this pretense. To not give into temptation and say to hell with the past or the future. It was reckless and stupid and oh so foolish, but my heart didn't seem to care. My body certainly didn't as I could still feel the effects of his kiss all over my body. The goosebumps on my skin. The tingle on my lips. The wetness between my thighs. I felt it all, which is why I forced my legs to move and to take that temptation further away from making the wrong decision.

One I felt like I had already made.

"Upon my word, girl, but you sleep like the dead!" I woke with a start after feeling myself be shaken and seeing a face I didn't recognize. Although she was dressed like a housekeeper and someone who most definitely looked higher up on the food chain, as Lucius had put it, than me. She was older than I was and looked to be in her fifties but at least she had kind eyes, even if she did look unimpressed with me at the moment.

"I am sorry, I must have overslept."

"Yes, well there will be none of that in this household, girl, we are here to work and work hard at that, something you will find yourself out of if you don't get a move on. Our Lord's guest is not to be kept waiting for he takes most of his meals in his room and according to my Lord, you are to be his new maid… upon my word, it is unheard of for a woman to replace a footman but nevertheless, this is what I have been told," she said, and all this while I was out of bed, splashing water over myself from a bowl I filled from the jug. This just so as to get clean the best I could with the freezing water that literally took my breath away when it touched my skin.

"I am sorry, but I don't know your name," I admitted to the woman who was immaculately dressed, wearing black like I was, only in a much finer fabric. Her light brown hair was twisted back from her face and secured in a bun with streaks of grey at the temple. Like I said, her hazel eyes were kind as they saw me struggling with the dress, making her bat my hands away so as she could help me.

"My name is Mrs Price and I heard what that brute of a man did to you yesterday." I froze at this and asked,

"Which man do you speak?"

"But Mr Jacobs of course, why child, who else had raised a hand to you in this household?" she asked pausing her hands to look at me in the mirror we faced.

"Oh yes, him… I'm sorry, it's been a long few days. I am not used to working for such a grand estate," I said, making my excuse and happy to hear that no one thought Lucius was the brute, as I had been ready to defend him.

"Yes, someone said you were new from the village. What is your name?"

"Lia Earhart," I replied before she finished with my dress and handed me my bonnet.

"That injury looks nasty, you should have…" I quickly cut her off with a dismissive wave of my hand.

"It's alright. I promise you, it looks worse than it is, and the bonnet covers it," I said, now twisting my own hair up and using the pins from yesterday to keep it in place.

Last night I had managed to find another maid on her way to bed when I had been looking for Pip in hopes that she had a plan for that night. However, after no joy, the maid thankfully showed me the way to the servants' quarters. Two other girls were already asleep inside, so I had only needed to take off my dress and let my hair down enough so as it didn't give me a headache throughout the night.

But it now looked as if my hopes for an abrupt departure were not to be, because both Pip or Sophia where nowhere to be found and like Mrs Price had reminded me, I still had a job to do.

Which meant that ten minutes later, I was nervously walking to Lucius's room once more and, this time, with a breakfast tray in my hands. One that consisted of slices of buttered toast, boiled eggs and slices of cold pork, along with a tea set that I was desperate to use by pouring myself a cup. I had obviously missed the first meal of the day due to my over-sleeping, so my stomach was growling at me. Especially seeing as the last time I had eaten was when Pip had found us clothes to wear and brought with her an apple and a piece of crusty bread for me to eat.

As soon as I got to his door, I tried to balance the tray the best I could, while simultaneously trying to knock. But in the end I could only manage to make a slight sound with my foot, hopefully alerting him to the fact I was about to walk inside. Although I waited for him to respond to this but when I didn't hear anything, I decided his food would be getting cold and my arms were killing me by this point. So, using my elbow I carefully opened the door and walked inside, seeing the curtains were still drawn, meaning it was still quite dark inside.

So, knowing he was most likely still asleep, I walked across the room as quietly as I could. I wanted to look to the bed but in the end I chickened out, thinking it best to keep my eyes to the table near the window. This was in hopes that I could do my job, drop the tray and sneak out of there before he realized.

Something I thought I had managed to achieve until I heard him speak directly into my ear behind me…

"Good morning, my little maid."

CHAPTER 5
IN ALL HIS MORNING GLORY

As soon as he said this, I froze. My hands even tensed on the handles of the tray before I was made to jump when Lucius suddenly whipped back the curtains, flooding the room with light.

"Ah!" I shouted in shock making him chuckle.

"You seem very nervous this morning, Miss Earhart, any reason for that?" he asked me as he leaned in close from behind, now practically pinning me to the table edge as he reached around me so he could pick a piece of the toast off the plate. Then he raised the bare arm to his mouth above my head and I heard him take a bite, making me instantly jealous. In fact, I could hear my stomach rumbling at just the thought of eating.

"I am not... not nervous," I told him, now needing to do something with my hands, so I started fussing over the china cup. He leaned around me again and dropped the bitten slice on the plate as he swallowed his mouthful. Each time he made sure to get as close to me as possible and I couldn't help but hold myself still whenever he did, and I could feel his muscular torso pressed against my back.

"No? Well, you are most certainly hungry. Here, sit," he said, now taking hold of my hips and moving me aside so he could pull out a chair for me. This made me take a step back, now bumping into the corner of the bay window in order to put space between us.

"I am… I mean no, it's not… wait, you're… you're not dressed!" I shouted after finally looking up and getting my first sight of him today, and good gods almighty, I was quickly forgetting about food. Lucius was standing there shirtless, in nothing but his breeches that he had slept in from the night before. With his half bare legs and muscular torso on show, he looked as hard and unyielding as he always did, proving that Lucius worked out physically no matter what the time period. In fact, for some reason I could just see him bare knuckle fighting in a muddy pit somewhere getting dirty while he was at it. Even his hair was loose and flowing unruly around his shoulders.

Suddenly his chuckling brought me out of my lustful daze,

"Erm?" I asked, making him laugh again.

"I asked for you to take a seat, although now I do wonder if there is something else your body requires besides food." At this I flustered, knowing I had gotten caught staring.

"I am sorry, My Lord, I am not used to… well, erm… such a display. No, wait, not a display, I mean such a body… being on display that is," I said, flustered with my words and making him laugh even harder as if he was thoroughly enjoying my reaction to him.

"Here, sit and let me pour you some tea before my display gets too much for your innocent eyes." I would have laughed at this, thinking back on the not so innocent things Lucius and I had done to one and other. But then I focused on the tea part of that statement, and I swear I actually moaned at this. Just the idea of a cup for myself sounded like heaven, making him a raise a brow at me as he took me by the arm and led me to the seat.

"I really shouldn't… I am here to serve you… tea! I mean to serve you tea, absolutely nothing else… erm, serving wise," I said making a complete balls of this! Again, he just seemed amused by this and a little shocked also, because I wasn't exactly playing a very good part right now.

"And yet I still must insist, for if only one of us is allowed to serve the other… *tea, of course*… then let it be I." The way he said this was both teasing and also insinuating he actually meant serving me in another way. Oh, and with half his body on display like that, then I almost begged him to do so. Of course, it didn't help the way he continually made any excuse to touch me or be near my body. Like as soon as I sat down, he decided to pour me a cup from behind, so he had no choice but to crowd around me to do so. Then he placed his hand at my shoulder before placing the china cup and saucer in front of me. After this he leaned down close and told me,

"Please, eat, Lia." I couldn't help but shudder at both the way he said this and the sound of a fake name coming from his lips.

"No, I really shouldn't, as it is your breakfast and if someone were to find out and…"

"And they would do nothing, for you eat at my request and as my maid, I insist that you are well looked after," he said, interrupting my concerns and brushing them off as something he would simply take care of.

"But I am…"

"You are hungry, for your stomach has been growling at me this entire time, so please, do not finish that sentence with a lie and displease me further." I frowned at this before turning to look up at him where he still stood behind me.

"Displease you further?" I enquired, making him fold his arms and lean back against the bedpost. Then he gestured towards the food with a nod of his head, telling me he wouldn't divulge further into that comment until I had started eating. Well fine, if he wanted me to eat, then I would finish the whole damn plate. At least it would give me an excuse to stop drooling over the way his biceps bunched as he still kept his arms crossed. So, I picked up his bitten piece of toast and made a show of eating it, giving him my best, 'see smarty pants, I'm eating' look. A smirked played at his lips before he relaxed his posture.

"You were saying?" I prompted making him chuckle.

"You left last night, the fact displeased me and kept me from my sleep for quite some time." I swallowed down the toast like it was a lead ball.

"But you knew why."

"Knowing the reasons and liking them are two entirely separate things," he told me, making me sigh before remaining quiet as really, what could I say to that? But then he pulled out the chair opposite me and I couldn't help but pause mid-bite and ask,

"Would your Lordship like me to get you a shirt?" At this he raised a brow at my sassiness, making me realize I had slipped into teasing wife Amelia and not nervous maid Lia.

"That depends, do you dislike what you see, Miss Earhart?" he asked brazenly.

"I… well, I… don't think about you… it… your body, I mean," I flustered again making him smirk.

"Do you prefer I not have one?" he teased.

"A body, well that would make this conversation look rather odd, for I am not sure where I would put your head," I said over the rim of my teacup making him grin.

"Mm, and there is that quick wit once more… I see food

must be the key," he replied making me grin with him this time.

"Then I should continue to eat as you suggest, for we don't want you getting bored with our conversation."

"I think there is little chance of that, Miss Earhart," he replied smiling, and this time it was such an easy-going grin that it stripped him suddenly of his mischievous playfulness and made him even more handsome, if such a thing were even possible.

"Perhaps it is I that will get bored then, for I hear men of rank do love to talk politics… tell me, are you such a man, Lord Septimus?" His grin turned playful once more.

"When faced with a beautiful woman I found myself dreaming of most the night… then no, politics are the very last thing on my mind," was his smooth reply, making me blush and look down at my plate before thinking of something witty to say.

"Ah but who is it that speaks of untruths now, for not long ago you told me you hardly slept."

"Clever girl you are but you twist my words, for I recall saying that you kept me from my sleep but not that you kept it from me entirely," he replied making me tip my cup his way as if to say a silent, touché. But then I thought of something clever in return and made a point,

"Ah so your displeasure wore off at some point… interesting."

"Is it, how so?" he asked now covering his mouth with his hand as if trying to hide his grin, as clearly, he was enjoying this banter.

"I am merely trying to judge your character as the Lord of this castle suggested I do."

"And what have you surmised?" I lifted my teacup up and before taking a sip, I said,

"You mean other than being an easily forgiving, sleep deprived, half naked man that pours a good cup of tea… very little as of yet," I teased, finally drinking and making him throw his head back and laugh as he often did. Gods but I adored the sight of him laughing, always had and always would, no matter the time period.

"I see I will need to be quick on my feet as well as my tongue when you are in my company, Miss Earhart," he replied with a grin making me realize that on that note, I had most likely stayed too long already. Which was why I cleared my throat and pushed my chair back before saying,

"Yes, well speaking of company, I fear I have stayed too long as it is, as I really should…" At this he made a quick move so he was standing before me.

"No, please stay… I implore you," he said, raising his hand out to stop me.

"Well, I really…"

"Besides, you have yet to finish your breakfast," he quickly interrupted nodding down to the remaining food on the plate.

"You mean *your* breakfast," I corrected.

"What is mine, is yours," he stated, and my mouth opened in surprise.

"You… you cannot mean that, sir," I said quietly, sounding as shocked as anyone should hearing that being said from a Gentleman to a maid.

"What can I do to get you to stay?" he asked ignoring my outburst and making me feel guilty. As clearly, he was trying to woo me, and the irony wasn't lost on me considering what my own past with Lucius had been like. As let's just say that Lucius and the word 'wooing' are two words I didn't think would ever be matched together in a sentence. Which was why I sat back down and said a single word,

"A shirt." He grinned at this before he made a show of bowing before me.

"As the lady wishes." Then he ran the backs of his fingers down my cheek and along my chin before whispering softly words that shot straight to my heart.

A nickname Lucius would end up calling me throughout the ages…

"Eat my sweet, funny girl."

An hour later and I swear Lucius was trying to kill me with sexual frustration because he was definitely succeeding in making me fall in love with him all over again. Gods but if I had met him in this time period for the first time, then I wouldn't have stood a chance. Hell, I would have most likely lost my virginity last night, throwing the damn thing at him like a fan throws knickers at a lead singer at a rock concert!

Because Lucius was charming, funny, witty and charismatic all wrapped up inside a handsome roguish shell that held that hint of danger and dominance. A personality, that after experiencing it first hand, now had a girl like me just begging for that rough control in the bedroom as much as I was his gentle touch.

And all these things combined, its why I knew I needed to get away from him as soon as possible. Because I was weakening by the minute. Pip's warnings were now less like alarm bells and now more like soft tinkering sounds fading off into the distance.

So once I had eaten, I told him that I had to take his tray back to the kitchen or people would get suspicious that something scandalous was happening between us. Of course, this was like waving a red flag in front of a bull as he pulled me back against him, now thankfully wearing a shirt, and said seductively,

"But what if I want something scandalous to happen."

"It just did, for my belly is full having just consumed my Lord's morning meal," I said, and gave my belly a little affectionate pat with his hand.

"And in that I am satisfied at least, for it is no longer growling at me like a wild beast," he replied playfully. But as much as I wished to stay and continue our time together, his touch was only serving as a reminder of how forbidden this was. So I told him,

"Please, My Lord, I must get back to my duties."

"And what if I say your duties are here with me, what then say you?" he asked making me sigh.

"Then I will ask you what is required of me upon my return from the kitchens." At this he released a breath before whispering in my ear,

"Then hurry along, little maid, and be quick with your return." Then he ran his fingers along my belly before getting to my side where he gave me a squeeze before letting me go. I said nothing more but hurried out of his room, only taking a breath when I was free.

Which brought me to now and why I was practically running out of the castle desperately needing some air. I had already taken the tray back to the kitchens and gained gossiping looks from some of the other maids. But with an exasperated roll of my eyes, I simply left out of a servant's entrance now in search of solitude. I knew that Lucius would be expecting me back, but I just needed space between us. It was getting too much, playing this act and trying not to just give into impulse and throw myself at him.

In fact, I was just walking around the front of the castle and towards where a stunning green vista was opening up in front of me, when a sight stopped me dead. Soon the green valley in front of me paled in the distance because sitting in a huge chestnut tree situated at the entrance of the castle was a man I recognized.

A man that chuckled the moment he saw me.

A man dressed like a jester.

Oh, and it wasn't just any jester.

No, it was…

Marcus.

CHAPTER 6
A FOOLING TOM

"*Marcus?*" I hissed his name, forgetting myself and making him smirk down at me.

He was dressed in a blue and gold checkered pattern jacket that was of a style I was used to seeing him wear. It looked almost like a military jacket, it was longer in the back with rectangular tails and a V of gold buttons at the front. A bright blue waistcoat was worn underneath, and light-yellow breeches completed the look.

But of course, with this being Marcus, this wasn't without his elaborate clown make-up on, always making me wonder what he would look like without it. Either way, you could still tell regardless that he was a handsome man, despite the creepy aura he always managed to give off.

I also had to wonder what he was doing here? I knew a very vague amount of information about him, mainly because he was known as Jared's second in command. He also managed the Devil's Ring fight club and was known as a sort of ringleader there, he was usually the one who announced the acts as well as the fights. But regarding his early history, I didn't know when he had met Jared. Which I was guessing must have been after this point if he was still here.

I also knew he was classed as being one of the Seekers and had been trained by a man on my father's council, Takeshi. But he was an odd character to say the least and looking at him sitting up in that tree now, then I would say he most likely always had been. He also still held a cane, one that he was currently swinging between the branches with a carved skull at the handle. But this accessory wasn't surprising as he was rarely seen without a cane or staff of some kind. Most likely because he was well trained with one, thanks to Takeshi, who taught him not only how to hone his supernatural gifts but also how to fight.

Marcus had a natural arrogant air to him, thanks to his striking facial features, with his slim nose, square cut jawline and high cheekbones. He also had high arched brows with one that always seemed to be raised as if he was judging every single action you made. But those elongated red diamond shapes that ran through his eyes and curved slightly an inch above his brows reminded me of horns. The opposite ends were drawn down in long points that reached his jaw until they were nothing but a thin line. A set that mirrored the same triangular design starting from under his bottom lip. This thin red line continued all the way down his chin until it disappeared under the shadows of his long neck before it dipped under a crimson red cravat. A colour that matched his unusual hair, with its strands that were twisted back from his face into sections with the ends pointed with little bells attached. All of which adding to the theatrics that rest of his outfit provided. Piercing dark blue eyes studied me as I approached.

"Now that is a curious thing indeed," he stated in his arrogant tone.

"What is?" I asked stupidly instead of just getting straight out of there.

"That there are few here who would call me such as most from these parts would refer to me only as a Skelton."

"A Skelton?" I asked, taking even more bait and making him grin. A creepy look thanks to his painted face.

"You're not from around here are you, little dove?" I shook my head thinking it best not to say more on this.

"In fact, I would go as far to say that time is not on your side." I gasped at this making me wonder what he knew exactly. Did he know of my own Fates, being a seeker?

"But enough of all of that! Some like to call me just another Tom's Fool, but to others, like you and I, then I am indeed known as Marcus."

"Tom's fool?" I asked because I couldn't seem to help myself.

"Ah but that is a tale of over some hundred and fifty years prior and a time when there was previously a name... let's pretend that it was once mine for fun... was a fine young fellow known as Thomas Skelton and it may or may not have something to do with a blacksmith losing his head on account of a pretty lady sought after by another. But the poor bastard didn't stand a chance... um, kind of reminds me of another blacksmith tale I have heard whisperings of before and one, I am still yet to meet. But alas he is in the city, and how I do loath the stench of a city." I frowned at all of this, making me wonder if he was talking about Jared, who I gathered he hadn't met yet, not if he was currently hinting to me of his past lives. Which was why I foolishly asked,

"You mean Jared Cerberus and the Devil's Ring?" At this he smirked, looking even more intrigued.

"Now I could ask you, how you yourself know such a name, but then again, you are no more a simple maid than I am a simple man. So perhaps our secrets are all the amour we need. Although I confess that talk of the man is making me want to meet the beast all the more, so perhaps I will venture to the big city after all and make my services known... besides, not sure how long it will be again until the village folk take up their pitchforks and pikes against me," he said this last part behind his hand like it was a secret.

"What did you mean by others like you and I, for what if I am just a simple maid?" I asked, trying to hide whatever ideas he may be having but at this he laughed.

"Oh, I would say you and your situation in life is far from simple, as like I said, you are as much a maid as I am naught but the fool villagers take me for... but alas, we all have our parts to play, do we not... speaking of parts." He nodded behind me, making me turn and hiss a curse the second I saw the angry strides of the butler striding towards me. At this, I turned when Marcus commented,

"The old dog looks vexed and like death's head upon a mop-stick if ever I saw one."

"He doesn't like me all that much," I commented before trying to make my escape. "Goodbye, Marcus."

He bowed a head and I started to walk faster in the opposite direction to where the butler was coming from, however I wasn't fast enough.

"You! You troublesome little rat!" he snarled, making me start to run because the last thing I needed was to have to explain how I put this guy on his ass. Oh, and what's worse, get into trouble for it. However, I was suddenly grabbed from behind with a painful grip on my arm, making me turn and try and push him off me.

"Get off me!" I shouted as I was tossed to the ground, making me thankful that it was at least a dry day, or I would have been covered in mud.

"You cost me my position!" he accused, making me bite back a curse.

"You lost it through your own actions!" I snapped back, instead of calling him the fuckwit I wanted to, now gaining my feet and the moment the butler named Jacobs was back at me, I watched as Marcus reacted.

"Well, that's this fool's cue to dance," he said before jumping down and landing on his feet as agile as a cat. Then he tucked the cane under his arm and clapped his hands as if dusting off the bark before striding over to us. However, because I was watching him approach, I had taken my eyes off Jacobs and the next I could see, was him pulling his arm back ready to strike out at me a second time.

However, unlike the first, he never got there as suddenly there was a red leather gloved hand wrapped around his wrist before he said to me,

"Fly away, little dove, and leave this one to me." Then before I had chance to do that, he twisted his hand and snapped Jacob's wrist. But before he could scream out aloud in agony, Marcus covered his mouth with his other hand and hushed him with a big grin.

"There there, old chap, do try and take it like a man." Then he winked at me and jerked his head to tell me to get going. I nodded and mouthed a 'thank you' before doing as he suggested and getting away from any drama. One that would no doubt just land me in trouble or shed an even bigger spotlight on me, and more than the one named Lucius I already had shined my way.

I quickly made my way down the side of the castle opposite the way I had originally come, and back towards the stables as I recognized the road the carriages had used the night before last. In all honesty, I was just hoping to find somewhere to hide for a bit, already knowing that I would need to make up an excuse as to what to tell Lucius. Because he was no doubt expecting me to return to his room like I said I would. I had also been hoping to find Pip or Sophia somewhere nearby, I was getting worried this was all taking too long.

Of course, the problem with trying to find Sophia or Pip also meant running the risk of who else I would find. Which was why the moment I walked through the stone cobbled archway; I stopped dead. Because there now was Lucius mounting his huge stallion, one all glossy black and looking almost as unruly as he did.

He wore a double-breasted black jacket with two lines of buttons in the same fabric that was shorter at the front and longer at the back. This split into two square tails that reached the backs of his knees, as was the common style. Bone colour breeches met high black riding boots and the white cuffs of his shirt beneath could be seen peeking out at his wrists, along with the same black leather gloves I had unpacked. Along with the usual strip of material around his neck like a tie and the waistcoat that matched the jacket, the only other item added to his outfit was a striking black top hat that made him look like he had just stepped from one of Jane Austin's novels.

He was breathtakingly handsome.

Of course, the moment he mounted his horse he raised his head up and found me standing in the middle of the arch transfixed by the sight of him. His grey-blue eyes drank me in and for a few startling moments we both remained unmoving as if equally locked in a suspended question in time. As for me, I was asking myself, do I run? Lucius was no doubt asking himself would he make chase if I did.

The answer for us both was yes, as I suddenly snapped back to my senses. I turned and quickly started running away from him, making me jump in surprise when I heard him shouting behind for his horse to move,

"YAH!" Then I heard the galloping behind me getting closer and closer. Meaning he was only seconds away and I glanced back knowing I had no chance as he was already leaning to the side ready to grab me. This caused me to scream out the moment I felt his arm curl around me and for a few scary moments, I felt my feet leave the ground as the horse continued on. I was then lifted up with the strength of only one arm around me until I then felt myself positioned in front of him with my ass to the saddle.

"Let me down!" I shouted, making him hold me tighter as he urged his horse to gallop faster into the countryside. He never said a word, but I could feel him breathing heavy behind me. This as I was forced to ride uncomfortably side saddle, with my ass pressing against the leather that was not designed for a second rider. But when I started to shift awkwardly, he finally slowed down his horse and whispered in my ear,

"Spread your legs." I froze as he did and he must have felt it, believing it to be from fear and not excitement.

"Easy now, I simply suggest you ride as a man would, so as to ease the burden of your…"

"Yes, yes, I understand," I snapped before he could refer to my ass, making him chuckle. A sound that stopped abruptly when I lifted up my skirt and expose my simple white cotton stockings that were tied with a bow above the knee. Then I threw a leg over at the same time Lucius put a hand to my belly and pulled me flush against his front, so we both now fit snug in the saddle.

"Now is the lady more comfortable?" he asked flexing his fingers along my belly where he kept his hand.

"She would be more comfortable on foot and nearer to the

castle like she had intended to be," I replied, speaking of myself in the third person and making him sigh.

"You never returned to my chamber. I was displeased," he told me and I scrambled to think of something quickly.

"I had other duties expected of me, it would not be seen as proper if I am alone in your room with you for so long, for the others have already started to gossip."

"I care little for the idle chatter of others, nor do I care for what is thought of me," he replied arrogantly, making me huff.

"That may be so, but I care about my own reputation, for I wish to ensure any future employment is upheld and can be obtainable within the county," I replied, thinking this would make sense surely. I mean he was rich, he was also immortal, which meant that he could do what he liked. But had this situation of mine been real then it was far easier for him to walk away unscathed if he cared little about tarnishing his own reputation.

Of course, this didn't please him as I felt him grip me tighter and I had to wonder if the thought of me working elsewhere was what sparked the possessive action.

"Your future is no longer your concern," he stated making suck in a quick breath. Was this Lucius deciding that I was his now? Did he really feel that strongly for me, enough to break the laws of his people? Or did he truly believe I *was* his Chosen One, despite Pip's best efforts?

"It will always be my concern, for I am free of mind, free of heart, and free of soul enough to make my own choices," I told him making him scoff behind me.

"You think to ridicule me for this belief?" I asked as he started to lead the horse into a wooded area.

"It is not ridicule but knowledge."

"Knowledge?" I asked hoping he would elaborate. However, when he did, I was left even more shocked.

"Knowledge that I will soon rule all three." My mouth dropped at this, making me snap,

"Then your arrogance deludes you, sir, and leads you astray, for I will always be… wait… *what are you… doing?"* This last part was whispered after he dismounted his horse and was now reaching up to drag me off it. It was done in such a way that I was dragged slowly down the front of him, stealing my breath in an instant.

"You were saying, Miss Earhart?" he hummed in my ear as he could no doubt hear the way my heart was pounding and the way I still held my breath captive in my lungs.

"I… I… was erm…" I tried to voice a witty comeback but with him now being this close, and the way he tilted my head back with his gloved hand, it just sent me hurdling into our own past. Those leather hands were doing things to me and reminding me of earlier times with Lucius, every touch on my skin was making me want to moan at the memories.

"Just as I thought, little maid, your mind can be possessed and owned by thoughts of another, no matter the arrogance in which you think lies at its core," he said jarring me back to the now.

"But I…"

"I am not finished. For I know this and say this, not through that arrogance, but through experience, for my own mind also can be possessed and owned by thoughts of another, even when I know that innocence is what lies at her own core," he said, surprising me yet again as he admitted to having me on his mind, just like he knew with certainty that he was consuming mine.

"I… I don't know what to say," I admitted.

"Then I will take your silence for what it is," was his

response, and at this I foolishly felt myself leaning forward before asking in a breathy tone,

"And, what is that?"

"Acceptance," he stated firmly before finally moving away from me and giving me space to breathe, which also forced me to take a step in order to regain my balance. Then I watched as he took his horse by the reins and walked him over to a nearby tree as I looked around to see we were standing in a clearing of sorts.

"Where are we?" I asked, deciding it was best not to address the conversation we had just been having anymore because it was dangerous ground for sure.

"We are still on Muncaster grounds, but far enough away from all those prying eyes that worry you so," he said, securing the reins so his horse wouldn't just wander off.

"If I am gone too long, Mrs Price will be vexed and I do not wish to get into trouble," I said, now backing away when Lucius started striding towards me, cutting the distance between us far quicker than I could retreat.

"No one would dare…"

I stopped him. "I am merely a maid, My Lord, and you exaggerate my importance greatly," I said making him frown.

"Then your importance to me will soon be known." I released a sigh and shook my head before trying to walk away, but he snagged me around the waist and pulled me back to facing him.

"Do not walk away."

"I walk away from a fantasy you build," I told him, trying to remind him of his own duty. He was destined to find his Chosen One just as all the Kings were.

"It is not a fantasy if it is built on truth," he replied firmly as if he were sure about our future together, making me question yet again if Pip's ability to hide my true nature from him wasn't as powerful in this time period. Was it because it was closer to our own, with only a few hundred years between and not thousands like it had been the first time they used the Janus Gate?

"Your truth is flawed," I said before moving away, and he let me this time. But what I had really wanted to say is that our time was flawed as it was not truly our own.

"How is it flawed, what makes you speak so?" he demanded to know.

"Please, can we not speak of this now? If we are here, then let us just enjoy the moment before the beast of gossip will once again be roused from its cage." At this bowed his head, clearly deciding there was a time to push and a time to pull back.

"It is beautiful here," I said, turning away from him and taking in the rolling fields through the tree line for as far as the eye could see. I placed a hand at the tree next to me and tried to focus, not at the man I could feel approaching behind, but on the sense of calm the sight of the countryside brought me. Ella would have loved it here, she was always so happy outdoors. It made me think about her and, not for the first time since all this had happened, it made me worry about her. If only I could know for certain that she was safe. If only I had a sign.

"Beautiful indeed," Lucius said behind me and the way he said it, I didn't think he was talking about the view like I was. That's when I felt him pull my bonnet from my head, dropping it to the floor before I felt him leaning in so he could smell my hair.

"What are you..."

"Ssshh now, just be still," he said, now leaning his head closer until he could run his nose up the side of my neck, using his leather clad fingertips on the other side. He was so

gentle, so tender in his touch I couldn't help but close my eyes and sigh out a moan.

But that was the power of Lucius, because with each touch that protective shell around me started to crack.

The only question now was…

When would he make it shatter completely?

CHAPTER 7
THE FIGHTER IN ME

I shivered at his touch, and I felt his lips turn into a knowing grin along my skin.

"I know I affect you, little maid," he hummed against me, and I swallowed hard wishing he knew the inner turmoil he was causing within me. But then again, would he care? Lucius was now and always would be a man who was used to getting what he wanted. And foolishly, I was tempted to see just how far he would go to getting it.

If he knew who I was… if it was finally confirmed to him, what would he do if I ran? Would I become a prisoner to him? A slave to his desires? Gods, why did that thought make me squirm? It was like I was burning up, a mistake I knew I made instantly as Lucius suddenly scented it.

Scented my lust.

I knew that when I felt him grip my dress in an unyielding hold, the material bunching in his fist he now positioned at my side.

"I know you want me," he purred again, and this time without giving himself away by confessing he could smell it on me.

"I want a lot of things in life, sir, but wanting something and being in the position to gain it, are vastly different," I told him, making him groan against me before growling,

"Tell me what you want and let me gain it for you... *let me give you all you ever desired,*" he told me, and I sucked in a quick breath at the offer he made freely. Surely Lucius would not be this way just for one night to get me in his bed. Not unless he truly felt something... *something he perhaps didn't fully understand.*

Gods, how easy it would be. To turn in his arms and kiss him. To tell him exactly what I wanted. Exactly what I needed. What I truly desired.

I just wanted him.

But what would happen when I did? How would I have the strength to stop it before it went too far. Just thinking about last night's kiss and how I had lit up for him. How I had let my passion soar until being forced to grant him my painful rejection, one that was made even more cruel as it was clear I wanted him. Which meant that I couldn't lead him on any further.

It wasn't fair... *to either of us.*

So, I told him,

"I wish to return." I felt him sigh against me and finally his fist uncurled from my dress before I felt him stepping away.

"As you wish, but before we go, I want to teach you something," he said, making me turn to face him and I frowned when I saw him removing his jacket. He then folded it up and placed it over a nearby log that looked to have been chopped down at one point and left due to its size. After this, he then removed his gloves and placed them inside his upturned top hat after first removing it. This too was then placed on his folded jacket, and I couldn't help lust after the way he looked.

Bellowing sleeves of his white shirt were a contrast to the way his tight black waistcoat outlined his slim waist and his powerful shoulders. His white cravat was perfectly in place at his neck and his bone-coloured breeches finishing just over the knee met black riding boots that were polished to a high shine.

"What are you doing?" I asked, hoping like hell he wasn't getting naked again. This morning was all I could cope with and I knew that if I saw even the hint of muscle once more, I would be a goner.

"Come here, Lia," he said using my first name, something that was said in a soft, gentle tone. It was also one that made me do as he asked as he held his hand out to me. He then looked gratified when I filled his hand with my own, taking a moment to look at our fingers curling around one another, before using his hold on me to pull me closer.

"I want to teach you how to defend yourself against anyone wishing to strike you like that bastard Jacobs did." I shook my head a little and blurted out,

"Wait, you know about that?!" Of course, I had foolishly been thinking back to earlier and not the more obvious first time Lucius was referring to. I knew that when Lucius narrowed his eyes and said,

"I was there, of course I... *That fucker!*" he snarled, stopping himself mid-sentence before he started storming over to his horse.

"Wait! What are you doing!?" I shouted after him, making him turn and ask in a dangerous tone,

"When did he touch you!?" I stopped dead and raised a hand,

"I..."

"Answer me, girl," he snapped making me swallow hard and shake my head.

"You know for you were there," I said lying.

"And the last time, when I clearly wasn't, what of it then?" he asked, and I took a step back when he came at me. Then he gripped the top of my arm to prevent me from retreating any further, but he never hurt me.

"When?" he asked again, however when I didn't reply quick enough, he yelled at me,

"WHEN?!"

"Please stop! You're... *you're frightening me,*" I pleaded, knowing this would be enough to calm him down and it worked. He took a deep breath and released my arm, however, when I turned my face away from him was when I felt his softness. He lifted my chin with a curled finger and brought my head back around to face him.

"Please just answer me... Did he hurt you, Lia?" he asked me, making me shake my head telling him no.

"But he tried?" Lucius assumed next, and I swallowed hard before nodding, telling him yes this time, knowing he didn't deserve another lie. I watched his eyes glow crimson for a single second before he looked away, obviously able to feel himself losing control. A muscle jerked in his jaw as his anger was spiking higher, making me say,

"Nothing happened. Not really. Marcus intervened and stopped him before he could strike me. I believe he even broke his wrist." At this he whipped his head back around to look down at me.

"Marcus? You met the fool?"

"Well, that's a little harsh, I mean he is odd yes, but I wouldn't call him a fool as he seemed quite intelligent to me." At this he then looked at me as if I was the odd one. As if he was doing a double take.

"He is extremely intelligent, as most household fools are, or do you not know this, for he is no court Jester that is to be sure, as alas the two are vastly different." I quickly realized my mistake here, as obviously Lucius's little scholar didn't know everything about history like she thought. I laughed this off nervously and said,

"But of course, my mistake." He raised a questioning brow to this, and I knew he wasn't accepting my brush off the way I hoped.

"It matters not, for the issue was clearly dealt with," I said as he just continued to look at me like he was trying to unravel all my secrets.

"It is far from dealt with, as the cretin still breathes." At this my eyes widened but then true panic set in when turned and started walking back to his horse once more.

"Wait, My Lord! Where are you going?" I asked, now rushing to catch up with him.

"To handle this myself, like I should have done after the first time he took a hand to you!" he snapped, just before I could grab hold of his arm trying to stop him from taking hold of the reins of his horse.

"Please don't do this!" I pleaded, trying to think of something to stop him as the last thing I wanted was him committing murder of a mortal and kicking up a fuss with my father. Something that could potentially lead to even more difficulties for our eventual planned escape. However, Lucius just ignored me, shrugging off my arm and making me quickly rack my brain for what I could do to stop him. Which was why the moment he started to mount his horse I tried again,

"So, you're going to leave me here?!"

"I will be back shortly for you, as you may trust my words, woman, this won't take long." Then he turned his horse and started to gallop through the trees when I suddenly shouted the last thing I could think of,

"I will kiss you!" The second he heard this he pulled back on the horse's reins and the fine animal stopped. Then he looked over his shoulder at me.

"Say that again," he demanded firmly, making me take in a quick breath at the intensity of his tone.

"I will kiss you but only if you come back," I reiterated and the second I did, he turned his horse back around making my heart pound when he tossed his leg over the saddle. Then without worrying about his horse this time, he took long strides over to me and cut the space between us in seconds. Which meant that it was only seconds later that he was cupping a hand to the back of my neck and pulling me towards him. This at the same time he lowered his lips to mine, doing so as if he wasn't giving me a moment to back out of our deal.

And suddenly I was home.

Home in his arms, in his kiss, in all that was Lucius.

Of course, I opened up to him instantly, moaning the second I felt his tongue caress my own. It was hard to describe the full intensity of kissing the man you loved, but what was easy to say was how near damn impossible it was to hold yourself back. Which was why I didn't even bother trying as I knew I would fail every time. It was also the reason that there would never be any doubt in Lucius's mind to how I felt about him. How much I wanted him. How I clearly craved for more. Because in that kiss, just like the one before it, I held nothing back, meaning it became one of the most truthful moments between us.

A truth without words.

Lucius didn't know me and what I had told him had all been a lie. A lie to keep myself protected. To keep the vow I had made and ensure it became fulfilled. But there were no lies between the way we kissed. And knowing that, no matter how dangerous, brought me comfort. To know that Lucius was getting a piece of me... *the real me.*

That was what centred my soul.

So, I kissed him back with a fiery passion that could never be extinguished. I turned my head to deepen the kiss instead of pulling back like I knew I should. I let him wind his arms around me and hold me to him like I was the most precious being in the world. Like he would never let me go. And as for me, well I gripped on to his waist with the painful knowledge plaguing the back of my mind that I would have no choice but to let him go, and soon.

"Gods," he hissed, placing his forehead to mine as if overcome with emotion and letting it slip that his religion was not what he most likely believed mine to be.

"The way you kiss, it feels like I am touching your soul," he told me in a deep, fervent tone. It was such a beautiful thing to say, I wanted desperately to give him something back in return, so braved to tell him,

"I believe such actions only occur with you, My Lord, for I confess no other has had such power over me, nor ignited such a response." At this he held me tighter, kissing my forehead before cupping the back of my head and holding me to him.

"This pleases me," he told me after releasing a happy sigh.

"It is unfortunate then that we must return before our absence is noted," I said, meaning the next sigh out of his mouth didn't sound as happy as the last.

"I do not like that you always seem to be trying to run from me," he told me, now pulling back and raising my face up to his.

"Speaks the man who moments ago was about to leave me stranded in the woods with naught but blood in his mind and revenge in his veins," I said, making him pull back a little so he could see me better.

"Upon my word, little maid, the manner in which you freely speak is perplexing as much as I find it liberating and fascinating," he replied, telling me I had gone too far with my thoughts of what should have been from a simple maid.

"Does this mean I will get my way and we are to return?" I pushed.

"No, it does not, for if you will not let me get rid of that cretin with the use of my hands or that of my sword, then I will at the very least teach you how to defend yourself against such delinquency."

"And you label me as being perplexing, when you are the one who wishes to teach a woman to fight," I commented despite knowing what I did, because he didn't know that I would have been able to put the asshole Jacobs on his ass ten times over. However, I had refrained for the very reasons I just mentioned as it would have looked odd when the guy went screaming in pain throughout the castle. Especially when telling all that would listen that a woman just broke his arm in the blink of an eye.

"Well, that sharp wit of your tongue will only get you so far, my dear," he replied with a wink making me smirk.

"Very well, My Lord, you may teach away," I said, thinking he was just going to show me how to punch someone. But then he made a mistake… or should I say, *I did.*

Because he said,

"First, I am going to test your reactions…" Then he pretended to lash out and hit me, and despite knowing that he would have never connected and hurt me, my brain didn't accept that fact in time. Because years and years of training overrode all logical thought and I just reacted.

Like muscle memory, I grabbed his wrist and instead of just batting it aside, I twisted my body under his shoulder, and took his arm with me, now holding it pinned in a way that meant I could have broken it. And because Lucius hadn't been expecting it, the most shocking thing happened...

I had beaten him.

But I had fucked up by doing so.

Fucked up...

Big time.

CHAPTER 8
MEASURE OF A GREAT MAN

I instantly let go of his arm the moment he growled and backed away with my hands raised, fearing the hard look in his eyes when he turned slowly to face me.

"I am so sorry... I... I... don't know what came over me," I stammered, fooling myself by thinking this would ever be enough. I knew that when he continued to come at me as I too continued to walk backwards, soon needing to look down so I wouldn't fall over. But then I felt myself be grabbed and walked towards where he wanted me. Meaning as soon as I felt the tree against my back I knew why because, clearly, I already had a record of running from him, something he wanted to prevent.

"Who are you?" he growled dangerously, making me gulp before shaking my head.

"I...I am a no one, My Lord."

"Lies," he snarled into my cheek before I felt my hands being raised above my head.

"Please..." I tried when he held both hands there shackled with only one of his own secure around my wrists.

"Now I will get my answers and they had better be of the truthful kind," he warned, now using his other hand at my neck just like last night. The prime place he would feel my pulse and detect my lies. Which meant I was going to have to get real creative with my answers. I nodded quickly, telling him I would and doing so enough that his hold on me would allow.

"How did you know to defend yourself in such a way?" he asked, making me release a sigh before answering,

"My father taught me." His gaze narrowed slightly but then he must have been satisfied with my answer as he relaxed his grip just a little, seeing as I hadn't lied.

"And this father, why would he do such a thing?"

"For the same reason you wanted to teach me I can imagine," I pointed out the obvious.

"A strange inclination for a father indeed, especially for what I assume were aspirations in a well-bred daughter." I laughed without humour at this.

"I am a maid, My Lord, or did it skip your memory?"

He growled at this, making me snap,

"Meaning any hopes that I would marry a gentleman of significant rank was naught but a wasted effort on his part, for despite having a sharp wit and a pretty face, I believe a substantial dowry is usually the price for such a wife!" Now this did anger him, as he got closer to my face, putting more weight against my hands and pressing them into the tree.

"You push me too far with that statement!" he retorted in return before pushing from me and walking away. I lowered my arms slowly and rubbed at my wrists as if I could still feel the pressure of his hold there against my skin.

"But is it not the truth? For we both know that it is," I replied, making him look back at me over his shoulder.

"Your sharp wit is shadowed by your lies and you're not fucking pretty!" I sucked in a startled breath at this, having not heard Lucius speak this cruelly to me since the first time I ever stepped foot inside his club. It felt like a verbal slap and one look back at my face and he knew it. Which was why he reacted and stormed back over to me, making me try and get away from him.

"No! Get off me!" I shouted the moment he reached for me, making him wrap me in his arms from behind, taking hold of my wrists and holding them prisoner across my chest.

"You mistake my meaning, Miss Earhart." At this I lost it and shouted back at him,

"Fuck you and your meaning!" At this he stilled in shock before he growled,

"You're not fucking pretty, *you're fucking beautiful!*" Then he spun me around and I instantly stopped struggling the second he took my face in his hands and kissed me hard. I felt my hair pulled tight as one of his hands slid from my cheek to the back of my head, and the other wrapped around my waist to pull me in tighter against him. I practically sighed into him, giving myself willingly and secretly wishing he would never let go.

But Lucius had something on his mind. I knew this when he pulled back and as was his way, his forehead lowered to mine, so he could tell me,

"Gods be damned, woman, what is it you do to me?"

"The same you do to me, My Lord," I told him squeezing him tighter. But then he said the most beautiful thing, making me gasp,

"Speak of me not as rank, for you should only ever speak of me by my name, as I am not your Lord... *no, for I feel more like a slave to your heart."* Naturally, I didn't know what to say to this, because letting him know my true feelings would have been dangerous. I was just glad that he had closed his eyes to say this, and they remained that way long enough for me to blink back the tears. I did, however, raise my hand up and cup his cheek to let him know with my touch what his words had meant to me.

How they had meant everything.

Gods, but what it was that this man did to me, it was almost too much to bear. Because all I wanted to do was get lost in all that was Lucius. His touch, his words, his arrogant, knowing smiles and his piercing blue-grey eyes. I wanted it all and I knew if I simply just let myself, then I could have had it all.

It made me wonder, had my mother gone through the same temptations when it had been her own prophesy to live through? Was she going through it all over again right now with my father? Did she struggle as I did with the guilt and all the lies? Did she feel as if she was going against nature, against her very soul, by holding herself back?

"Come, it is time I grant your wish to return," he said finally breaking away first and despite wanting to stay with him longer, I knew the danger of doing so. So, I tried to gather my wits about me and followed him to his horse but then I paused.

"Oh, my bonnet," I said but before I could make a step to get it, Lucius stopped me.

"Allow me," he said, leaving me next to his horse, and when it nudged me, I could help but grin before giving him what he wanted, which was a fuss.

"You're a good boy for waiting around without running off," I told him, forgetting that Lucius would hear this.

"Strange, he is normally wary of others, but he seems to

like you," he said, coming up behind me and handing me my horrible white bonnet that made me feel like some old woman wearing it.

"What is his name?"

"His name is Sleipnir," Lucius told me and before I could think, my mouth started talking before my brain engaged quick enough to stop me.

"Mmm, an unusual name for a black horse, I always thought Sleipnir was described as being grey." At this he turned me away from his horse and the second I saw his face, I knew the mistake I had made. This was confirmed when he said,

"Now that is curious, for how would someone, who is often described by your own lips as being nothing more than a simple maid, know of such things?"

"I do read," was my only explanation, although it most definitely came out as sounding more like an excuse.

"Then tell me more and prove your knowledge of such." I released a sigh before telling him what I knew.

"Sleipnir was known in Norse mythology as an eight-legged horse used by Odin and as his steed, was sometimes ridden to the location of Hel. He was also known as a child of Loki and Svaðilfari. As I said, he was also described as being grey in colour and was considered as the best of all horses," I said with a shrug of my shoulders like me knowing this was no big deal. Although for Lucius, well he looked more than a little impressed.

"You are well educated for a commoner," he stated, and I could tell he was trying to pick holes in my 'simple' origins.

"My father taught me more than just how to fight," I said hoping this would be enough.

"And your father, where is he now? For I would greatly

like to meet such a man." Oh yeah, I bet he would, no doubt just to gain confirmation to his suspicions about me. Although just what would he have thought knowing the truth, that my father was in fact his friend and King. Well at the very least I could be certain that particular truth would be the furthest from his mind. But as I walked away, turning my back on him, I told him only a half-truth this time,

"He is no longer of this time." At this I felt his fingers curl around my arm, to hold me back.

"Then I am truly sorry, for he sounded like a great man, and one to be admired." I looked back at him and asked,

"Even for a commoner?" At this Lucius bowed his head once and told me after a sigh,

"My words will seem empty, for there are only personal thoughts to give them merit, but where I am from, I believe that the destiny of a man is not bred from wealth or rank, but from the strength of one's heart and the power of will they hold. For a great man is led by their integrity and the bravery to make difficult decisions for the greater good... *this is what I believe, Lia.*"

After he said this, I couldn't help myself or my reactions. I threw myself into his arms and hugged him to me, feeling the tears start to rise. Because what he hadn't realized was that he hadn't just described my father but more importantly...

He just unknowingly, described himself.

Of course, my reaction had taken him off guard, as he first tensed in my arms before relaxing. Then because he didn't want to be trapped by me, he pulled his arms free from where I had them held so he could wrap them around me.

"Thank you, Lucius," I whispered into his chest where I rested my head against him, and I felt him lay a cheek to the top of my head before whispering back in return.

Whispering another name I hadn't yet heard coming from his lips since being here and honestly...

It tugged at my very soul when he said...

"You're welcome, sweetheart."

CHAPTER 9
UNDERCURRENT OF TRUTH
LUCIUS

Gods.

My Chosen One.

I had finally found my Chosen One.

I knew it for certain now. I knew it with every breath I took, for the girl consumed my every waking thought and even those I could not control in my slumber. She was everything and she was now all mine. Or at least...

She soon would be.

From the very first moment I saw her across the room, I felt myself consumed by just the sight of her. Naturally, I had thought it strange at first, the pull she had on me, where no other before her ever had. It was like two pieces of silver thread entwined around us both, with her unknowingly tugging on the end. It drew me closer and closer to her, until I found myself staring down at the most beautiful creature I had ever seen.

Never in all my years had I believed anyone having enough power over me to bring me to my knees but in that moment, I very nearly willingly fell to them. Already knowing of her beauty, having seen but a glimpse of it from across the room and quickly forgetting the woman I had been passing the time with. I couldn't even recall her name, for it seemed as if every single detail in the room fled me in an instant.

There was only her.

Even hearing her chastising herself had me beyond intrigued and I found myself unable to hold back from teasing her. My desire for her to know that I had heard her muttering about her own clumsiness was combined with the hand I offered so as I may help her to her perfect feet. And if I recall, a hand she did not so willingly take and the only part in our meeting that vexed me so.

I remember willing her to raise her head to me, so as I may at last take in much more detail and ultimately my breathing hitched within my chest the moment she finally did. Those stunning cobalt blue eyes like the sapphires mined from the orient. The hint of raven black hair and perfectly shaped lips naturally tinted red for I couldn't see a maid having the inclination to apply rouge. As for her stature, she was much smaller compared to my own, for I was a full head higher than her giving me no choice but to look down at her. Even the width of my chest was near double to hers, despite all the temptingly delicious looking curves I could see under such plain garb. Gods but I just wanted to get her in my bed, so as I may strip away each offending layer that kept her true form hidden from me. This so as I could drink her in and memorize every last inch of her before tasting the journey I had made first with my eyes.

Although the first challenge set against me had been to get her to actually accept my hand, something she had disappointingly seemed reluctant to do. I even remember the way my jaw had hardened when she refused, forcing myself to keep my response light and teasing her about it when being called kind. However, my failings came at the end when I couldn't hold back the order clearly given in my tone, having no choice but to force the issue.

I had needed that first touch.

So, despite being in the presence of a stunning and rare creature, and one I could have beheld in my sights all night, it was in that moment that she finally placed her hand in mine that I knew of our Fated connection. The scorching heat was not one that burned but more like painlessly branded the feel of her to my skin. I was so stunned by the effect that I failed to react in time. For when she snatched her hand away from me, it made me want to growl, making it clearly known of my displeasure of being denied the right to touch her. Of course, her fearful, shy glances around the room told me the root of her fears. As a man of rank, my station in life was vastly different to her own and even holding her hand would have been seen as scandalous to onlookers.

Not that I cared or as my dear Pipper would say, I didn't give a shit or a fuck, for my faithful little Imp was forever the wordsmith. But the sentiment rang true, for all I cared for was knowing who this mythical goddess was and questioning how long before I could get her behind a locked door. But not only had she denied me the right of her hand still held in mine, she also had denied me the right to knowing her name. A rebuff that infuriated me enough that I felt my eyes heating to an unnatural glow, surprising myself at the ease in which I had momentarily lost control. Even my gums had split making way for my fangs to elongate and to such lengths that most mortals would consider a frightening sight indeed.

But what was troubling was that, usually, I never lost control. In truth, I was known for my lethal, calm persona, and as a man and supernatural being who prided myself on making the killing blow without barely a quicken to my pulse. But as for this enticing beauty, well, all my pulse seemed to want to do was quicken. Gods but it was astounding that she had the audacity to dub herself as a person of little consequence when she could not be further from the truth!

However, gaining her trust and ease I knew would not be easy, for it was clear I intimidated her, as she looked as if she could not get away from me quick enough. Well, I knew I would have been damned to even further depths of Hell should I have been foolish enough to let her get away from me that easily. Although what I hadn't expected to see when finding her was seconds after she had been struck by another's hand! Fuck, but I could have drained him there and then, doing this by ripping out his fucking arteries, carrying blood away from his heart permanently.

In fact, it had only been the power of her touch that had made me drop him in the first place, and he was lucky it wasn't after simply snapping his fucking neck. Although letting the bastard bleed out would undoubtably have been more fun to watch.

But that would have left its scars on her mind and memories forever tarnished when thinking of me. For no matter how much I had tried to control her mind, alas to my utter astonishment, it hadn't worked. Her mind was an impenetrable wall erected against me. In truth, I had never encountered anything like it, and it wasn't often for there to be an occurrence for me to be shocked by. Not for a being as old as I.

However, the second I scented her blood, I quickly regretted my decision to let him live. This despite her trying to assure me it was her own clumsiness that caused the injury, I knew that it had been by his hand that had made her healing skin open once more.

Had made my Chosen One bleed.

A declaration of Fate I had confirmed, turning hope and assumption into fact the moment she had finally been given leave of me. But first, I had removed my handkerchief to gain such proof, as I used it to soak up her blood and stop the bleed. Of course, this wasn't without its own difficulties on my part as once more my fangs ached within my gums, desperate to make an appearance, and one that would most certainly frighten her. Because I knew that I would have no choice but to gently ease her into my world and couldn't let her discover who I was at my core. Not before I could first ensure she could not escape me.

I had no doubt that she would understand in time, but that time would be a lot longer in coming should she accidently discover my true self before I could prepare her for such a sight. This being said, it had made holding back even the slightest of reactions near impossible. Meaning, I gave myself leave to scent her blood further, feeling my eyes heat as the near taste of it on the air caused me to lick my lips in anticipation. Anticipation for when I would finally be free to feed from her life source as I pleased, knowing the pleasure it would bring us both when I did.

But for now, all I was granted was a single piece of her, as the moment I was forced to take a step away to make way for the King, I pocketed the blood-soaked handkerchief. I also had to confess how difficult it had been to take a step away back and allow another so close, despite it being that of my King and good and loyal friend. In fact, had he not only so recently been granted God's favour enough to find his own Chosen One, I most likely would not have let him. In the end, all that was left for me to do was bare it with a fist to my side and the scent of her blood coming from my pocket.

Although the moment the King's impatience cut to the

quick, I couldn't stop myself from coming to her aid, pointing out his flaw when trying to get her to answer him and crowding her when doing so. And the arrogant bastard knew it the moment I let slip my protectiveness, as he looked back at me with a knowing smirk. This before asking me that Fated question,

'Did she mean something to me?'

Of course, my answer had not needed time for thought, as instinct guided my lips, for there had been no answer other than yes. Thankfully, this had been all that Dominic had needed to hear as his demeanour towards her instantly warmed, putting me more at ease. It also helped for he had the power to command her duties be passed on to me, and in that moment, he could not have gifted me with anything better. Not when it would ensure our paths now entwined, giving me cause to keep her firmly within my grasp.

Yet despite being happy for this rapid turn of events, it did not bode well for me when she tried to back out of the corner the Lord of this castle had put her in. No, in fact, I was both angered and amused by it, for watching her squirm would no doubt become a favourite pastime of mine.

"It looks like congratulations are in order for both of us, my friend, for we are favoured by the Fates and envied by the Gods this very night," Dom said, clasping me on my shoulder before whispering in my ear,

"Now best get rid of your footman." I scoffed at this and answered as I usually did,

"Indeed."

The King walked away laughing at this, no doubt as eager as I was to get back to his own Chosen One. But like he said, I had a footman to excuse before that could happen for me. Yet I couldn't help but add my thanks just before he went out of sight, as he had most definitely aided me in getting me that step closer to claiming her. As there had still been one important piece left for me to unravel and that had been her identity. The reason being why I prompted such from my friend, as we both knew it was a request that she could not deny us both.

Her name.

Miss Lia Earhart.

Now I had to confess that after hearing this, the truthfulness of its origins didn't ring quite as true as I would have liked. For if this was indeed her name then why did her heart quicken whenever it was spoken if it in itself was not a lie? I confess, that despite feeling the victory of being granted a name, I still felt as if I did not know her any better, for she continued to be not only a surprise but also a mystery.

However, the little I knew of her past mattered not, for it was only her future that concerned me, and it was now an absolute, for in it…

She was mine.

Something I knew for certain the moment I had dispatched my footman, giving him enough coin to drink himself through a few good nights at the local inn. I had finally been free to make my way up to my bed chamber. This knowing there was little chance of her finishing her chore of unpacking my things and therefore assuring that she would still be there. And if I had my way, for the rest of the night at that.

Fuck, but if the Fates had been on my side, then I would have it that she would not leave my bed for the week I intended to be here. Of course, I would not be leaving here without her, but I just hoped that it would be as a willing body and not a reluctant prisoner. Because the moment I had the first chance to do so, I took the blood-soaked handkerchief out of my pocket, and held it to my mouth.

I then let my fangs grow and bit into the material, needing only the barest hint of a taste to know for certain. Which was why my eyes had heated instantly and my body grew taut like the strings of a bow were being armed with an arrow.

I growled into the cloth before it turned into a deep animalistic snarl of want and need.

For it was in that moment I knew without a shadow of doubt that I had found her…

My Fated One.

My Khuba.

CHAPTER 10
SURMOUNTING GLORY

As I guided Sleipnir from the wooded area I had ridden us into, I had the greatest of urges to turn in the opposite direction to the Castle of Muncaster. I could then steal my beautiful little liar away from the world she obviously feared I would discover. Because no matter what excuses Lia had given me in her answers, I knew the hint of the falsehoods she told.

The question I asked myself was why?

What was it that she was hiding from me and why did she feel the need to continue to hold her true self back? Of course, I would be a hypocrite should I think to hold this against her, as I knew I was doing the same. But she was mortal, there was no doubts about that, making me question whether her reasons could be some law breaking on her part. Was she in fact escaping some dark past and feared exposure? I simply did not know, for the only frustrating fact awarded to me was that she was an enigma. A mystery I planned on discovering by any means necessary.

The night just past I had pushed her into answering my questions, challenging the recognition I had seen in her eyes across the ballroom. Of course, it stroked my ego to hear from her own lips that she found me handsome. As I could use this attraction she harboured for me as a tool in getting what I wanted. Did it make me a bastard? But of course it did. Did I give a fuck? No, not in the slightest. The girl was mine, despite the past she held from me and aspects that she must have believed too important to divulge.

But I also knew when to push and when to back off, as scaring her into trusting me was a fool's errand. It was like the Greek philosopher Epicurus once said, *'The greater the difficulty, the more the glory in surmounting it.'*

No truer words spoken, for just holding her in my arms and using the excuse to keep her from slipping from my horse as we rode already felt like glory won. Although the closer we came to the castle, the heavier my heart felt, and I longed for the day we would ride like this on the way to my own. For every time I was forced to let her go from my grasp, it felt like the shell of my patience was cracking until I would be unable to control my actions any longer. It was also an emotion I was not familiar with. Not enough to know how to act or, in this case, how *not to act*... not without anything other than irrational thought.

I was known to be a calculating bastard, only striking out at an opponent when the timing was perfect, aimed to achieve the greatest outcome. I was calm, even in my rage, and I was lethal. But around her, I felt as if I had been stripped bare of these well-known traits and reborn into an ever-questioning thought, one barely in my right mind enough to make decisions.

Like when I had been forced to let her leave my bedchamber for the night, never before had I known such a battle within my mind. I had not lied when I told her sleep did not come easy that night. However, I had refrained in disclosing what happened shortly after she left. When I had growled the word,

"Enough!" Then hammered a fist to the wall, needing to pull my fist from stone before I stalked the hallways searching for her scent like a man fucking obsessed!

Naturally, I had found where she slept, took over the minds of those she shared a room with and walked inside. The ache in my chest only settled when I saw her sleeping form, easing the pain of being apart. Gods but how badly I had wanted to scoop her up into my arms and walk away with her. To feel the comforting weight of her in my grasp before laying her down in my bed and keeping her there until such an ache fled me completely.

If it ever did.

But in the end, all I gave myself leave to do was to caress the escaping strands of hair from her face before running the backs of my fingers down her cheek.

'Until the rising of the sun, little maid,' I had whispered down at her before laying a gentle kiss on her forehead and forcing myself to leave. Only after this moment shared, was I finally granted the solace of sleep, as my fears that she would be using the darkness of night to escape had been eradicated.

But then morning blessed me with the sight of her once more and I had to grin to myself when she entered my room in clear hopes that she would not wake me. Of course, I had wanted to lead her into that false sense freedom, making my move when I deemed it would make the most impact on her, purposely sleeping half naked. I had been tempted to show her all, if only to be granted the gift of the blush upon her skin. A natural sun-kissed complexion that made little sense in this climate. Especially, seeing as the wildness of the mountainous region in Northwest England offered little in the way of sun. Perhaps her origins of family would offer an explanation for her olive skin? And despite how she tried to hide it, there was no getting away from the hints of a foreign accent that was not entirely English and held an undercurrent of something else. Something I was hoping to discover as she was sure to slip up, especially if I continued to disarm her like I had done this morning when breaking my fast.

Something accomplished when seeing that knowing blush of hers creep along her skin, and one I had been aiming to obtain in response to how I greeted her. For the moment her eyes had taken in my muscular physique, I had all but nearly needed to place a fist in my mouth to prevent the laughing trying to burst out of me. Her stunning blue eyes widened like a doe in the sights of a hunter and her small, feminine hands twisted in her white linen pinafore, one pinned to the front of her plain dress.

But then her stomach had signalled its need for substance and all other thoughts had fled me, for I only wanted her cared for. I even found myself furious at the thought that she had gone without, vowing that it would not happen again. For she was mine to care for now and I would not have her neglecting herself.

Yet, what surprised me was the interest I found in the simplest of things. Just watching her eat had me transfixed, but then this combined with her light-hearted and teasing conversation, her opinions spoken freely… *fuck, but I was lost to all that was her.* It was like being awarded with a glimpse of the future and I found myself as excited for the mundane things equal to if I had been about to go into battle. Life, it seemed, would no longer be dull and unfulfilling for the most part, but now would be full of moments like this simple meal shared. Moments that no matter how simple would bloom into the excitement of new, for I would be sharing them all with her and seeing the world once again with new eyes.

She was clearly a woman of high intelligence, despite the feeling that she held herself back and no doubt did so to keep up the persona that she was of simple origins. Yet I doubted this more and more the longer I was in her company, for she was extremely well read and didn't speak like the commoner she claimed to be.

Therefore, my suspicions were leading me down a path that was likely to lead to a destination of a noble birth. That she was choosing the simple life whereas she would be free to make her own choices without duty or obligation getting in the way of what she wanted. Of course, the thought of her engaged to be married to another was enough to have me wanting to commit murder, as she belonged to no man but that of this jealous Vampire King.

But it did not negate the fact that if this turned out to be the truth, then it explained most of her behaviour. Like why she would want to keep her true identity from me, no doubt amassing her fears to the exposure marriage with a noble man would open her up to. Which meant that I would have to reassure her that this would not be the outcome, for I would do all in my power to protect her from anyone who would think to try and steal her away from me. But also, at the core of the matter, I ultimately wanted her to fall in love with me, as the match between us relied on much more than just Fate.

For Fate would never be enough.

Not when I aimed to possess her heart.

Which brought me back to now and being forced to help her from my horse as soon as we reached the stables. The excuse to watch her blush as I gripped her slim waist, now spanning it with my large hands, was considered too much a lost opportunity to miss. An action that made her gasp as I purposely dragged her down my body, just as I had done so back in the clearing. The satisfaction I gained knowing she was not immune to my touch nearly outweighed the frustrations I felt in letting her go, as she was soon free to hurry off back to the castle. Of course, I had tried arguing her reasons, but this was to no avail, as her concerns of getting into trouble with the head housekeeper continued to vex me.

I simply could not wait until she was known as the lady of whatever house we occupied, for her days as being known as my maid were certainly numbered. However, before I let her go, I reached for her hand and pulled her back to me, putting a stop to her escape.

"I have to go." She tried once more to deny me, making me grip her chin and force her eyes to mine.

"And for now, I will let you go, but only after the vow of return, for be warned, if you do not keep your promise this time, I will be inclined to steal you away again." At this she nodded, but it wasn't good enough.

"Words, little one... *grant me your words,*" I urged, making her sigh in defeat.

"Don't worry, My Lord, I won't let you go hungry... for food of course!" she shouted this last part the moment she saw the way my eyes heated as I was most certainly hungry, and she knew with one look that it wasn't for food.

No, it was now and forevermore...

Just For her.

CHAPTER II
WANTING PIE
AMELIA

By the time I finally managed to free myself from Lucius's grasp, I made my way out of the stable yard and back to the castle down the gravel path. But as I was glancing behind me, checking Lucius wasn't chasing after me, I wasn't looking where I was going so ran straight into Mrs Price who was very flustered.

"Good heavens, where have you been?!" I instantly looked back up the path I had come to see Lucius now striding masterfully from the stables and towards us. Mrs Price followed my gaze and was forced to clear her throat as she started to guess the wrong thing... *or was it the right thing?*

Even I didn't know any more.

"I must apologize, as I did not intend to be gone for most of the day," I said while trying to think of an excuse and buy myself time with my apologies.

"And pray tell, Miss Earhart, just where did you spend most of the day when your work is here... *indoors,*" she added this last part as an obvious slight rendered on my part but even then, I knew she was being lenient with me. A reason that might have had something to do with the irritated looking Vampire coming our way. In fact, I was just opening my mouth to speak when Lucius did so for me.

"Miss Earhart, please allow me to thank you for assisting me today on the errand that was imposed upon me by Lord Draven, he will be most pleased by the outcome, I am sure. Of course, I do not need to remind you for your discretion on this matter," he said, clearly coming to my aid and leaving Mrs Price without any doubts as to why I had been absent most of the day.

"But of course, My Lord," I said bowing my head respectfully.

"Excellent. Now as for my evening meal, I will take this in my chambers, for my research continues and if I may impose upon you once more, then I will be in need of your assistance in this also. For I am sure Mrs Price can survive without you for an evening," Lucius said, posing this more as direct order than that of a question. Something that meant it gave her no choice as she too bowed her head and replied,

"Certainly, My Lord, I will free Miss Earhart of any duties she had assigned to her." Lucius looked smug in this outcome, making me wish I was free to sigh as it looked like he was trying to manipulate another night out of me. One where he could watch me squirm in his cat and mouse game. And damn myself for continually wanting to be that mouse!

"Very good. Miss Earhart, I will take my leave of you but, *J'ai hâte de te goûter ce soir,*" Lucius said, ending this in perfect French and I failed once more in my pretence of being nothing more than a simple maid when I couldn't help but react as I started coughing on a breath. This made him walk away grinning to himself as he had, yet again, discovered even more proof that I was not exactly who I said I was. Not when I knew mythology, clearly spoke French and knew how to defend myself.

But then again, I knew being around Lucius was dangerous and each minute spent in his presence was only adding strength to that belief.

"What did he say?" Mrs Price asked, making me blush and shrug my shoulders as if I didn't know. Of course, the problem was that I did know, and that meant now all I could think about was what lay in store for me tonight, especially when he had just told me,

'I look forward to tasting you tonight.'

∼

"Come on, Pip, where the Hell are you?" I hissed under my breath as I had spent the rest of the daylight hours searching for her. Because she was the only one I was free to speak with. Especially seeing as I had already bumped into my aunt Sophia, only to find myself unable to say anything other than excuse myself. Because my father had been within easy hearing distance and therefore, I had no other option than to set down the tea tray and get out of there with haste. She did, however, grant me a comforting smile before mouthing a single word,

'Soon'

Something that made me even more eager to speak with Pip, because it seemed as if they had a plan at last. But as for me, well I had not one single clue how to get out of taking Lucius his evening meal. It was clear that if I didn't show up, he would simply come and find me, already threatening to steal me away again. Something that coming from anyone else, I would have believed to be nothing but an empty threat. However, this was Lucius we were talking about and if there was anything I knew with a certainty when it came to him, it was...

He never made empty threats.

Which meant that by the time his tray was handed to me, I was left with no choice but to take it to him. And with every step I made though the castle, I tried to think of an excuse that would save me the temptation the night ahead promised. Of course, my hussy of a brain came up with nothing, meaning that by the time I reached his door, my heart was hammering in my chest. So much so, he must have heard it as the door opened for me before I had chance to struggle with knocking while holding the large tray.

"Good evening, Miss Earhart," Lucius said in such a way I swear my toes curled and heat bloomed in my belly. His words felt more like some sexual caress than that of just a simple greeting.

"My Lord," I replied, something that had him smirking once more as if he knew, just like he always did, what it was he did to me. Then he took the tray from my hands and frowned at it as he walked over to the window and placed it down at the table. A strange reaction that prompted me enough to ask,

"Is something wrong?"

"I was expecting two plates," he said, making me react before thinking.

"Oh, I didn't know you were expecting someone," I replied, worried now that I had missed something but then he burst out laughing and said,

"But of course, for she is here now and looking nervous as always." I blushed at this and told him,

"Yes well, the last time I was here you locked the door, so I... wait, what are you doing?" I asked when he walked to the door and did exactly that before turning to me as he made a point of pocketing the key.

"I would hate to disappoint," he replied cockily, causing me to narrow my gaze when he said this.

"That's not what I meant." However, he simply grinned at this, and it was a knowing smirk that told me I had little say in the matter.

"No, but it was always my intent and very good of you to remind me of such. Now if you please…" he replied before holding an arm out towards the table, motioning for me to sit.

"I already rid you of your morning meal, so I think it would be unfair of me to do so again."

"Then you will do me the honour of your company." I looked back at the door when he said this, knowing this was a bad idea. But seeing as it also looked like it was one I couldn't get out of, I let my feet lead me closer to where he wanted me. However, it was when I was looking over at the table near the window that I took pause. Just knowing that I was now trapped had me chewing on my bottom lip, and it became clear to him that I was unsure of what to do. Which was when he made the decision for me as I felt his presence close enough behind me that his lips were soon at my ear,

"Relax, little maid, for I do not bite." I almost choked at this and nearly forgot myself when I wanted to shout bullshit. But I felt his hand come to my side and squeeze, making me shiver at his touch. This before that same hand slid to the base of my spine and applied pressure. So, I did as he asked and took my seat, one he held out for me, making me sigh as I lowered myself into it.

Then I watched as he took the one opposite me, leaving the tray in the middle between us. Seconds later and he lifted the silver dome, also known as a cloche, off the plate and awarded us both with the delicious smell of venison pie.

"Mmm, I hear that the cook here is famous for her pies and there have been many a lord trying to steal her away from the castle." I laughed at this.

"Yes, well they would have a job on their hands with that," I muttered, making him enquire in an amused tone,

"How so?"

"Clearly you have never seen Mrs Wheeler with a rolling pin in her hand," I said, thinking about the large butch lady that was head of the kitchens, with rosy cheeks that she would puff out in annoyance on the few occasions I had seen her making demands of her staff. He laughed at this and said,

"Fair point, Miss Earhart." Then he picked up the fork and used it to dig into the round pie that, I had to admit, had my mouth watering at the sight. Which was why I didn't hesitate when he held the fork out to me, making me lean forward to take a bite.

"Oh Gods, that tastes soooo good," I said, forgetting myself and feeling my eyes roll up as my tastebuds started to sing. However, the moment his eyes heated showing me the hint of crimson, I quickly looked away, making me mutter,

"Forgive me, My Lord." But I quickly felt my hand being taken as he reached across so as he could gain my attention ready for his words.

"Never apologize for the pleasure you find, for I fully intend to gift it to you... and often." I swallowed hard at this and just because I needed to clear the sexual air, I said,

"Then in that case, maybe you should brave the rolling pin and steal me the cook." At this he threw his head back and laughed heartedly, making me bask in the handsome sight. He was utter perfection, as always, but made to look more roguish now he had removed his jacket and only wore his black waistcoat. His longer hair was still tied back from how it had been on the ride and the temptation to reach out and pull the tie free was almost too much to resist. Damn, what I wouldn't have given in that moment for a lake and the opportunity to create my own wet Mr Darcy moment.

After this, the conversation continued to flow, despite Lucius taking every opportunity to try and gain information from me on my past. Naturally, I was purposely flippant with my replies as I didn't want to lie to him but then Lucius wasn't stupid. He knew exactly what I was doing. Every time I evaded a question or answered one with another question he simply gave me a pointed look. Just like when he suddenly asked me,

"Were you ever engaged to be married?" I nearly choked on the wine he had poured me.

"Have you?" I asked as he walked back over to the glass decanter so as to pour himself a glass.

"No," he instantly replied, and I couldn't keep the bitterness out of my tone when I reminded him of when we first met in this time period.

"What, not even to that woman I saw you with? Surely, she was promised more than just a single moment kissing a Lord?" At this he grinned before leaning back against the sideboard and shrugged his shoulders, now looking smug before telling me,

"I never make promises I am not assured to keep." I scoffed at this and clearly, he was enjoying the idea that I was jealous. This was confirmed when he pointed out what we both knew was an obvious fact,

"You seem to be fixated on how we first met, for you have mentioned her twice now… so tell me, Miss Earhart, are you jealous?" At this, I made a frustrated sound and got to my feet before making my way across the room towards the door.

"I think it best I get back to my duties." At this he had the arrogant audacity to laugh and made no attempt to try and stop me. But then again, he didn't need to. I was reminded of this when the door wouldn't open.

"Unlock the door," I ordered sternly, something he simply continued to look amused by.

"And pray tell, why would I do that, little maid?" he asked light-heartedly. So, I stormed back over to him and held out my hand.

"Because I am a free woman who wishes to leave your presence. Now give me the key," I stated firmly, wishing I could wipe that smirk off his handsome face with a swipe of my leg and put his overconfident cocky ass to the floor. At this he put his hand in his pocket and pulled out the means to my escape, holding it out in his palm.

"You mean this key?" he asked in that same playful tone, making me angry.

"Yes!" I shouted before trying to get it, but damn him he was too fast and closed his fingers around it before I could grab it.

"And once again, why would I do that?" he asked, making me growl in frustration, something that had him biting his lips as if trying to stop himself from laughing at me.

"Because I demand you give it to me!"

"Oh, you demand it of me, is that right, little one?" he asked, emphasizing the height difference between us when he held up his fist above me, doing so the moment I tried to take the key from his hand.

"Just give me the damn key, you big brute!" I shouted, and when I started trying to climb him like a tree, he simply wrapped an arm around my waist and picked me up off my feet. Then he held me off to the side while laughing as if this was the most fun he'd had in years.

"Big brute, am I?" he asked cheerfully, making me growl again.

"If the manhandling shoe fits!" I snapped back, making him raise a brow at me after putting me down.

"I have heard if the cap fits, but nevertheless, either fits me well enough." I snorted a laugh at this, and muttered,

"Oh, I just bet it does... now if you will kindly give me that key!"

"And what do I get in return?" he asked, now crowding around me until, soon, I was the one with their back against the sideboard. His hands now lying flat against the top, caging me in so I had nowhere to go, keeping the key firmly under one of them.

"What... what do you want?" I asked, now losing my anger with him being this close. But that was the power he held over me, the power he always had... the means to render me completely under his spell.

"What do you think I want?" he asked seductively.

"Another pie?" I asked, making his lips twitch before he shook his head and then leaned in close and said,

"No, little maid..."

"I only want you."

CHAPTER 12
BARGAINS AND BATTLES

The second he said this, I lowered my face so as he wouldn't see the yearning in my eyes to let him have me. How badly I wanted him to simply take me in his arms and never let me go. But I had to keep reminding myself that my own Lucius was back in my time and, there, he was husband. He would be there waiting for me to come home. A home I would never return to if I gave *this* Lucius a Fated reason to keep me.

Which was why I replied in a soft voice,

"I can't give you that."

"Cannot or will not?" he asked, making me sigh.

"Are they not the same thing, My Lord?" At this he lifted my face, forcing me to take in his dissatisfied gaze.

"No, they are not, for the root of one is denying yourself what you truly want, and the other is refusing me of what I truly want and for reasons not yet known to me."

"I have already explained why," I reminded him quietly.

"You explained nothing, for if it is not a lie that comes from these lips, it is a twisted version of the truth, lips I wish to punish with the force of my own!" I gasped at this and tried to pry myself from him, but I was too late, he was already lowering his head and claiming what he wanted. This not only rendered me speechless, but it also ignited within me the very same passion that I was powerless to stop from being released. A passion I knew would only spur him on to take more and because I would let him, it made me a liar in his eyes every time I tried to deny him.

Because he knew, *I was only denying us both.*

But without him understanding why, then it wasn't exactly surprising he would push for it, no doubt trying to break through the barriers I had tried to build against him. His question about me being engaged before terrified me because I didn't want to give anything away. Like the fact that I already was married and was currently cheating on my husband with… well, technically, *with my husband.*

Yet despite how amazing it felt to be in Lucius's arms, tasting his lips and getting lost in the sensation of belonging to him, I knew I had to stop it. Especially when he suddenly lifted me up and wrapped my legs around him before he started to make his way to the bed.

"No, we ca…"

"Yes, we can!" he growled back before leaning in once more and kissing me, reclaiming my lips as if he were a madman desperate. Which was why as soon as he started to lay me down, caging me beneath his body, I shouted the first thing I could think of the second I had freedom to do so when his lips found my neck.

"I'm a virgin!" This made him freeze above me before releasing a heavy sigh. Then he pulled back and told me,

"I am happy to hear it and even better, for I won't have to kill anyone for touching what is soon to be mine and mine alone." I gasped, knowing that this was not having the effect that I had hoped for.

So much for Pip's advice.

"I am not this type of girl," I said, trying to reason with him in another way.

"And pray tell, what type of girl is it in which you speak?" he asked, now framing my face and pushing my bonnet back from my head before gently stroking around the area the cut was slowly healing.

"I will not lay with a man, a Lord at that, only to be cast aside when he has taken what he wants," I said despite knowing that he was not that man. But it was the only excuse I had left to go with, after all, the person I was claiming to be was someone who had only known him twenty-four hours. And well, all things considered, this shouldn't have been a great surprise to him. Not seeing as my first sight of him had been from across the room locked in the embrace of another woman.

"Then you mistake me greatly, for trust me, little maid, having you only once will never be enough." I sucked in a quick breath at that, knowing how nice it was to hear but equally as frustrated, as it wasn't serving my purpose in trying to get out the room.

"And how can you be so sure? For a second time might be enough," I challenged, something that made him grin before asking,

"Are you bargaining with me, little one?" He seemed amused by the idea. But as for me, well I was sticking with my original plan and still trying to talk my way out of this. Something he was not making easy with the way he kept undressing me with his eyes and caressing me softly with his light touch. Which was why I asked,

"What do you want with me?"

"I think that's more than obvious considering you lay beneath me on my bed. And as a woman that's able to kiss with such a fevered passion, well I think you intelligent enough to know what the hard line and heavy weighted feel of my cock pressing against you means… *and where I would like it to go,"* he whispered this last part down at me, making me blush.

"I know what it is for a man to lay with a woman despite never experiencing the pleasure for myself," I replied, now squirming beneath him, wishing I was not having this conversation in such a vulnerable position. Because yes, the feel of that very obvious cock of his pressed heavily against me was most definitely making the virgin act harder to play. Especially when I knew exactly what I wanted to do with it before begging him to do exactly what I knew he wanted to do with it.

"But you have kissed before?" he asked, and I was about to open my mouth to answer him when suddenly two fingers prevented me from doing so as they pressed against my lips.

"Actually, do not answer that question, not unless you wish to render me murderous." I would have smiled at this but chose to tease him instead.

"Now who is the one showing their jealousy?"

"I have no problem revealing my thoughts or showing the obvious distain I feel when thinking of you being with another, nor am I ashamed to admit that these thoughts render me jealous to the point of madness… which makes me question why I have those feelings at all for someone I have only known but a day." I swallowed hard at this, knowing I was walking on dangerous grounds just by having this conversation. Yet despite this, I couldn't help but give him something, letting my feelings slip through my barriers.

"Only you are able to answer that, My Lord, but perhaps…"

"Perhaps?"

I took a pause, knowing this was going too far, but one look at his face and I knew he needed something from me to explain my behaviour towards him.

"Perhaps it is the same feeling or reasoning I too felt when I first saw you, beholding your image above all else across the room." At this he granted me a soft smile, before agreeing,

"Perhaps indeed, but I refuse to presume that you kiss with such passion of the likes you have bestowed upon me with just anyone and again, I do not want details." I smirked at this and gave him what he needed… *a slither of the truth.*

"Then I can grant you this and put you at ease, for I vow that I have never kissed anyone that way before, nor have I ever been kissed with such passion returned."

At this his eyes widened in surprise before suddenly a hand was collared at my throat again, and his next demand was almost snarled down at me.

"Say it again, so as I can hear the truth from not just your lips alone, but also feel it as a shuddered breath and thundering pulse against my palm." I nodded once before giving him this easy truth.

"I have never kissed anyone the way I have with you, My Lor…" I never finished, because suddenly his lips claimed me once again and like all others, I had no way to stop the sexual fever that burned between us.

His hand disappeared from my neck, moving to my hair and gripping it in his fist to lock my lips to his. The kiss was just as fervent and the moment I felt his free hand slipping down my side and grazing my breast along the way, I knew again I had to stop this.

So I pulled back, panting this time and quickly reminding him,

"I thought we were going to bargain."

CHAPTER 13
ESCAPE IS KEY

"I thought we were going to bargain."

At this he let his forehead fall to my chest as he too dragged the much-needed air into his lungs. As if this was what he required to force a moment of clarity into his lust-induced brain.

Oh, and of course, he wasn't the only one.

"You want to know that you are special to me before I claim your Maidenhead?" he asked, and I nearly choked on a breath as I started coughing. *If only he knew why.*

"I want to know that I am not like the woman I found you kissing," I said after clearing my throat, hoping this would buy me the time I needed to think of enough of a reason to take things slow with me.

"You are nothing like that woman, nor would you ever be, for that you can be sure of. And despite the lies I know in which you occasionally speak, I know that your soul is pure. Which means I would only be damning my own if I was to darken its light in any way, despite what I want to do to you."

"Dare I ask what those things are?" I stupidly asked,

wanting to kick myself the second after I let the question leave my mouth.

"You may dare, but as of yet, it is not an answer I'm willing to give." Of course, his cryptic reply wasn't half as cryptic to me as his wife and someone who knew him better than anyone else. But to someone who just met him, I knew it would be strange if I didn't respond to this.

"Why not? After all, it's like you pointed out, for you already have me in your bed and the key firmly in your pocket to prevent me from leaving."

"That may be so, but I do not want you frightened of me, as it is not your fear I want to taste, but your passion, unrestrained and free… that is what I want… *that is what I crave from you, my little servant girl."* I swallowed hard and he watched every motion with rapt interest.

"Now for one so pure, it does surprise me to see that you do not look frightened as perhaps you should by the cravings I speak of." I decided to keep my mouth shut on this matter as I already knew of Lucius's dominant tendencies in the bedroom. I knew of his preferences to have me tied to his bed and at his mercy of his hands, teeth, and tongue before granting me the delicious brutality of his cock. Whether it was being held in my mouth for longer and deeper than I thought myself capable of achieving or it being pounded into my core making me feel every hard inch.

"I think we should speak of the bargain we are to make," I said, wisely choosing to steer the conversation back to safer ground. Especially with the way his hands kept stroking down my side or caressing back my hair.

"Tell me what you want, Miss Earhart." I bit my lip thinking about it, wondering what I could possibly say that didn't include the word marriage, *unless*…

"I will not become your mistress," I stated firmly, making him jerk back a little as if shocked by my statement.

"I believe that is you telling me what you *do not* want, despite me giving you no intention of making you my mistress of anything."

"I could not possibly become your wife!" I shrieked, at the same time I shifted up from being underneath him and thankfully he allowed me the freedom to do so, meaning I was now sitting with my back against the headboard. But that raised brow of his prewarned me for what came next.

"No? Pray tell me, why not, am I that hideous a prospect?" he asked, sitting back and folding his arms as if somewhat insulted by my outburst.

"No, but I am," I said, making him growl back at me, and the next bite of his words was said through gritted teeth.

"Never speak that way of yourself ever again."

I swallowed hard before nodding, taking the threat seriously.

"Now when you speak next, I suggest you use logical thought I know that clever mind of yours is so capable of conjuring."

I released a sigh to this and told him what he should have known as an obvious fact. One that I was starting to think he was purposely refusing to acknowledge because he did, in fact, believe me to be his Chosen One. Because there was no other reason for him to behave this way. Not unless he really had fallen in love with a human, saying to Hell with prophecy.

"I have no dowry," I reminded him.

"That matters little to me, for I am a very rich man and care little about adding to an already substantial pot." Well, I knew this to be true as even back in my own time he made no secret about how he felt about me trying to earn my own money. Oh no, not when he believed his vast fortune was now my own to do with as I pleased.

"I have no status, no family name to align with your own," I said, pointing out another fact that should have concerned him in this charade we were both playing.

"You may think I care for such things as a family alliance, but you must know that my last name is not one you'll ever hear shared upon these shores. Nor do I care for what society thinks of me."

"But that can't be true?" I said, even though I knew it was. But if I hadn't shown shock by this statement then it would have seemed odd on my part.

"I can assure you it is. Despite what most would consider as the advantages of being rich being that nobody really cares for what you are, not if you have enough money to buy opinion, which I do… and still, I choose not to," he said making his point and adding to the fact that he really didn't care what people thought of him. But then again, for a vampire who was thousands of years old, then why would he? How many more lives would he see come and go? How much of society was constantly changing, and changing as quickly as fashioned did?

"So, you're talking about a scandalous love match, is that what this is to be?" I asked, making him grin before reaching for my hand, now holding it firmly in his own.

"All I know is that I want you like I have never wanted another before and you may not understand this, but trust me when I say that I have lived long enough to know what a rare gift that feeling is, indeed. Just like the Lord of this castle has also recently felt it, and when people like us do, we are not so foolish as to ever let it go again," he said, reminding me of what my mother was also going through in this moment and how, like Lucius, my father never had any intention of letting her go. Which begged the question, did I really need any more confirmation than this? It was becoming clearer by the second that Lucius did in fact believe me to be his Fated.

"I... I don't know what to say," I replied honestly, a rare response I didn't need to fake.

"Then do not speak but, instead, listen to what else I have to say for I hope I will only need to say it the once. I want you, not as some passing fancy to warm my bed for the time that I am here but for always."

"My Lord, I..." I tried to interrupt him, but he clearly had much more to say on the matter.

"I will be heard in this, Lia, for it is time you know your Fate, for I fully intend to be taking you with me when I leave here. You will be well taken care of, for in that let there be no mistake, as I can assure you, I take care of what is mine," he said sincerely and I couldn't help but reply,

"What is yours? You make me sound like a possession, Sir."

"My most precious yet," he agreed and, once again, I didn't need to fake my response of shock.

"I..."

"I understand that this is a lot to take in, for you do not know me well enough and therefore perhaps think these empty words in some scandalous attempt to get you in my bed and keep you here for the night. Which is why as part of my bargain, I will allow you to leave it for the night." At this I sucked in a quick breath, and I was not ashamed to say that only half of it was relief. The foolish other half was most definitely disappointment and I stupidly let this be known in the tone of my reply.

"You're letting me go?"

"Ah now, is that disappointment I hear in your voice? For I could quite easily take it…"

"No, no, I'm just surprised, that is all," I said hastily, knowing this was my chance to save myself the heartache of having to refuse him if he wanted more. Or maybe I was just afraid that I wouldn't have the will power strong enough to actually say no. But then again, if he truly did believe me to be his Chosen One, then was there any point in fighting it?

Damn it, but I just didn't know!

"Do not mistake me, for I'm not letting you go for long. I'm doing this to prove to you that this is not all about making you mine in this bed, but in fact making you mine in every bed from here on out. Making you mine on every path we walk along, in every country we set foot in, and I am allowed to be graced with your presence and beauty. For you will serve me only as a wife and never as a servant again. Now do you understand the future I have in mind for you?" he said, making my heart beat faster and faster.

I had to admit, hearing the way he was declaring me as his for the second-first time in our lives was of course going to have the same affect. He was the man I loved, no matter which time period he was from and to hear how much he wanted me in return warmed my soul, just like it had the first time.

"Lia?" He spoke the wrong name and it was enough to jar me back into the situation.

"I understand your words as much as they confuse me," I confessed as this wasn't a complete lie, not when I no longer knew what to do.

"Then I will also give you the time to understand them, but know this, little maid, and heed my words, for I am not a patient man, so I will not allow you the time you may think you need... no, for I will be the judge of that."

Well at least he was giving me time, and hopefully enough of it so I could make my escape. It was clear now that our window of opportunity was closing fast. Especially when Lucius planned to steal me away from this fake life as a maid and quickly make me his wife... *again.*

"I think I should be awarded more than a day to think about the rest of my life and what may become of it," I said, trying for more time as a backup.

"In that case, I will endeavour to think of a way to convince you that I am as sincere with my offer as I am equally hoping that you accept it."

"I don't know you... you don't know me," I pointed out as this was most definitely true, if not a little one-sided considering I was his time-traveling wife from the future. Jeez, but even that one would make Doc Brown's head spin.

"I know enough and as for everything else... well, time will award us all we need to know."

"But how can you be so sure?" I asked, wondering if he would open up to me about Fate.

"There is a way, I can assure you, despite it paining me to even suggest it." I frowned at this, wondering what he could possibly mean and making me ask,

"Which is?"

"I vow not to take your virginity, until I have wed you and made you my wife under the eyes of God."

I gasped, knowing for Lucius this was big and no doubt meant that he was already planning the wedding in his head. Especially if sex was off the cards with his Chosen One until we had said the 'I do's'.

I also questioned Lucius's motives. If he was willing to

make me his wife, to make me this offer without telling me the full truth of what he was, how did he ever intend for that to work in our future? Was he really going to be that deceitful by letting me marry him, so as to tie myself to him so fully, that by the time he did reveal his true self, I would have nowhere to run?

I knew this time was vastly different for these kings, and that caveman thought process was still clearly following them over from some barbaric time zone. Somewhere that should have been long ago left in the past, as clearly my father keeping my mother locked to his bedchamber was evidence enough of that. But I couldn't help but feel disappointed at the betrayal, despite knowing his reasons.

"That looks like a heavy mind, little one," he commented, running the backs of his fingers down my cheek and along my jawline.

"You've clearly given me a lot to think about," I stated, hoping this was enough of an explanation for what I knew must have been a worrisome expression.

"Don't think for too long or too hard, sweetheart, or you may not like the outcome," he warned, making my eyes snap back up to his.

"Dare I ask again?"

"And once again, you may dare, but from the lips of a man that wants you to accept the offer you have been bestowed, I will refrain from revealing my true nature just as of yet." I frowned at this, knowing just what he meant by that. Which was why I couldn't help myself when poking the Demon.

"Your true nature? Pray tell me, My Lord, will you turn into a beast of a man once we are married?" I asked in jest, despite knowing what he truly was. Thankfully, he took this playfulness as what it was, an impasse in battles of the heart.

Which was why he leaned forward and growled playfully in my neck before nibbling at the flesh there. Something I knew would soon turn into something more and as I closed my eyes, basking in the feel of his lips on my neck, I forced myself to say,

"I think it is time for me to leave, as like you said, I have a lot of thinking to do." At this he narrowed his gaze a moment, before telling me,

"Actually, I think I have changed my mind."

"What?!" I gasped, and the disappointment was easy to hear in my tone despite knowing foolishly I should have been happy. My goal by coming here was not to remarry my husband or to make him fall madly in love with me for a second time.

Yet despite all logic telling me this, I couldn't help the bitter sting that gripped my whole being. But then I was suddenly pulled down the bed, making me quickly slide underneath him and back to my original position.

"I see no reason you can't think right here in my arms," he told me and I, irrationally, released a sigh of relief that again should not have been allowed passed my lips. Not as it gave him false hope as this was not our time despite a foolish piece of me wishing it was.

I had to say, it was the romanticized dream I'd always had when meeting my Chosen One for the first time. To have them fall madly in love with me at first glance. Which meant this had kind of been more like a fairy tale to experience, and far from my own past filled with the dark tale of woe Lucius and I had started off as.

"I cannot sleep with you in this bed," I stated in a scandalous tone.

"And why not? For when you accept my offer you will be in it every night."

"If I accept your offer," I countered, making him do the same.

"When you accept my offer… for mark my words, I am not leaving here without you," he said purposely making me shiver.

"And what are you going to do, Sir, pack me into one of your trunks and sneak me out of here?" I only half teased, as knowing Lucius, well then, I wouldn't have put it past him.

"Don't give me ideas, for I quite like the idea of you locked in a cage." I couldn't help but laugh at this.

"Then I certainly hope that you jest, or you might find me running for the hills screaming like a mad woman trying to escape you."

"Ah but I would give chase… and given the prize I would win at the end of my hunt, I would therefore enjoy it immensely," he told me, making me suck in a much needed breath. I then nervously laughed, because despite it being said in jest, I also knew the undercurrent of truth that came with it. Especially when knowing from past experience that Lucius had once before hunted me, and quite successfully at that. This despite all my best efforts. Because he was right, there was no other answer that he would have accepted than agreeing for me to be his. Not when he was a King used to getting his own way and letting nothing stand in his way when there was something he wanted. And clearly, *that something was me.*

"I can't stay," I told him, making him sigh before pulling the one card in his time period arsenal.

"Then I commanded it of you as your Lord."

"You cannot do that," I stated firmly, making him grin down at me before reminding me of one very important fact.

"I think you're forgetting something, little dove…" He

paused so he could lower his lips to my ear to tell me exactly why he could do that and, in fact, fully intended to.

Words that meant far more then even he could imagine them to mean…

"I still hold the key to your escape."

CHAPTER 14
FOOLISH BLOODY MISTAKES

After he said this, Lucius made it abundantly clear that I was going nowhere and therefore felt the freedom to get off the bed. I then slowly sat up and watched him as he removed his waistcoat, needing to bite my lip as the thin material of his bellowing shirt did nothing to hide the perfect physique underneath.

"Erm… what are you…?" This was said in response to him gripping my ankle and pulling me down closer to him before he removed my shoes. This also left me no choice but to rest my weight back, now propped up on my elbows.

"Isn't it obvious? Getting you comfortable, of course," he replied with a knowing grin, as once again, he just loved to make me squirm.

"Yes, well as long as it stops at my shoes." At this his heated eyes found mine and held my gaze when his hands caress up my leg and pulled on the ribbon that kept my simple stockings in place. Then he tantalizingly started to pull one down my legs, making me nearly sigh with need as his fingertips grazing my skin only made me want to feel more. I swear by the time he moved to the next leg I was near purring!

"But why stop there? For this also looks as though it provides little in the way of comfort," he said once finished with my legs, now crawling his way up me and tugging at my dress.

"Then fine, you may rid me of my apron and that is all, My Lord." At this he smirked at my reply before he did just that, purposely grazing my breasts when unpinning my pinafore. Then after gripping the material in his fist, he tossed it aside before lowing himself down over me, keeping his weight rested more on one side so as not to crush me with his weight.

"You don't play fair," I whispered, closing my eyes as he ran his nose up my cheek and down again where he breathed deep at my neck.

"I never claimed I would, little one," he whispered in my ear before letting his body fall completely to the side of me, allowing me to release a held breath. Then he tucked me close to his body, spooning me from behind and after moments of feeling my tensed body against his own, he whispered,

"Relax, sweetheart, for I only wish to hold you throughout the night." Naturally, I let his words take effect and felt my body ease into the cradle of his own and for a few blissful hours, I allowed myself to bask in the comfort of his arms.

Which meant that as I lay there after he had tucked me close to his frame, my mind was left to wander long after he had fallen asleep. I couldn't help but focus on my mission and the very reason I was here. The vow I had made and the added weight I felt pressing down on my soul. Because no matter what happened after this point, I knew I would be crushing his heart as I had no choice but to run. Something I had promised to Lucius I would never do again. But then what other choice did I have?

Pip hadn't had any problems masking what my mother was to my father when she went back in time. This despite obviously feeling something for her and enough to make her part of his… dare I say it, *harem*. Which made me think about this logically, could the reason for Pip's powers not having as good of an effect on Lucius be that our time was closer together? Could it be that if I had managed to get back to the year 1202 like I had intended, Lucius could have possibly walked past me in the street and not felt anything thanks to Pip's influence?

Despite all these questions plaguing my mind, in the end it was pointless as it was all too late now. And Speaking of Pip, the moment I felt something touching my nose, I batted it away only to open my eyes and find the naughty Imp staring at me. A grinning face I could see thanks to Lucius leaving a single candle burning in its glass lamp and the fireplace that still had plenty of logs to burn.

Although, the moment I did see her, I was surprised enough that it didn't matter when she held up a finger to her mouth to silence me, because I couldn't help but flinch slightly in Lucius's hold.

Thankfully, however, other than his arms tensing a moment around me, he didn't stir enough to wake. My wide eyes tried to tell her that if I moved, he would most definitely wake up. In response to this and knowing my worries, she nodded once. Then she held up a finger and like magic, started to twirl it round and round before a faint green light made a circle six inches above her fingertip.

Her eyes then started to glow the same intense, forest-green colour as her magic, making me realize that the more concentrated her gaze became, the more intense the ring of power started to get. A circle quickly grew in size and as soon as it was the dimensions of a bicycle wheel. She then used her other hand and maneuvered it slowly so that it floated across me, only coming to rest when it hovered above Lucius. Her fingers were constantly twisting and turning as if she had two invisible orbs she was manipulating in her hands, and I was stunned by the beauty of it.

Because it was very rare to see Pip's power, meaning that when you did, it was enough to take your breath away. In fact, thinking about it, I knew as much about Pip equally as I didn't. Of course, she had told me the tale when I was a child of how she had met Adam. I even knew how she had met Lucius. Admittedly, I seemed to have been fascinated even at an early age whenever I heard his name and naturally trying to learn everything I could about the Vampire King. But I vaguely remembered a time shortly after that where Adam went missing and her story never finished. Which meant there were pieces of Pip's life I still didn't know, and this power she possessed was one where I knew even less.

However, right now, it was one that obviously worked as I felt his arms relax and slip from me before he rolled to his back. I was then finally free to shift from the bed. I turned to look down at the ring slowly circling his head and chest area, seeing now the magical inscriptions rotating within the band of power.

"This should keep him asleep for long enough, but who knows how long it will sing its zombie lullaby for... so we best be quick, come on, we have a plan." I shifted over him gently and the moment it looked like I was about to have my wicked way with him, Pip said,

"Yeah, that's not what this spell is for, you know." I shot her a pointed look over my shoulder, before fishing out the key from his pocket with my other hand then gently shaking it at her.

"Oh right, well that makes much more sense," she agreed, making me roll my eyes before suppressing a giggle.

"Yeah, I guessed as much. Besides, if I don't take the key, then he's going to think I just vanished out of thin air, and I think that would mean a lot more explaining to do on my part," I added as I got off the bed, grabbed the cap he had taken from my hair and the rest of my clothes that he had rid me of to make me more comfortable. Then with a lot more speed than it taken him to free me of these things, I put them back on before rushing over to the door.

I then reached over to pick up the lamp, only stopping when she said,

"Don't worry, I came prepared for your mortal eyes." I rolled those mortal eyes at her yet again, making her wink at me before she plucked the key from my hand. Then she slipped it in the lock and waited at the door for a few seconds before giving me the go ahead. This I knew was so she would be able to pick up any sounds and wait just in case anyone was lurking outside. I couldn't help but look back at Lucius, wondering if this was it... would I see him again after this point?

"Come on, little bean, he will be fine," she said after seeing my reluctance and picking up the lantern she had left outside the door. Something that would have no doubt look suspicious to anyone that had been still awake, but I chose not to point this fact out. Instead, I simply nodded before we slipped through the door and closed it behind me. Doing so as gently as I could, just in case her spell could slip without giving us the time we needed to get away.

"I never knew you had that type of power, to be able to

keep Lucius in his sleep like that," I said after we were far enough away from the door.

"Trust me, if he hadn't already been asleep, then it would have been near mission impossible, as I don't have the ability to control his mind mojo, only to be able to keep his mind in the state it's already in. Unfortunately for us, it won't last forever, meaning Caveman Vampy will be up and running in no time at all." I winced at this.

"That was reassuring in no way whatsoever." At this she laughed and said,

"Yeah, no shanizzel." Not sure what this meant but at a guess it was a no shit moment.

"Then we better be quick, where's Sophia?" I asked, making her nod and answer,

"This way." However, the moment I turned a corner I was faced with a very large portrait of a… well, there was no other way of saying this… *a very ugly man.* However, it wasn't the fact that he was unattractive that made me stop in my tracks. No, it was that there was something about the painting I recognized. One that was hung on the wall under a glass hexagon section of the roof therefore allowing the moonlight to shine down enough so I could see it.

Pip noticed I had stopped and walked back towards me, now holding her lamp up and enabling me to read the long scroll that was in the painting. It was attached to a table and nearly the full length of the table leg and as for the man himself, he wore a floor length jacket of none other than blue and gold check. Exactly the same pattern like the one I had seen Marcus wearing earlier in the day. Strangely enough he even held a long staff in his hand, but this was where the similarities abruptly ended. Because despite his strange make up, Marcus was far from ugly, and his athletic physique was easy to see even when hidden by his flamboyant choice of style.

But as for the man in the picture, well he looked a little potbellied with the buttons on his jacket lay open around his stomach. His face was weathered and cast down, with bulging dark eyes, and sagging cheeks reminding me of the drooping jowls on a dog. Which was why I couldn't understand at first what connected the two.

"Wow, now he had a face only a Demon's mother could love, poor fuggly guy," Pip said as I started to read the scroll of paper, one named as…

Thoms. Skelton late fool of Muncaster last Will and Testament

Be it known to ye, oh grave and wise men all,
    That I Thom Fool am Sheriff of ye Hall,
    I mean the Hall of Haigh, where I command,
    What neither I nor you do understand.
    My Under Sheriff is Ralph Wayte you know,
    As wise as I am and as witty too.
    Of Egremond I have Burrow Serjeant beene,
    Of Wiggan Bailiff too, as may be seen
    By my white staff of office in my hand,
    being carried straight as the badge of my command:
    A low high constable too was once my calling,
    Which I enjoyed under kind Henry Rawling;
    And when the Fates a new Sheriff send,
    I'm Under Sheriff prick'd World without end.
    He who doth question my authority
    May see the seal and patten here ly by.

The dish with luggs which I do carry here
Shews all my living is in good strong beer.
If scurvy lads to me abuses do,
I'll call 'em scurvy rogues and rascals too.
Fair Dolly Copeland in my cap is placed;
Monstrous fair is she, and as good as all the rest.
Honest Nich. Pennington, honest Ths. Turner, both
Will bury me when I this world go forth.
But let me not be carry'd o'er the brigg,
Lest falling I in Duggas River ligg;
Nor let my body by old Charnock lye,
But by Will. Caddy, for he'll lye quietly
And when I'm bury'd then my friends may drink,
But each man pay for himself, that's best I think.
This is my Will, and this I know will be
Perform'd by them as they have promised me.

Sign'd, Seal'd, Publish'd, and Declared in the presence of
   HENRY RAWLING
   HENRY TROUGHTON
   THS. TURNER

THS. SKELTON, X his Mark

"He died?" I asked shaking my head wondering now if Marcus had something to do with his death.

"Yeah, well from the sounds of those last words, Mr Jowly face there drank himself to death. Come on, little Bean, Sophia will be waiting." I released a sigh knowing she was right, I was only wasting time here, so I let her lead me in the opposite direction to the painting. We walked down some stone stairs and turned right at the first landing, to only walk up some more and along a wood panelled corridor. I let Pip lead as she carried the lantern and the large bay windows on the left-hand side didn't offer much light, not like the skylight above the painting had.

Then as soon as I saw a door open up ahead, I tensed until I saw Sophia's head pop out, ushering us in quickly. As soon as we were inside she shut the door and turned the lock.

"I'm close enough to my brother's rooms that I don't want to take any chances but with that being said, he shouldn't hear us," my auntie Sophia said the moment she listened to check that nobody had followed us. Then she turned to me and grabbed me to her so she could hug me and, boy, did I need it.

"How are you holding up?" I released a deep sigh, especially when Pip said with a giggle,

"More like holding out." I cast her a wry look, making her wink at me while sticking her fingers in her fist and rolling her eyes back as if in the height of pleasure. I tried not to laugh at this and instead focused on Sophia's question.

"I'm not going to lie, it's not been easy."

"I'm gathering your husband is currently fast asleep?" she asked looking to me and then to Pip, obviously silently asking if she had used her magic green wheel mojo on him.

"Yeah, he is… oh and fun fact, he also wants to become my husband for a second time, so I would say Pip's 'just a regular girl' spell isn't working as well as it did back in Persia, or Lucius has just lost his damn mind in this time period, and he's actually fallen for a mortal he knows isn't his Chosen One and just doesn't care." Sophia looked to Pip before releasing a sigh. She sat on another huge, carved four poster bed, joining where Pip had already made herself comfortable sitting crossed legged and looking like a maid had taken up meditation.

"Hey, don't look at me, as far as I'm concerned, I think my Imp ass is doing just fine," she said, straightening her bonnet on top of her wig.

"Perhaps it isn't working as well because of your own connection to Lucius or maybe there just isn't enough time in between when we meet?" I asked, making them both shrug their shoulders.

"I mean, it's possible I guess," Pip admitted.

"Yeah, I mean it's not like you guys have done the deed… right?" Sophia asked, making Pip sit up as they both now sat forward waiting for my answer.

"What?! No, of course not. That was one of the rules I most definitely remembered."

"Okay so if it's not that then I don't know what the Hell is wrong, I mean it's not like he had been feeding off you and could have tasted any of your blood, so that's out the… oh wait a minute, now what is that face for?" Pip asked, wagging her finger at me the moment she saw my eyes get wide.

"Oh shit," I muttered after visibly wincing.

"Now that right there is not a happy oh shit," Pip pointed out.

"When is an oh shit, ever a happy oh shit?" Sophia asked, making Pip reply,

"When I walk into my bedroom to find Adam wearing nothing but tight leather pants, all his big muscles on show and a whip in his hand." At this I closed my eyes and muttered,

"Way too much information about my uncle."

"Okay so moving on from… *well, that…* how did this happen?" Sophia asked, making me sigh back onto a large truck at the end of the bed.

131

"After I saw him in the ballroom, I got into an altercation with the butler."

"What kind of altercation?" Sophia asked in a dangerous tone like she was about to murder the man.

"Don't worry, Lucius more than handled it, but the wound I got from being knocked out in the cottage must have opened up and because I was bleeding, he held a handkerchief to it to stop the bleed."

"I think I see where this is going," Sophia muttered, rubbing her forehead.

"I didn't think he would pocket it and keep it for a snack to suck on for later," I pointed out, making Pip burst out laughing before we shot her a look. She held up a finger as she continued to giggle before explaining,

"Sorry… just got a mental picture and well… Lucius saying in a corny Dracula voice, 'I want to suck your hanky' was just the funniest shit." I had to agree, that was pretty funny and therefore took all my willpower not to burst out laughing. Something Sophia noticed, warning,

"Oh no, not you too. I already have one comic genius to contend with, I don't need a geekier one."

"Why thank you," Pip said, tipping her imaginary hat to her.

"So, you think Lucius knows I am his Chosen One then?" I asked with a sigh, knowing I had messed up but even worse, I had done it without even realising. Plus, it wasn't an important factor, but it did also annoy me to know that I could have been giving into temptation after all.

"Erh, yeah, and most likely from the very beginning." I shrugged my shoulders at Sophia's reply before dropping them again like I was deflating.

"Okay, so please tell me we at least have a plan," I said getting us back on track to the point of this conversation.

"I do, but it might include some outside help." This was the exact moment that somebody knocked on the door, making me narrow my gaze at Sophia as she hurried over and unlocked it. However, the moment the door opened, I couldn't help my gasp of surprise.

"What is he doing here?!"

He huffed at the sound of my disbelief before dropping a bombshell,

"Now is that any way to welcome an accomplice..."

"Little Princess."

CHAPTER 15
THE PERFECT PORTRAIT OF A PLAN

My mouth dropped open in shock in sight of Marcus now standing there looking smug.

"You told him?" I hissed in an accusing tone towards Sophia, who was now relocking the door.

"I'm a seeker, Miss Draven, or should I call you Miss Earhart? Either way, I had already foreseen your arrival," Marcus said with his creepy yet weirdly handsome smirk and just like earlier in the day, he was wearing his blue and gold chequered-pattern jacket. Something that must have been associated with his role as a Fool of this house, as he had been wearing something similar in the portrait I had passed. But suddenly this thought fled me as another took its place.

"Wait, you told my father about my mother, didn't you? That's how those men knew to take the blonde." At this he raised both his hands.

"Guilty as charged." The second I heard this I narrowed my gaze and let my anger take over. Which meant I quickly picked up the nearest object, one that just so happened to be a stone statue, before raising it up and walking towards him with my unconventional weapon. Sophia quickly intervened and grabbed my arm before I could batter him to death with it.

"Wait, Amelia! Just hear him out," she said throughout Pip's laughter, who thought this scene was hilarious as she muttered,

"Double whammy dose of ironic being beaten in the head by that chick." In the end I wasn't surprised by her comment when I finally looked at the statue and realised it was Ate, who was the Greek Goddess of mischief. Of course, she was also the known Goddess of delusion, ruin, and blind folly, rash action, and reckless impulse who led men down the path of ruin.

So double whammy indeed.

"Fine!" I snapped before allowing my aunt to take the statue from my hands and unsurprisingly, Marcus smirked.

"Well, let's hear it and it better be good, considering you're the one who got us into this mess," I bit out and I had to say, his smug expression was not exactly helping in cooling my anger, no matter how he had come to my aid earlier in the day.

"Yes, and before you judge me too harshly, young one, I am also going to be the one who gets you out of it," he replied, twirling his cane before catching it up in the air and making Pip clap like he was there solely for her entertainment. Something that made him bow his head in her direction before tucking the stick under his arm. One that was topped with a Demonic hand clutching a black onyx, glass sphere.

"And just how are you planning on achieving that?" I asked, folding my arms and granting him my best sceptical look.

"All in good time, my dear."

"Well, see, that's just the thing here, Marcus, we don't really have much time on our hands, something you would know being a Seeker and all," I said pointing out this obvious fact and, again, his grin was a little unnerving.

"Ah but I disagree, for time is all any of us have and as its new weaver, then this applies to you more than most," he replied, making Pip mutter,

"Ooo, Amelia the Time Weaver, I like the sound of that… what? It's got a kick ass superhero ring to it." Pip added this last argument when Sophia and I shot her a look.

"And what, pray tell, is a *Super Hero?*" Marcus asked, using a tone like he was speaking these last two words in a foreign language.

"Not importa…"

"We are!" Pip shouted at the same time I said this, making me sigh and resist acting like my father by holding the bridge of my nose in frustration.

"What is important is why, if you had foreseen all of this, would you get us into this mess in the first place?" I asked, still trying to understand the crazy fool's logic!

"Ah, little Princess, but you are not the only one who is acting under the mercy of the Fates and as one of its Seekers, well I am, more than most, under the foot of the God Janus and it is forever a boot he holds firmly at my neck." I rolled my eyes and muttered,

"You're almost as cryptic as Pip."

"Hey! I resent that like a piss in the sand," she said making Sophia frown as I just threw out a hand and said,

"Case in point there, Pip."

"Oh, come on, everyone knows that if they are going to be forced to take a piss outside then they want to see something for their accomplishment and make a puddle." At this Sophia and I looked at each other, both of us showcasing the same bewildered expression.

"I don't think…"

"Uh… yeah, no I don't…"

"Actually, she is right, as personally I do enjoy trying to write my name on the dry stone… nor is it as easy as it sounds," Marcus said interrupting both I and Sophia.

"Yes, and very near impossible for a girl… *trust me, I have tried but I can never seem to dot the I's,*" Pip said, making Marcus grin when she whispered this last part behind her hand. At this I felt like smacking my own forehead seeing as I didn't think we could have gotten any further from the 'planning our escape' track.

"Okay, so moving on and trying once more to make the most out of this limited time I have away from Lucius… so what you're telling me, Marcus, is that this…" I paused to roll my wrist around, indicating to us three currently up shit creek without a paddle, "…All that is happening right now, is all Fated, is that what you want me to believe?" I asked, now granting a look to Pip and Sophia who seemed just as interested in that answer as I was.

"Surely you must have questioned by now why you are currently occupying this point in time and not exactly where you thought you would be?" Marcus pointed out, making me wonder how he knew that but then again… perhaps the Fates also provided him with a manila folder on us, one with a red 'Top Secret' stamp on the front.

"So that's your answer, you're telling me this is all Fated and that my mother and I were destined to meet our possessive, domineering Kings in this time, so as to what exactly? Get kidnapped and…" He quickly cut me off from my rant and said,

"I'm telling you to trust in the Fates, for they have clearly placed their trust in you. The one true God that even all other Gods must follow."

"Okay fine, I get it… so moving on from this Fated mess… how are you going to get us out of this time-traveling fiasco, one that you yourself have said to have been charged by the Fates into putting us through?" At this he grinned again and this time, it was prime evil.

"The same way that the late but genius, Thomas Skelton once used to lure those he did not like to their deaths by simply whispering the wrong way."

"Thomas Skelton… wait, so it was you in the painting!" At this he dropped his smirk and scowled.

"Yes, and that damned artist did enjoy making me the ugliest of Fools."

"Yeah, and if I recall, he did catch you fucking his wife," Sophia added, gifting us with this insight and bringing back his smirk at the memory.

"Ah yes and almost worth the immortalized slight on my image… but then, *she was great at sucking cock,*" Marcus said with a wink that was clearly aimed at Pip, who whipped off her wig and started fanning herself with it… *unsuccessfully I might add.* By the Gods but that was all we needed, Pip with a crush on this crazy Fool. One who's eyes widened the moment he saw the colour of her mad hair.

"So, you're most definitely going to help us?" I asked, needing to be sure I could trust this guy.

"Like I said, when you're under the boot of Janus, while he is whistling to the flute of Fate and signalling for you to come running, what else is this fool to do, but enlist his cunning." My face said it all, because noticeably I wasn't as impressed with his act as a now giggling Pip was.

"That's very poetic, Marcus, but what exactly is the plan here?" I asked cutting to the chase.

"It's simple."

"We doubt that, but go on," my aunt Sophia replied, clearly unconvinced.

"I will create a diversion," Marcus replied, nodding at Pip when she muttered in a dreamy tone,

"Genius." I shot her a look, making her mouth,

'What?' with a shrug of her shoulders.

"I don't see how that will get us out of here," I said focusing back on the plan.

"The diversion will be of such that your Vampire and the King of Kings will have no choice but to deal with it themselves. And while trusting no one else but that of his kin, he will have Sophia here, at her own suggestion of course, be standing guard over the King's Chosen One, *your mother."*

"And what about me?" I asked, thinking it couldn't be this simple.

"Ah yes, another possessive King, for he will no doubt lock you in his room, so I suggest making a fuss about not wanting to be alone and that's when we will suggest putting all the chickens needing to roost in one place." I had to say, for a half assed plan, it wasn't sounding too bad.

"And then?" I prompted.

"Then I suggest you all learn how to fly with the wings you have been given."

"Chickens can't fly… too fat for their wings… but then that does beg the question, why those fat chubber bumble bees can, as I swear those little dudes just defy gravity," Pip pointed out, making Sophia shake her head at her, silently telling her not now as I can imagine this wasn't the first time my aunt had heard this conundrum coming from Pip's mouth.

"Nor can mortals, but horses can, for they ride fast enough," Marcus pointed out, making me release a relieved breath because at least now we had a plan.

"Sounds simple enough, so when is this to happen?" Sophia asked, now sitting down at a stylish high-backed, padded chair that looked covered in an oriental pattern.

"Your best chance at escaping is naturally at night, for it will make your success slipping from the castle unseen more likely," Marcus said, making me nod and voice the decision.

"Tomorrow then." At this he bowed his head in agreement.

"Then I have work to do and mischief to make. Ladies, it has been a delightful distraction from the bore of immortality. I bid you all well for the journey ahead," Marcus said, taking steps towards the door and making me follow, so as I could see him out. However, this was when he took my arm and whispered down at me,

"Trust the stones even when they break, trust the Fates and what they can make, for only the strength of your heart not its ache will get you home."

I pulled back the moment he said this, shocked to how much he truly knew about this quest. Yet after this, he simply winked at me before bowing at the waist and leaving me to digest his cryptic words. Then I closed the door behind him and leaned against it, now folding my arms before asking,

"Can we really trust him?"

"I would say yes, but I am not the most reliable seeing as I might only being saying that because I am horny and missing my pookie bear," Pip said, slapping her wig back on and twisting it so the bangs were to the front.

"He's odd, to be sure, but Kings have trusted him for centuries, and like he said, he is a Seeker and is ruled by a single God Janus."

"So?" I asked making my aunt sigh.

"So, if he's saying this is all Fate, then I believe him,"

Sophia replied and to be honest, I couldn't argue much with that.

"Come on, time is getting on. Now that we have a plan, we better get you back to your Vampire," she added, now getting to her feet and placing a hand at my shoulder but before Pip could shift herself fully from the bed, I stopped her.

"It's okay, I can make my own way. Besides, I don't want him sensing your presence in case he wakes." Pip gave me a girl guide salute, making me smile, and as for my aunt Sophia, she pulled me in for another hug and told me,

"Alright, my niece, but be careful and try not to worry, we will be through this soon." I nodded after hugging her back.

"Get some rest, aunts, tomorrow's going to be a big day." After this I grabbed the lantern that Pip had placed by the door and left creeping my way back the way I came. And with every step I took, I did so hoping that Lucius was still locked to his dream state so it would be easier for me to sneak back inside.

However, like most of my best laid plans, it didn't exactly go my way, making me hope this wasn't a sign of things to come. Especially when I heard the furious voice behind me coming from Mrs Price.

"And just where do you think you're going!?" Her voice hissed behind me making me whip around and nearly drop my lantern, before finding myself faced with the displeased face of the head housekeeper.

"I was asked to…"

"I do not care what was asked of you, for it definitely is not warranted at this hour, now come with me!" I gulped at this, now seeing even greater distance being put between me and Lucius's door.

"Where are we going?" I asked, letting her take me as I knew it would be uncharacteristic to do anything else at this point. Because what was I to say? That there was a Vampire back there that would be really pissed off to find out that his 'little maid' wasn't in his bed and still in the room that he had locked her in?

"To the servants' quarters, where you are meant to be sleeping." Again, I decided not to argue at this, as it would have been fruitless. So instead, I followed her to the same room I had slept in last night and as soon as the door opened, I could see the other maids in there fast asleep just like the night before. And well, at this late hour, I wasn't exactly surprised that they didn't even stir. Not with the amount of work that they did. I could imagine they were exhausted and slept like the dead the moment in their heads hit the pillow. And no doubt stayed that way until the moment they were forced from it only to do the same thing all over again.

"Now, this time, make sure that you are up with the others, as this late hour is no excuse for tardiness," she said before shutting the door and making me exhale a breath.

"Well, come tomorrow, we will see just how possessive one Vampire King is," I muttered to myself before stripping out of my dress and keeping the underlayer on, as it wasn't exactly like I had anything else to wear. I took off my bonnet, my stockings, and then my shoes, already missing my boots and the rest of my clothes that we had kept hidden in the stables.

Then after this, I lay down and gave way to exhaustion with my mind still wondering what tomorrow would bring.

Although, no sooner had I closed my eyes did it feel as if seconds later and I was opening them again and the peace of morning was shattered. Because I was suddenly roused from sleep when I heard a furious growl coming from outside the door.

My angry Vampire had awoken and, clearly, there was only one thing on his mind…

"Where is my maid!"

CHAPTER 16
A TASTE OF IMPATIENCE

I flinched at the same time my eyes snapped open and were glued to the door.

"My Lord, this is unproper!" I heard Mrs Price argue, seeing her silhouette standing guard in front of the door with its small, frosted glass window nearly completely blocked by her form.

"Is she in there?!" Lucius demanded to know, his tone sounding furious and terrifying.

"She is and will be rising shortly to bring you your breakfast, My Lord," Mrs Price said, trying to keep her tone steady.

"Make it quick, woman, for I want my maid in my chambers in no less than ten minutes!" he snapped, making her sigh in return before arguing,

"Which is barely daybreak, sir."

"Then you better make it quick before it breaks any further… am I understood?"

At this I watched her bow her head and I had to give it to her, in the face of such an imposing figure, and a furious one at that, well she certainly knew how to hold her ground. The moment he left was finally the moment I could breathe but I knew it wouldn't be for long. No, not when Mrs Price slipped inside wearing her dressing gown and with her hair still wrapped in curling rags as she rushed to where I lay.

"Quick, girl, up you get now, as you need to be ready, for I do not know what has gotten into that tyrant the master calls his friend, but he is asking for you… truly a brute of a man… now come on, get yourself presentable and I will have his breakfast tray ready before anyone else's… what a state of things, breaking his fast and before the hand even strikes ten," she muttered, shaking out my dress before handing it to me and reminding me that historically, breaking your fast usually happened a lot later in the day than it did in my own time.

I nodded, not knowing what to say but my fearful gaze made her features soften, as she patted my hand reassuringly and said,

"Do not fear, girl, for the Lord of this Castle would not condone such actions," she said, making me want to laugh at this seeing as he kept my mother behind lock and key and would, no doubt, be tearing the place apart to find her if she had been the one to go missing.

"I assure you that those who work within its castle walls are protected, so be sure that if Lord Septimus should harm you in any way, then you must tell someone."

"He will not hurt me," I told her quietly as the other two had not yet woken, making me surprised that Lucius's ruckus hadn't roused half the house, let alone the two I shared a room with.

"No, I should think not," she stated firmly before walking to the door and granting me one last warning.

"Nevertheless, you must hurry, girl, just in case, for I have never seen Lord Septimus so angry before… no, I had once believed him to be a composed, mild-mannered man. Upon my word, I do not know what has come over him," she said, shaking her head at herself as if speaking her mind aloud and I wanted to mutter, *if only she knew.*

Once she had left, I did as she suggested and got ready quickly, pouring the jug of water into a bowl and splashing it on my face for a quick wash before putting on the dress Mrs Price had handed me.

Which meant that just as I was leaving the other two were starting to stir, and I most definitely wanted to be out of this room before they were fully awake. I didn't have time for conversation and besides, it was better they not even know who I was, let alone give them more reason to gossip. This all meant that by the time I had finished, Lucius's breakfast tray was waiting for me to carry to his room just like the morning before. The only difference, of course, was the sun had barely started to rise.

It was an odd sensation, to be apprehensive and nervous about meeting with your own husband. But then, I kept having to remind myself who he was to me in the future was not who he was to me now. Of course, he would always be my Fated King but seeing Lucius like this, experiencing him this way, was like stepping back into my own past. One where the few occasions we had met, he had regarded me with nothing but disdain or open annoyance.

But I knew these thoughts wouldn't do me any good and only make me more nervous. So, I tried to cling on to what happened last night and to the memory of him freely declaring me as his. However, that had been before I made what was potentially a grave mistake by escaping his clutches, if only for a night.

Well, it was time to face the beast, I thought with a sigh the moment I was faced with his door. This also meant knowing my place once more, so I set the tray down on the floor before knocking.

"Enter!" the single, sharp word was snapped as if said after the grinding of his teeth. I swallowed hard as I opened the door and then picked my tray up from the floor to walk inside with it. I purposely didn't look at him, deciding to forgo all pretences of intimacy from yesterday in favour of doing my duty.

Although, I had barely managed to set down the tray on the table before I was grabbed from behind and, this time, when he collared my throat, it wasn't to detect whether I was lying or not. No, it was purely a hold that screamed possession, and one that displayed his anger that I had gotten away from him. I knew that when he yanked me back into his frame, one that towered over me. And despite the fact that he wasn't hurting me, I could still feel him breathing heavy at my back. I gasped in surprise as he banded another arm around my front across my torso. Only then did he speak, and each word was said with lethal calm.

"Tell me, little one, did I lose all good sense last night and give you permission to leave?" The question was loaded and heavy with furious intent.

"I..."

"You had better give me your reasoning for such foolishness, and make it good, for my patience is nil at best!" he shouted, making me flinch in his hold.

"You're scaring me," I told him quietly, hoping this was enough to jar him from his anger.

"Good! Then let your fear feed your truthfulness… now answer me, why and how did you escape me?!" I gulped at this, and it was an anxious reaction he felt against his palm.

But then, this was also when something inside me flipped, making me snap back as my own anger ignited.

"I wasn't aware I was your prisoner!"

"Then that was a foolish assumption on your part," he stated firmly, making me try and squirm out of his hold at the same time saying,

"And how and why should I have assumed I was your prisoner?!"

"You're a smart girl, little maid, for were you not under my lock and key?" he snarled this, almost growling at the end of his words.

"I could have not made it any clearer had I put you in a gilded cage," he added, making me try and twist my way free even more before ordering him to release me.

"I demand you let me go!"

"No," he stated firmly, and I swear I was close to breaking his hold on me the old-fashioned, kick ass way, damning the consequences and giving him even greater reason not to trust me.

"I said, let me go!" I bellowed this time, seconds from reacting by first squatting down, stepping out behind him so I could grab him behind the thighs with both hands. Then I would pistol squat on my right leg and let my left leg go straight behind his ankles so as to valley drop him to the floor. He would not have known what hit him if I had done, although admittedly this would have been a hard move to achieve in my dress.

However, before I could react in any way, Lucius had other ideas as suddenly he spun me to face him and pushed me up against the wall, before snarling his answer down at me,

"Never!" Then before I knew what was happening, he crushed his lips to mine and I found myself, once more, a

willing prisoner in his arms. His kiss totally disarmed me, which was not really surprising as it usually did. But this then left me no choice but to act on impulse, for I kissed him back with as much fever as I always did. The moment he felt my compliance, he gentled his touch, along with his hold on me.

This in turn eased the pounding of my heart, knowing the effect we clearly had on each other was not one-sided, despite my pissing him off. Because I also I knew the root of his anger, and this was one mingled with his fears.

He feared I had run from him.

Run from his proposal.

Which was why the next time he pulled back, he lowered his forehead to mine and now when he asked me why I had left, he did so in a much calmer tone.

"Why did you leave me?" I released a heavy sigh.

"People would have noticed had I not returned to the room I was allocated. I do not want such talk surrounding our potential union," I answered making him sigh himself.

"You truly left me because you feared I would give heed to gossip?"

"If we do this, I want it done properly, and not because others believed I had trapped you into marrying me, coerced you with my body." At this he finally smirked.

"Coerced say you, upon my word, my reputation in this household must be lacking indeed if others are so willing to believe I was the one coerced and not the one doing the coercing." At this I scowled at him.

"Taken many of the maids to your bed, have you?!" I snapped and in turn, his grin deepened.

"I do believe that was quite a bite of jealousy, and something I find so very, deliciously endearing… despite there being a lack of evidence to support such. And in answer to your venomous tongue, one I will soon dominate with my own once more... No, I have never taken a maid to my bed, nor have I ever lost my temper so badly when finding the only one I want in it, leaving it so abruptly!" he retorted back, finding his anger once more at the memory.

"You were sleeping," I argued back.

"I believe you also had the same ability to sleep," he said with sarcasm lacing his words.

"Even a nun gets temptations of the body... I couldn't think with you lying next to me. I told you... *I needed time."*

He seemed pleased by this response, so pleased, in fact, that he framed my face with his hands and peppered kisses along my jawline before reaching my ear.

"Is that so... well then, my little nun, let's feed those temptations, should we?" This was the only warning I received before I was up in his arms, now crying out by the sudden movement. Then as soon as I was dropped onto the bed, he slammed the door shut with the power of his mind and I knew the logical thing in that moment would have been to question how he had done this. However, all thoughts and feelings went out of my mind the moment his hands reached up my legs and started to gather up my skirts.

"Wh...what are you doing?" I asked, stumbling for the words.

"Giving in to temptation and forcing you to now do the same."

I gasped at this, focusing on that one word.

"Forcing?" I asked as he started to crawl over me slowly, holding himself above my core.

"Coercing," he said, changing his wording and looking up at me with that bad boy grin as he lifted my skirts even higher until they rested up at my belly. Then he looked down at my underwear in a curious way. And this wasn't surprising, not considering I had chosen to keep my original panties on.

A pair that I had thankfully managed to wash the once, despite being forced to put them back on damp. However, the skimpy black scrap of silk would no doubt look strange to him as these were as far from the era of bloomers as you could get.

"Now isn't this a curious little thing?" he said, referring to my underwear before running the backs of his fingers over the triangle of silky material. I gasped at the feeling of his knuckle as it grazed me as gently as the butterfly's wing over my clit. A sexual touch that made my back arch ever so slightly, and his eyes heated as they took in every single movement my body made. He was like a predator watching his prey squirm before making a meal out of it. A puppet master playing with its new doll and enjoying every second that he pulled at its strings.

"But I thought you said..." I started to ask on a breathy sigh the moment he hooked the side of my panties and started to slide them down my legs.

"I will not take your virginity, but there are other things I can take and oh, my sweet girl... *I am oh so hungry,"* he growled this last part, giving me a hint of the darkness I knew lay within him. But then his eyes grazed down to my bare mound, and his features took on an even more curious note.

"You are bare?" he asked, making me feel so hot, I thought my cheeks would melt down my face!

"I... I shave it off, I prefer the feel..."

"Ah yes, I believe I agree with you, for it is soft indeed," he purred, running his fingertips gently down the sensitive flesh making me shudder.

"I believe I am going to enjoy this immensely and as for you... *I will make sure that you feel the same."* I took in a deep breath, one that hitched the second he grabbed the backs of my thighs and pushed my legs up and outwards. Then at the first swipe of his tongue up the centre of my sex, I curled my fingers into fists, gripping onto his bedding so hard I knew my knuckles would be turning white.

"Oh Gods," I whispered, knowing I was giving away even more by letting slip that I didn't believe in a single God, not like most mortals around him would do. Now as for what Lucius thought of this I didn't know and, in that moment, nor did I care. Not when he was lighting me up from the inside out and setting me on fire. I swear that with every swipe of his tongue against my clit I was close to flying off the damn bed!

"Yes… yes, yes… Gods, don't stop!" I demanded, making him chuckle against my flesh before sucking that little bundle of nerves into his mouth and making me cry out louder this time,

"AHHH!" The sound of my pleasure made him growl against my soaked flesh, before he gripped my legs in an even tighter hold and spread them as far as they would go so he could dive in deep. He started to fuck me with his tongue, and I tried to writhe beneath him despite being pinned in place.

"Yes, yes, please yes, Lucius… grant me my release!" I begged and the moment I said his name the sound of satisfaction coming from him was easy to detect. But knowing I needed him back on my clit, he exchanged a finger for his tongue, making my back bow off the bed when he started to fuck me with it. This at the same time gifting me his teeth and lips where I needed them the most. Naturally it was not long that I came screaming his name after he had latched on to my clit and vibrated his tongue against it.

"Lucius! I am… I am… AHH OHH YESSSS, LUCIUS!" I shuddered beneath him as wave after wave of sensations hit me, making my sex quiver and pulsate around his finger.

After this, he lapped at my dripping core like a man obsessed with the taste of me, meaning I was a slave to his feeding, as no amount of begging stopped him before he was ready to release me.

But then the moment that he did and was now looking down at me spent on his bed panting below him, he must have decided this wasn't enough…

He wanted more of me.

I knew this when he started to drag my dress up and over my head, finding not what he thought he would when he then rid me of my undergarment. Something that had looked more like a long linen nightgown back in my own time. But whereas he had no doubt been expecting to see a corset beneath it, let's just say that finding my breasts covered in a matching lace and silk bra was the very last sight he had been expecting.

"This…*what is this?"* he asked dumbfounded, making me wonder if this was the reaction of the first man ever to see this type of underwear. I bit my lip nervously and shook my head, deciding it was best not to say anything at all. So instead, I reached behind me, unhooked the bra, and pulled it from my arms in hopes the sight of my naked breasts would focus his attention elsewhere.

Thankfully this worked well enough as his eyes heated before he ducked his head and started feasting on a nipple, making me press it further into his mouth as I arched my back once more. Which meant the next time I found my release, it was by his hand at my sex and his mouth on mine, as soon he was swallowing up my cries of bliss with his kiss.

A kiss that spoke of so many things and for just a single moment…

Had the power to bridge the gap of time between us.

"You didn't... you know," I said after I once again found myself in Lucius's arms. However, this time I was naked, with only the sheet covering my body as I lay back against his chest and in between his legs. The breakfast tray was situated next to us and he was now picking things off and feeding me like some treasured pet of his he had to take care of. He was also dressed as he was last night, wearing only his shirt and breeches, as unlike me, he'd had no reason to get naked, hence my question.

"Trust me when I say that I am more than content and find myself quite satisfied with the results of our argument." I scoffed a laugh at this, making him squeeze me tighter before relaxing.

"Here, eat, my sweet little maid... after all, you will need your strength," he warned playfully.

"With you in my bed, I believe I will," I said in jest making him chuckle.

"I believe this is my bed, well, for the time being at least, because I confess that I cannot wait to steal you away and get you back to my true home."

"And where is home, My Lord?" I asked before letting him place a slice of plum in my mouth.

"Lucius... call me, Lucius," he hummed in my ear.

"It is improper for me to call you by your first name, at least until we are married," I said, nearly laughing at myself considering where I was now sitting.

"What I did to you would also be classed as improper before taking you to the marital bed, but I confess, I am as equally unconventional as I am impatient when it comes to you... for I cannot wait to finally have you... *all of you.*" I tensed at this, for reasons he mistook. Because I knew that come tonight, I would be gone from his life and that final moment between us he spoke of would never happen.

Not until my own lifetime.

"Do not fret, for I will still honour your wishes and wait until our vows have been made before I take your virginity. Now eat, little pet of mine," he said, telling me that he did view me as a sort of pet of his when caring for me this way. Which was why I couldn't help the small smile now playing on my lips and, thankfully, it was one he couldn't see. Not as I took the next piece of fruit from in between his fingertips. Then he softly started to brush back my hair, making me moan in bliss just like I always did.

"I love it when you do that." The words slipped out before I could stop them and more importantly, before I remembered where I was in time. Unsurprisingly, his hands stilled for a moment, before he voiced my fears.

"You make it sound as if I have spent half my life doing this." At this I had to first clear my throat and make a conscious effort to sound light-hearted in my reply.

"Then good fortune has blessed me, as it seems I now get the other half of that life to gift me with your hands, so please don't stop now," I answered, feeling him relaxed at my back knowing I had said enough to stop the cogs from turning and questioning why I would have said something like that. Something so comfortable.

Damn it... but this was hard.

"Eat," he said again, bringing another piece of fruit to my lips, however, this time when I opened my mouth, he had a new order as soon as I swallowed.

"Now suck." I'm glad he said this after I had consumed the piece, otherwise it might have gotten trapped on the way to my stomach, along with the lust I was forced to swallow down. Lust that only managed to bloom in my belly as I

eagerly did his bidding. Meaning I opened my lips and took his fingers into my mouth, licking and sucking the digits deep. I also couldn't help moaning around them as I tasted the juice that had clung to his skin.

"Mmm," Lucius groaned behind me before granting me with his thoughts,

"Now I am looking forward to a long lifetime of experiencing this talented mouth of yours, my dear."

I smiled around his fingers before letting them go. But then his words started to seep into the reality of my future, and I realized…

By tonight, his fingers wouldn't be the only thing I would be forced to…

Let go of.

CHAPTER 17
ORIGINS OF A NAME

As soon as I stepped outside the castle, I couldn't help but take a deep breath, filling my lungs with the scent of the untouched English countryside.

"Shall we?" Lucius said stepping up next to me and bending his arm, leaving enough of a space in the crook of his elbow for me to put my hand. I bit my lip and looked around to see who was watching, making him take my arm and put it where he wanted, as clearly, he had no patience for my reluctance. Just like he hadn't when he suggested we take this walk and my first reply had been to express my fears about people seeing us. Of course, every time I said this was simply an excuse, because naturally I didn't give a crap in a chamber pot who saw us. No, my real concern was all the time that we had been spending together, as every minute spent was just another chance for him to discover who I really was. And if that happened, then it was game over for all of us. There would have been no way for us to escape.

Of course, I would have liked to believe that Lucius and my father would have been understanding enough when it came to this mission. That upon discovering our time-traveling secret, they would have understood what hung in the balance of Fate and aided us any way they could. But then Pip had made the point that if they thought saying goodbye to us meant that when she said 'see you later' that later actually meant in a few hundred years from now… well, then that's where that understanding would take a flying time-traveling leap out the castle window.

So there was no other way. Keeping our secret was crucial, and our escape even more so. But as for Lucius, well his only concern at the moment was my continued reluctance to be seen together and it was an act I was sticking to. Especially seeing as it had half worked in my favour so far.

"I do not care who sees us, so they are welcome to challenge me on my actions for I guarantee they will not like the outcome of doing so," he said making it clear how he felt, and I wasn't exactly surprised considering Lucius was the type of man to take what he wanted and answered to no one. Well, no one other than my father. Someone who, in this time period, he still considered to be his King.

"Come, Lia, please allow me to show you the grounds," he said before leading me around to the front of the castle and towards the gardens beyond. He had also taken to calling me by my first name since the intimate start to our morning. Something that pained me to hear every time he said it. Just once I would like to have heard my actual name coming from his lips. A foolish wish, and one I forced myself to let go of instead focusing on the surrounding countryside.

"It's so beautiful here," I said and unfortunately, the flaw in this simple statement prompted his next question.

"So, you are not from around here after all?" he asked, giving me no choice but to tell him the truth.

"No, My Lord, I am not from around here." Of course, I couldn't help the way that it was said, knowing that it was loaded with so much more than I was ever willing to give him... *than what was ever safe for me to give him.*

"That sounds like a story waiting to be unraveled... tell me, pretty girl, *which thread do I pull on first?"* he whispered making me shudder.

"Ah but your silence only speaks of your fear, one that stems from what you think will be revealed, no doubt."

"You think I'm hiding something?" I asked trying to act shocked, to which he raised a brow and gave me a sceptical look in return.

"Oh, but I know you are, for you may not know this, but every time you allow yourself to speak freely around me, your breath catches when you realize your mistake and the beat of your blood becomes an excitable rhythm for my senses, as does that little heart that flutters within your chest." I would have sighed at this but knew that any response would only feed into his suspicions and give him greater reason not to trust me. And of course...

He would be right.

"Then that would make you quite the witch, for I do not know any other name to grant someone who can hear someone's blood sing."

At this I watched as a smirk played at the corner of his lips while the truth was held firmly behind a caged door. One he looked near desperate to open. Which was when I realized more than ever before that we both had our secrets. Secrets we were desperate to tell the other but couldn't through fear of what the reaction would be.

"It's true that I have... certain talents, should we say," was his diplomatic response.

"Or you just enjoy teasing me greatly, and this game you play is merely one of assumption and the root of your skills simply lay in the art of perception."

Again he seemed amused by this comment and patted my hand in a condescending way in the crook of his arm.

"Whatever helps you sleep at night, my dear."

I laughed at this.

"With you in my bed, I don't think I will sleep at all," I replied and suddenly he stopped walking. As if my brazen reply had utterly shocked him before he threw his head back and the laughter that erupted from him seemed to take even himself by surprise. Which made me wonder when was the last time he had laughed like that?

"I would pluck holes in your argument, however I fear there none to find for I am wholeheartedly inclined to agree with you, as such temptation in my bed, well... in truth, sleeping will be the last thought on my mind." I blushed at this and allowed myself to grin back at him.

"And you act as if my reply had been shameless enough to shock," I pointed out, making him return my grin with one of his own.

"Yes, but I assume by now you expect it to come from me." I raised my eyes up to his and said truthfully,

"By now I would expect no different, My Lord."

At this he stopped our movements once more, before taking hold of my chin between his gloved hands and lifting it so he could look at me with a tender gaze.

"Your Lord wishes for you to call him by his name, Lucius... call me Lucius, my dear sweet Lia." I smirked at this before nodding once and taking the first step to continue our walk.

And just like that, it once again started to feel like a scene plucked right out of Jane Austen's world. Despite at its core, I knew it was more like Bram Stoker. This was much more like Dracula finding his Mina than Darcy finding his Elizabeth.

But I couldn't help still being hurt at the idea that if we

ever had met in this time under different circumstances, and I hadn't been the daughter to one of the most powerful supernaturals on Earth, that he would not who have told me who he was. Of course, I was keeping secrets, but mine were for the good of the mission and ensuring the vow I had made.

But his excuse was worse.

Because he would allow me to marry him, despite not knowing who he truly was. He would have allowed me to run away with him, something made infinitely easier with me being a mere maid in his mind. Now had I been anyone of consequence or nobility then surely this would have made it harder for him. There would be family to consider as one would surely notice the daughter of a noble man disappearing more than a simple maid who lives in a village.

Which was no wonder why Lucius seemed almost pleased by this fact, as clearly my low stature in life was only making this far easier for him. Would this be his plan then, to entwine me so deeply into his life that when the time came for him to reveal his true nature to me, it would be too late for me to escape? That I would have no choice but to accept that side of him or was he simply just bidding his time by getting to know me? Giving it time so as he could try to show me a gentler side of him, like he perceived himself to be on this casual walk through the grounds?

I decided to test the theory,

"Might I enquire about your name, My Lor… *Lucius,*" I said, and when he granted me a knowing look, I quickly said his name like he had asked I use. Which meant the pleasure in his face when doing so was worth it because his handsome smile nearly took my breath away.

"My name?"

"It is quite unusual, and like you said, you are not from these parts, so I was just enquiring more about its origins," I said giving him the chance to open up to me, making me wonder if he would lie or try to be as truthful as he could be. He raised a single brow at me before responding.

"I suppose I am not to be surprised that you are curious. But you are right, my origins are far more, exotic should we say."

"But you reside in England, do you not?" I asked making him smirk this time.

"Ah, I take it that my little bird is curious to discover where she will be when spreading her wings and breaking free the duties of being a maid." I gave him a wry look at this and said,

"You forget that I am yet to accept your proposal, Sir, so I merely wish to…" I paused as his eyes heated the moment I reminded him that I had not yet said yes, and without even looking around to see if we were still alone, I suddenly found myself being cornered and pushed up against the castle wall.

"My Lord!" I shouted, knowing that if I didn't react this way it would seem unnatural. Of course, back in my own time and I would have eagerly hitched up my skirt, braced my hands at his shoulders, and wrapped my legs around his waist while inviting him to give me more.

"Lucius," he snarled his own name, reminding me of his earlier demands before warning me,

"You will accept, for I am not leaving here without you by my side."

"My mind is my own, along with my own free will," I argued, not wanting to give into him so easily.

"You really believe a maid is truly free?" I frowned at this, quickly informing him,

"I was not born into slavery and have not been bought by anyone last time I checked, so yes, even as a maid, I am free to choose under which master's household I may find employment," I snapped back, making his eyes heat once more and I wondered exactly how far I would need to push him before I got him to show me those crimson depths.

"I claimed your passion only this morning, and you speak to me as if there were choices laid at your feet like several pairs of shoes waiting for you to merely slip your feet into in order to see which one fits you best." Oh yeah, he was now pissed alright.

"And you? Have you not taken many women to your bed, tried them out, searched the room for the prettiest girl at the ball before asking her to dance…? No, you will not judge me, Sir, for taking stock of my life and wishing for time in order to make the right decision when faced with the first man to show interest in me!" I said, pushing him back and surprising him enough that he allowed it. He also seemed to take a keen interest in my words, clearly mulling them over before forcing his body to relax. Then he bowed slightly at the waist and told me,

"Forgive me, but you are right, you should take time, but only if that decision leads you to accepting me, for any indecision left between us I would like to have it known now, so as I may fill that gap with only the reasons of why you should accept. To spend my time commandeering your own, so as to convince you that no other answer but yes will do." I released a heavy sigh at this as I never would have believed that being pursued by Lucius was something I would class as a burden.

But the truth was, with how eager he was to move things along, I feared that the moment I agreed, then I would find myself standing in front of an alter and a priest before I knew what was happening. Because there was always the fear that tonight didn't play out the way we hoped or was, for some reason, delayed. But it was also more than this. It left a sour and bitter taste in my mouth saying yes to him when I knew I was only planning to run.

"And you're solely convinced that you and only you can provide me with my future happiness?" I asked, already knowing the answer to this as he had already proven it to me time and time again. But I was literally running out of reasons to keep putting him off.

"Without question," he said sternly enough that even if I was from this time period and this was our first-time meeting, I would have believed him.

"If I asked you questions, would you answer them honestly?" I asked, trying a different route.

"I feel like I am being interviewed for a position," he commented dryly but I raised a brow, telling him I wanted an answer.

"Ask away and we shall see," he said with a motion of his hand for me to proceed.

"That's not a very comforting reply," I pointed out, making him lean forward a little and say again,

"Ask it of me, little maid." The rumble in his voice almost made my toes curl. It was getting harder and harder to keep my hands off him when he spoke like that.

"From the short time I have known you…" I paused, making him take a step closer and run his knuckles down my belly, and I shuddered as he purred out a question,

"Mmm… and what say you, little Lia… what is your appraisal of me, I do wonder?"

"You have a very changeable nature." At this he laughed.

"Then indeed it would surprise you to know that I am normally known to be a calm and composed sort of man." I couldn't help but laugh at this myself, prompting him to repeat,

"As I said, it would surprise you."

"It has indeed, as you have been anything but since being in my acquaintance."

"Then perhaps you should ask yourself why… why would a man known for his calm countenance be so riled and passionate in his emotions ever since meeting you?" I blushed at this, and it was a sight that didn't go unnoticed as he ran the backs of his fingers along my cheek.

"A non-verbal answer, for I think this blush tells me that you know perfectly well, why."

"But like I once said, you don't even know me," I answered softly, pained by the truth of those words.

"I know enough to know I want more," he said in a husky tone and with lust in his eyes.

"Come, for there is something I want to show you," he said, now holding an arm out for me to take, and one I didn't hesitate to give him. We then walked the grounds at the front of the castle before we were near the stables once more. However, instead of continuing up the way we had travelled on his horse yesterday, he led me towards a different path he called *the green walk*. He then explained it was a half mile walk that offered breath-taking views of some of England's highest mountains and had been described by many as being a 'Gateway to Paradise'. But then as we walked along this south terrace, Lucius took my hand to stop me, pulling me back to him as clearly, he had something on his mind.

"Will you dine with me again tonight?" he asked making me chew on my bottom lip, a sight that looked like it distracted him as his gaze homed into my mouth.

"I really shouldn't, not again," I answered, however he started to draw me in closer before tilting my face up with a hooked finger under my chin.

"Why ever not?" he asked, as if surprised.

"Because it is improper... I am still your maid, remember?"

"Improper? Even for a man who has already tasted the ambrosia between your legs and feasted upon it like a wild beast?" I knew I blushed at this.

"Ssshh... you should not say such things," I scolded, looking round to check that we were still indeed very much alone. However, he just looked amused by this, and I realized that even in this time, Lucius would always find a reason and a successful way to tease me.

"Then I should only do them, but not speak of them?" he mused light heartedly in response to my 'such things' comment. But then I couldn't help my reaction, despite it not being 'proper' like I was trying in vain to adhere to. I slapped my hand to his chest, and scolded him yet again,

"Will you quit being so incorrigible!"

He looked taken aback a moment by my action, making me quickly try and remove my offending hand. Yet before I could, he held it grasped tightly in his leather clad fingers, now keeping it firmly to his chest.

"Upon my word, striking a Lord now... indeed you are more feisty than I gave you credit for... that, or I am rubbing off on you. But now I do wonder what punishment it should be," he said, tapping his lips with a finger and making my eyes widen at this before he leaned closer and said,

"Perhaps this time, it will merely be an improper feast." He laughed when he saw my expression before taking my hand and putting it back to the crook of his arm, telling me,

"Of course, I speak of the one we will share and gained substance from this eve... come, little maid, it is time I feed you, if only to cease the sound of your stomach growling at me like an angry bear."

"My stomach isn't growling," I argued even though I was pretty sure this was a lie.

"No? Then perchance your body is in need of some other substance, perhaps something I could be ever useful in providing you?" he teased again, and I couldn't help it, but I rolled my eyes before telling him quickly,

"Food will suffice just fine." However, the moment I started to take a step away from him, he stopped me suddenly by pulling me back. Then before I could even ask why, his hand was in my hair yanking my head back as his face lowered to mine.

"Now that is a curious thing indeed, for an action I normally disdain in others, I find endearingly satisfying on your face, perhaps it is because of my want to punish you after all… so by all means, little maid, roll your eyes again, for I look forward to discovering where it will get you and the pleasure I will gain by bringing you to heal by my hand." I swallowed hard at the implications of this. However, the moment my lips parted as a breathy sigh left me, he swooped in, seeing it as an invitation to claim my lips. Now kissing me until I was breathless in his arms.

Because even in this time I knew that Lucius's sexual desires were lead with a firmer hand, one that always managed to spike my arousal.

It was just a shame then that in this time period it was… *forbidden.*

Or was it?

CHAPTER 18
LADY IN RED

We walked back inside Muncaster castle and I instantly pulled my arm from his before anyone could see us, making him growl in annoyance.

"I am going to look forward to the day I can openly express that you are mine... *in every way,*" he said pulling me back to him with his hands at my shoulders, towering over me from behind and making me sigh as I allowed myself a moment of freedom to relax into him.

"Soon, little maid, but until then, I wanted to show you something."

"What is it?" I asked, curious as to what he had up his sleeve this time.

"Something to feed that intellectual and inquisitive mind of yours," he said with mischief glistening in his eyes as he took my hand and led me into a room on the right-hand side that soon had me gasping at the sight. It also made me realise how little of the castle I'd had chance to explore as I hadn't yet seen the beauty of this room.

"It's a library!" I gasped making him chuckle.

"Your power of deduction does not fail you, for those are

books indeed," Lucius teased making me grant him a wry look, and one he laughed at before pulling me further into the room.

It was a stunning octagonal room with an incredibly elaborate ceiling painted like the night sky in between interwoven triangular beams. The lower part of the room was nearly entirely made up of carved in-built bookshelves that matched the wooden panelling and decorative fire surround.

This theme also matched the upper level as nearly the whole room was framed by a wooden balcony, with the walls above giving space for a gallery of oil paintings. Much like the library back in Afterlife, the whole room was a collection of different styles of furniture and what would be known as antiques back in my own time. There was a sculpture of an alabaster lady atop of a mahogany side table, along with other treasures clearly collected from my father's travels. A beautiful red clock stood proud, and was in the oriental style with its gold and red lacquer work.

But it was the extensive collection of books that drew my eye as the leather spines of each were pristine. Which, for an history buff like me, was like a moth to the flame as I automatically walked towards the nearest shelf.

"This is incredible," I said looking back over my shoulder to find Lucius watching me with avid interest. I ignored his heated gaze and went back to scanning the shelves.

"This is a first edition Robinson Crusoe!" I shouted as I was excited seeing it here instead of where I knew it now resided in Afterlife. Although, it was true that my father could have bought more than one copy seeing as it was one of his favourite books. He used to read it to me when I was a child, leaving out any violent parts like the cannibals who occasionally visited the island to kill and eat the prisoners they had taken.

"You act as if this is a rare book, yet its publication was only…"

"Before you or I were born," I said, already knowing that the actual book I held in my hand was at least seventy years old. At this he grinned, as clearly he knew the truth.

"I see I am going to have to invest in more books for my own library, for clearly I have just found your greatest passion," Lucius said and before I could reply, I tensed suddenly the moment I heard my father's voice.

"Did I just hear talk of passionate interests and these words being said from my second in command, and within the walls of a library no less?" His voice was full of jest making Lucius grumble,

"I do read, Dominic."

My father laughed at this before his eyes landed on me, making me so nervous, I dropped the book.

"Oh please forgive me, I can be so clumsy." I crouched to retrieve it when my father's hand came into view.

"Allow me," he said picking it from the floor and standing to his full height as he started to look down at the cover. Then he raised his gaze and looked at me in surprise.

"Robinson Crusoe? This book interests you?"

"I have read it, My Lord. My father also enjoyed the story and used to read it to me as it was one of his favourites," I said unable to keep that truth from him. At this he gave me a warm smile in return and said,

"Then your father and I share this in common, for I can also claim it to be one of my own favourites." I bowed my head a little at this, showing respect as was expected of me to do so. The whole moment also tugged at my heart because he was the father I spoke of, yet right now, it felt that our circumstances could not have been further from a lifetime of my own reality.

"A well-read maid it seems and perhaps one too intelligent to pick the likes of you, Luc… what say you, Miss Earhart, have you yet to soften the stern countenance of my oldest friend or will you run for the English hills as fast as your legs can carry you?" my father asked teasingly, only this made Lucius come to stand next to me, place an arm around my waist, and tug me closer to him before he snarled,

"She is going nowhere." To which my father threw his head back and laughed whereas I had tensed all over.

"I am glad to hear it! For I declare you will both dine with us tonight." At this my mouth dropped open and I started to say,

"My Lord, that is very kind, but I couldn't possibly…"

"I must insist, my dear, for I have a feeling my friend here will be stealing you away to his own estate soon enough. I fear I will not see him again for years, for I have no doubt you will occupy all his time," my father replied, making me blush and wonder what his real reaction would have been to Lucius stealing me away had he known I was his daughter.

"You will not be rid of me so easily, no matter how you try but alas, you are right, my thoughts and days will be occupied indeed," Lucius replied, and I had to say having them both talking about me like this was making me squirm. It was also making me blush uncomfortably just like the first time I had taken Lucius home and we had pretended not to be an item. As for now, however, my own father was once again playing matchmaker and the irony certainly was not lost on me.

"Excellent, I will instruct the kitchen staff that we have an extra two seats to dine and look forward to getting to know your acquaintance further, Miss Earhart. Good day to you both," my father said with a nod, before scanning the shelves and plucking a book from the collection with a smirk.

Lucius and I then bowed our own heads in respect, doing so slightly lower than he had done. Because my father was at this time still his King and to me, he was still the Lord of the Castle.

Of course, this did now pose an even bigger problem, as not only was I expected to dine in a room with my family and my husband but I was supposed to do this playing the naive little maid. Meaning the three of us, Sophia, and my mother would have to spend the evening pretending that neither one of us really knew each other, them knowing me even less.

Gods what was this, the family edition of Cluedo?

But above all, would I be the only one left holding the candlestick in the dining room, who knew everyone's secrets?

Worst yet…

What was I going to wear?

I also had to admit that the first time I thought of Lucius coercing me into anything, I thought it would have included a bed and a locked door. Not that he would have had to work hard at getting me in his bed as the longer I spent with him, the closer and closer I came to being the one doing the coercing. And when I say coercing, I pretty much mean throwing myself at him because Lucius was not exactly making this innocent virgin act any easier.

Making me wonder…

Would I still be his virginal little maid by the end of the night?

∼

"Wow, I look…"

"Like a maid no more but the kick Vampy ass Princess you truly are… man a mundo, how much would I love to see the look on his face when he sees you for the first time. I bet he will tent his breachers!" Pip said making me choke on a laugh.

As for her comment, this was down to me now being dressed in one of Sophia's finest dresses. As thankfully for her, she kept her wardrobes stocked with the latest fashions in each home they owned. A frivolity I was happy to exploit considering all I had was this days-old, worn maid's outfit and a pair of washed once panties.

As for Lucius, he had insisted I get ready for the evening in his own chambers and before I had chance to convince him otherwise, male servants were entering his room. Then I watched as they each gathered items of clothing and what I gathered was what he was intended to wear for the evening. After this he walked over to me, kissed me on the forehead and told me affectionately,

"Tonight, Sweetheart." Then he left, along with who I assumed was my father's footmen. Shortly after this a bath was brought in the room, along with maids carrying jugs of hot water. None of them said a word to me but this didn't mean I didn't gain some evil looks. Not that I cared, as I didn't know any of these people and neither did I give a damn what they thought of me. Despite what I had said to Lucius on many occasion, giving him this as an excuse, using it more than once.

But clearly, this bath was intended for me to use and I had to admit, I was more than ready for it. Washing with a scrap of cloth out of a cold bowl wasn't exactly an experience I would ever miss. Nor was using the chamber pot. No, I was just thankful I wasn't on my damn period or that would have made this more like a trip back to Hell!

No thankfully, I had gotten that delightful time of the month out of the way before Christmas and when I say delightful, I mean it in the most sarcastic sense of the word as obviously it always sucked to be a woman for this week. And I was not even going to begin to describe what it was like during this time while being married to a Vampire!

Nope, not going there.

It had to be said though, that I had started to panic slightly after being done with the bath and worrying that I would be joining the rest of the dinner party dressed as a maid. However, the moment Pip slipped in the room carrying one of Sophia's dresses, it felt as if my prayers had been answered. Even more shocking was that Pip told me this request had been made by my father, who I suspected had first come from Lucius.

Which brought me to now, as I stared at myself in the mirror and felt like any minute I was waiting for some director to shout, 'Cut!' It had also taken a good twenty minutes to actually get me dressed as there was so many layers, I didn't know where my body ended and material began!

It started with the linen chemise, one that I exchanged for another. I knew from my studies many years ago, these were worn as a way to protect the expensive clothes and silks from sweat and bodily odour as these undergarments could easily be washed. Another pair of stockings, silk this time that went over my knees and were tied with ribbon to keep them in place.

Man, but I never thought I would miss pantyhose or a suspender belt in my life but here I was. After this was another petticoat which was just a knee-length, white linen skirt to which Pip informed me was called a dicky. Not surprisingly, something that made her giggle.

However, if I thought she found this amusing, then soon after the boned corset had strapped me tight, she howled with laughter when the sausage log of stuffed material was tied around my waist.

"Butt burrito anyone?" she commented making me burst out laughing right along with her. Of course, I knew this was called a hip pad and was worn to lift the skirt enough that it emphasized a smaller waist. After this came another bloody petticoat making me groan,

"Gods just how many skirts can one girl wear!" She wagged her brows and said,

"You can see the appeal of a quicky by having your skirts flipped up, as trust me, trying to do a strip tease in this thing and your lover is gonna be passed out from boredom before you have even got down to the good stuff." Yeah, I definitely couldn't argue with that or when she pointed out,

"Unless your lover has claws that is." Then she winked at me as she tied the full-length skirt this time. After this came a triangular panel of fabric that was stiff and decorated to match the rest of the dress and needed to be pinned to the front of the corset. It was also called a stomacher and pointed down like an arrowhead towards my lady parts that Lucius wouldn't have needed any guidance to show him the way. Although I did fear that with the number of pins he might encounter on his way there, I would end up feeling like a pin cushion. That was, if my hopes of recreating this morning was on the cards.

Of course, the stomacher covered the front of me enough that when the last parts of the dress were actually put on, it meant it covered the corset underneath completely.

The fuller silk skirt was lowered over my head and tied at the sides of my waist, before ribbons were pulled and tied to raise the skirts up at the side to create what Pip informed me was a,

"Time for the polonaise puff."

"Ah so if I am late, I can just tell them I'm sorry, but my polonaise puffs just weren't right." At this she giggled and said,

"You're not puffin' wrong." Again, we started laughing as she held out the jacket style part of the dress, letting me slip my arms through before she then pinned the gold ruffled edges to the sides of the stomacher and basically created the classic style of the gown this era was known for.

As for the colour, it was a stunning deep red which I knew had been picked by Sophia on purpose, being it was Lucius favourite colour for obvious reasons. Layers of thick gold frilly lace extended the sleeves to my wrists, whereas the red silk finished at my elbows. Gold embroidery glittered in the light that decorated the front of the stomacher in a swirling pattern that continued as a boarded path down the front of the underskirt.

And Pip was right, never before in my life had I looked more like a princess than I did in that moment. Even my hair had been artfully coiled and curled so it was a mass of black spirals cascading down from the twists pinned high on my head. A cluster of red rubies in the shapes of stars and flowers were clipped in place at the side of the curls, completing the look.

"Seriously, little bean, the poor bastard isn't going to know what hit him." I grinned at her and despite knowing this wasn't a good idea, I had to confess to being excited to see what he would think of the way I looked. Because I had only ever been the plain little maid in front of him and even though he had clearly fallen for me, tonight I got to show him a different side of myself. Even if this evening was going to be the hardest test yet for our acting skills.

I gave Pip a hug and thanked her for helping me get ready as quite honestly, I wouldn't have had a clue. Especially not considering I would have had to be a contortionist to be able to tie myself in half of this stuff.

"Go get em, gorgeous!" she said winking at me as I walked out the door. I then made my way down to the main hall with my heart hammering in my chest as I heard voices coming from the dining room. So, knowing it most likely wasn't wise to keep them waiting and hearing the chimes of the clock telling me I was at least on time, I took a deep breath and walked inside.

I only had to scan the room a few seconds before my eyes landed on Lucius, who currently had his back to me and was, at present, talking with my father who was facing the doorway. This meant that he saw me first and slight look of shock was one that was follow by a smirk. One that emerged quickly and said that he was no doubt looking forward to the reaction on Lucius's face when seeing me.

Which was why I saw my father say something to Lucius, obviously alerting him to the fact that I had arrived as the moment he did, Lucius's head snapped around. Of course, the second he drank in the sight of me, a look of astonishment took over his features and it was one I promptly blushed at.

Especially when I don't think he even realised the hint of crimson he allowed to seep through in his eyes as he scanned the entire length of me. Then he muttered something I couldn't hear to my father before striding his way towards me. His long legs eating up the space between us in seconds.

Then before I could even say a word, my mouth barely even opened as he took me in his arms and with no shame at all…

His kiss ravished me.

CHAPTER 19
FOR THE LOVE OF CHEESE

I gasped the moment I felt his tongue teasing the seam of my lips, urging me to open up to him further. Something I didn't hesitate to do. His hand went to my neck as his other arm banded around my lower back, drawing me in closer as he governed the kiss. I sighed into him as his tongue caressed my own, completely forgetting where we were or more like… *who we were in front of.*

A reality that only came back to me when I heard a gasp behind me and a soft,

"Oh my." I froze in his hold before trying to pull back, making him growl low in his throat, a clear and distinct sound of displeasure. But then seeing as we now obviously had more company than just my father, he knew he couldn't keep me prisoner to his passion for long. This meant he allowed me to be the first to pull away, taking a step back after a few seconds of hesitation on Lucius's part, and I was worried for a moment that he wouldn't let me go at all.

But when he did, this was when my eyes went straight to my mother. I even took a step forward as if my natural instinct was to run into her arms. Thankfully, I remembered myself, and I wasn't the only one as my mum also looked like she had been about to do the same thing. But the same thing stopped us both in our tracks as my father joined our group, stepping up next to my mother and taking her hand in his own to kiss.

"You are simply breath-taking, my love." I couldn't help but smile at this, especially when my mum blushed like she usually did whenever my father showered her with compliments. But he was right, my mother looked stunning in her peacock blue gown that brought out the blue flecks in her blue-grey eyes. Her blonde hair was no longer in waves but now cascading in spiral curls just like mine was. It was also pinned up in such an elaborate style, it looked like spun gold thread and must have taken twice as long as it took Pip when doing mine.

As for my aunt Sophia, she was wearing an equally stunning gown that was layers of purple silk embroidered with a silver fleur-de-lis pattern. As usual, she looked exquisite with her natural black curly hair pinned high around her subtle silver crown encrusted with purple amethysts.

This purple theme continued with my father who, like Lucius, was dressed very similar to how they had been the night of the ball. They looked dashingly handsome with their double-breasted black dinner jackets, as well as both of them choosing to wear their longer hair tied back from their faces. My mother looked close to swooning and well, I doubted I was much better. Not seeing as I still felt the warmth on my lips where Lucius had practically ravished them.

"My beautiful Electus, Miss Catherine Williams, may I introduce my good friend, Mr Lucius Septimus and his…" my father paused in his introduction, now looking to Lucius for confirmation.

"Fiancé," Lucius said like this was already decided,

making me gape open-mouthed up at him. A look, I should add, he purposely chose to ignore. As for my father, he smirked at my reaction to this before continuing,

"His fiancé, Miss Lia Earhart." My mum's eyes widened a moment as she heard the name and as a coy smile formed at her lips, she curtsied towards me and said,

"It is a pleasure to make your acquaintance, Miss Earhart." I returned the gesture and replied,

"Likewise, Miss Williams."

"And this here is my sister, Miss Sophia Draven."

"Yes, I believe I have you to thank for loaning me this beautiful dress," I said after we have both also curtsied to one another.

"You are most welcome, and I must confess to being quite envious, Miss Earhart, for it suits you far more than it ever did me." I blushed at this compliment, especially when Lucius pulled me closer to his side and told the rest proudly,

"She is exquisite."

"A rare jewel indeed, Luc, for I do declare us to be the most fortunate of men and with much cause to celebrate… please come, let us dine," my father said, tucking my mother's arm in his own before leading her to her seat, which unsurprisingly was next to his at the head of the table.

As for the room, it was a lavish yet surprisingly cosy dining room, with the wall's half-panelled in varnished oak and the top half covered in lengths of embossed leather glittering with gold leaf. A large fireplace with a dark wood surround was ablaze and created a warm glow to the room. But it was the table that stood centre stage, one made from what looked like a whole walnut tree and was big enough to sit at least thirty people.

It was one that was also bursting with colour, because all down the centre were stunning silver urns overflowing with flowers and fruits arranged artfully. Large silver candelabras stood like Poseidon's Trident in between these colourful arrangements and flickered with the tall white candles that occupied them.

As for the table setting, this was a stunning Chinese porcelain crested blue and white dinner service, that looked to be from the Qing dynasty. It was painted with a scholar and attendant in a mountainous river landscape within a border of stylized flowers and a pair of tied branches topped with a crested bird. Too much silverware to mention framed the sides, lined up like soldiers waiting for the order to be put into action. Numerous crystal-cut glasses were also waiting to be filled and I had to admit, a drink would be a welcome distraction for my frayed nerves.

Lucius led me over to my own seat, making sure I was seated next to him, whereas my aunt sat next to my mother and positioned opposite me. As soon as we sat down, the servants all filed in, now standing at the sides and making me jump, there were so many of them. Men all dressed in their finest ready to serve us at the mere nod of the head or lift of a glass.

It made me glad that I had not been brought up by my parents in this era and my father had long ago forgone the formalities of royal life. As most meals were now served buffet-style in Afterlife, where we helped ourselves instead of being constantly waited on hand and foot.

But as for here, wine was soon poured and by this time, I certainty felt like I needed it. In fact, as soon as I started gulping it down, I felt Lucius take my hand and lean into me, whispering,

"Relax, beautiful girl, you are among friends now." I gulped down the wine in my mouth and nodded, granting him a small smile, saying in my head,

'More like family.'

The first course was soon served, with large elaborate china serving bowls being placed in front of us, filled with stews and soups along with platters of meats and breads. Servants then ladled out our choices into the bowls that were part of each table setting, making my stomach rumble the moment I inhaled the delicious scent of food.

"Pray tell me, Miss Earhart, where in which do you hail from, for I must confess, your accent escapes me?" my father asked, causing me to drop my spoon and making it clatter back into my bowl. I winced the moment I did this but thankfully my mum did the same thing on purpose and made the excuse for me.

"Gosh, this cutlery can be quite slippery, can it not, Miss Earhart?" I grinned big and nodded my head in agreement. However, the second Lucius cleared his throat, I realised I hadn't yet replied to my father.

"But you are correct, Lord Draven, I am not from around here," I said stalling for time and wondering where exactly I could say I was from. But then I thought what would make the most sense, so completely winging it, I said,

"I was born in Philadelphia, in the Americas but my mother was English, so I was shipped back to be raised by my mother's family when both my father and my mother became sick," I said, knowing I had to give reasons for why they were no longer here. I also used Philadelphia as I knew from history that at the time of the nation's independence, the total population in the U.S. was only over two and a half million, with Philadelphia being the largest city with near forty thousand residents.

Of course, hearing this, Lucius tensed next to me and as for my father, he bowed his head respectfully, before offering me his condolences,

"Then I am sorry for your great loss, my dear." At this my mother and aunt looked at each other and I mouthed a quick, 'sorry' to my mum knowing I had no choice but to give this lie. She shook her head slightly to tell me silently it was okay and that she understood. But it was Lucius who took my hand in his and raised it to his lips before granting me a kiss there,

"I did not know but I too am sorry to hear of such loss." I granted him a small smile in return and told the table,

"I confess it was a long time ago, but their memory never fades, as they were the very best of people and will forever remain deep within my heart." At this my mother got teary and had to use her napkin to soak up her tears. My father saw this, and his features grew soft, before he too took my mother's hand in his and kissed it before whispering something to her I couldn't hear.

After this, conversation moved on between Lucius and my father about the Quasi-War, making me near gasp when I finally had a far firmer grasp on what date we had actually fallen into. The Quasi-War was an undeclared naval war fought from 1798 to 1800 between the United States and the French First Republic. These naval battles were primarily fought in the Caribbean and off the East Coast of the United States.

It was also a war that started in 1793 when Congress suspended repayment of French loans incurred during the American Revolutionary War, basically deciding they didn't want to pay back what they owed. This war also ended up including the British when the French retaliated by seizing American ships trading with Britain.

Now knowing all of this, I started to quickly put two and two together, one being the war and the other being a significant date for the Rosetta stone. Meaning I now believed that we must have come back to the year 1799, just before when the stone was discovered by Napoleon's forces in his campaign in Egypt in 1798. But it was on the 15th of July in 1799, that French soldiers were given the command from Colonel d'Hautpoul to strengthen the defences at Fort Julien. A place that was only a couple of miles north-east of the Egyptian port city of Rosetta, hence how the stone got its name.

Of course, as soon as this light bulb went off in my head, I started choking on a piece of bread I had dipped in my soup. Lucius kindly rubbed my back as he passed me a glass of water so I could calm the burn at the back of my throat. My mum and Aunt then looked concerned after I made my excuse,

"Must have gone down the wrong way." Clearly this wasn't a common phase or if it was, then there was another reason that Lucius and my father were looking at each other quizzically. Thankfully though, our bowls were quickly cleared and the next course was served, which saved me from potentially having to explain myself.

"Oh excellent, my favourite, Gumballs and Cheese wigs," Sophia said making my father grin.

"But of course, I could not welcome you back any better way, sister." I smirked at this, after first stopping myself from asking what they were, although my mother didn't have the same restraint.

"You mean they have bubble gum in this…" Of course, my aunt must have kicked her under the table as my mum suddenly sat up and started clearing her throat.

"Bubble what, my dear?" my father asked.

"Oh erm… wine! I do love the wine, no bubbles in sight though." I couldn't help but laugh at this, choking quickly to mask it. It turned out that 'Gumballs' were most definitely not what my mother expected them to be. But in fact, made from eggs, sugar, flour, mace, aniseed and carroway seeds all mixed together to form a paste, which was then baked. And as for 'Cheese wigs', well these were small bread buns coated with cheese sauce, so they kind of resembled the shape of a wig resting on a wig stand. Of course, these were only a few of the many dishes served, as there were also steaming buttery vegetables, even more meats and fish, with the addition of crusty golden pies that made my mouth water.

As for Lucius, he knew of my love for Mrs Wheeler's pies and therefore chuckled to himself when he heard me moan slightly as the first mouthful found home in my belly. I quickly then guessed that it was also the reason his hand found my leg under the table. A hand gripping firmly at the top of my thigh, making me gulp down the next mouthful of food like it was stone. This was because history started to repeat itself… or can that even be said, seeing as technically, this moment came first.

Now that's a thought enough to make anyone's head spin if ever there was one. But seeing as it catapulted me right back to that night sitting at the head table in Afterlife's VIP, I couldn't help but tense.

"Lucius," I hissed, making him grin before turning and whispering,

"I confess to be quite envious of that pie, for I too do hope to have better skills at encouraging those same sounds coming from kissable lips." I nearly choked hearing this, but even more so when my mother suddenly forgot herself and knowing my love of cheese, said,

"Oh my God, this Cheese wig is so good, you're going to love this…"

"…Amelia."

CHAPTER 20
THE HEART OF WAR

The moment my mother said this we both simultaneously froze, and Lucius didn't miss it. Of course, it was my aunty Sophia who once again, came to our aid as she laughed and said,

"I believe the wine must be getting to you my dear, as our guest is named Lia, although very similar to Amelia and must be the friend you were telling me about." My mum's eyes widened momentarily before she started playing along.

"Oh yes, silly me, of course... but I do apologise, Miss Earhart, for Sophia is right, I have a friend I write to often by the name Amelia." I instantly relaxed and replied,

"It is perfectly alright, and I dare say an easy mistake to make and in reply, I will take your recommendation, for I do love cheese." Then I reached for a cheese wig to put on my plate, purposely trying to ignore the heavy weight of Lucius's questioning gaze I could feel boring down on me.

Shortly after this, a far easier conversation continued thanks to Sophia talking to her brother about travel and her plans to return to Italy to be back with her husband. I had to hand it to her, the ease in which she played her role was nothing short of Oscar-worthy, often leaving my mum and I in awe of her. But then again, she had lived through this time already and evidently, she also had the memory of an elephant, as she seemed to slip back into this time period with startling ease.

Soon, dessert was served by which time I felt the bones of the corset digging in painfully, alerting me to the fact that if I ate anymore, I was in danger of impaling myself on a snapping whale bone and bleeding out all over the dinner table. After this, coffee was offered, to which my father asked for it to be served in the drawing room, as clearly, he had something on his mind. I knew this when he declared,

"Lucius, there is business I would like to discuss and a conversation I fear our lovely company may find tedious and tiresome." Sophia waved her hand at this and replied,

"Then I suggest you leave us ladies to our own topic of conversation that the men in the room may find equally tedious and tiresome." I nearly scoffed a laugh at this as I very much doubt they would, not considering it would be us conspiring with one another about our escape. Lucius stood and like my father did with my mother, he helped me to rise from the chair before granting me a kiss on the cheek.

"I won't be long and will meet you back in our chambers."

"Our chambers?" I mocked in a teasing tone. To which his eyes narrowed before he confirmed purposely,

"Yes, *our chambers."* Then he nipped at my lope and growled playfully. Both of them then excused themselves and I swear, the three of us each held our breaths until they finally disappeared. After this Sophia dismissed the rest of the staff that had remained ready to serve us coffee, meaning that once the door closed, we let out a sigh of relief, my mum especially. I immediately ran into her arms, more than ready to give her a hug.

"Oh Amelia!"

"Mum!" We embraced and, in that moment, I felt my whole world centre once more.

"I have been so worried," I admitted making her laugh once.

"That's usually my line." I pulled back a bit and she cupped my cheek, making me lean into it.

"I've been fine."

"And Dad?" I asked and she knew what I meant by this.

"Oh, don't worry about him, I can handle your father in any time period," she said winking at me and making me chuckle, despite knowing she had said this to ease my worries.

"Yeah, well let's hope this escape plan works or you might be rephrasing that claim when we are dealing with a mad-man hunting us across the English countryside," Sophia said making my mother sigh.

"I gather she told you the plan?"

My mum nodded with a solemn look on her face. One I understood all too well.

"It will be okay, Mum, once this vow is complete, then we can go home, and you will be with Dad again." She sighed at this and agreed,

"And it will be like none of this ever happened for them... I know, I know, it's still hard leaving him like this."

"I know, I feel the same about Lucius... but wait, it will be like it never happened?" I asked.

"Yeah, that's what Janus told me the first time I did this."

I let out a relieved breath but then caught it before it could finish.

"But if that's the case, then what if none of this even

matters?! What if I am going to find this Hyperborea and whatever I do, it just goes back to the way it was after I leave, taking no affect?"

"It won't work like that," Sophia said confidently.

"Why?" I asked, feeling my heart hammering at the possibility this had all been in vain.

"Because Hyperborea isn't of this realm. It is of the Elemental world, meaning the same principles won't apply," she said, and still I needed more confirmation of this, making me ask further,

"And how do you know that?"

"Because we are here and this was all Fated, if not, Janus would not have allowed us to use the Gate in the first place." Okay so this made sense as she was right, this had all been Fated so it had to work...

It just had to.

"So, the moment we are back, Lucius won't remember any of this?" I asked, feeling like this should have been something I was sure on before leaving. Both my aunt and mother shook their heads and that heavy weight on my heart lifted some.

Because that meant...

It would only be one heart breaking when it was time to say goodbye...

And it would mine.

∼

Shortly after this brief conversation, I returned to Lucius's room, where he found me sitting looking out of the window as the darkness beyond provided a blanket of stars to grace the sky.

"What is it in the window that interests you so, I

wonder?" Lucius asked after entering the room, the distinct sound of him locking the door echoing straight after. I didn't answer, it would only be a lie as it wasn't like I could say, *I was waiting for the sight of whatever distraction Marcus would be creating.* But as for now, well I felt his presence in the room like the heat of the desert, one that only burned hotter the closer his footsteps brought him to my back.

"Please, Lucius," I whispered when I felt his lips at my neck, making me wonder how desperately he wanted to sink his fangs there and taste what he had claimed as belonging to him? Just how much was he having to hold himself back?

"Umm, now that is a dangerous realisation," he uttered against my skin.

"What is?" I asked in a soft voice as his own was luring me deeper into his spell.

"Just how willing I am to grant you whatever it is you ask me for, for one look into those deep blue eyes of yours and the scent of your skin filling my senses and *I find my will is lost to all that is you."* I turned my head at this and because I knew it could very well be my last, I said,

"Then maybe you should kiss me and indulge in the use of another of your senses... *taste."* The second I whispered this last word, his eyes turned intense as his hunger for me was easy to see burning in their depths. Suddenly his hand was in my hair as be bent at the waist, kissing me deeply as his other hand snaked down to take my hand so as he could prompt me to stand. I stood and curled myself into his arms so our union was made easier for him, not once losing his lips in the process.

I also tried not to think about this being our last kiss for too long, because I knew by the time he pulled away he would find tears in my eyes. A sight I knew he would have no doubt questioned. So instead, I forced the sadness away and focused on all that was Lucius. The feel of strength beneath my palms as I held onto a bicep with one hand and the other was around his waist, knowing of the rippling muscle there beneath layers of fabric. His own hands fisted at the base of my spine, twisting just as many layers of silk within his pale, thick fingers.

Gods, but what I wouldn't have given for claws to have grown through human nails so he could tear this dress from my body and I may then feel his hands upon my naked flesh. In fact, had the looming escape not been hanging over my head like a noose, I would have tried to take this kiss all the way to the bed. But knowing that it was getting way too heated as it was, I finished the kiss by softening my movements against his lips before pulling away gently.

We both breathed deep before I did something that I knew he would find surprising and yet enjoyable at the same. I placed my hands at his shoulders, reached up on my tip toes, and kissed him quick on the nose.

"Thank you, handsome," I said enjoying the surprise that washed over his features before I turned. However, my hand was grabbed, and I was tugged back into his towering frame.

"Where do you think you're going!" he growled passionately, before tipping my head back and kissing me once more, not allowing me to get too far from him. This time he buried his fingers in my curls and the bite of pain when they tensed into a fist only ended up adding to my arousal, making me bite his lip in return. He growled low in his throat as his arm snaked around my back, holding me tighter to him as if he feared someone had the power to rip me from his arms. Just like he often did back in my own time.

However, the only thing powerful enough to do that right now was Fate, one that quickly caught up with me the second I opened my eyes. This was because there, in the distance, was a strange glow getting closer and closer. One that looked as if it was crossing down the fields in front of the castle's steep banks. I stiffened in Lucius's arms and the moment he felt it, he pulled back.

"What's wrong, Lia?" I nodded to the window and asked,

"Outside… there is something…" I never finished as he shifted me behind him before approaching the window. I knew with his superior eyesight it wouldn't take him long in discovering what it was that I was now referring to. I knew it especially when he growled,

"Scheiße!" Lucius snarled the German word which I knew basically translated into 'Damn it'. Seconds after this and there was a sharp knock at his door. He stormed towards it and in his haste, unlocked it with his mind, obviously not considering how strange this would have looked to me. He wrenched it open in his clear frustration, only to find a servant waiting there, one I didn't recognize.

"My Lord requests your presence immediately."

"Where is he?" Lucius snapped making the guy flinch.

"He is in his chambers waiting for you."

Lucius said nothing more but simply nodded before closing the door. He then walked to his trunks, at the same time ridding himself of his jacket. I then watched as he got undressed, leaving on his shirt and breeches on, as well as kicking off his shoes. After this, he grabbed what I know was called a gambeson, which was a padded, quilted jacket that was usually worn under armour.

Then as he continued to get ready, I only had one thing in my mind when Lucius pulled his sword from the truck.

As he now looked as if…

He was getting ready for war.

CHAPTER 21
ESCAPE PLAN

I looked towards the lights in the distance before moving my eyes back to Lucius as I watched him getting ready for the potential fight to come. He was just shrugging a shoulder into the quilted gambeson, that looked like a padded jacket. It was black with leather bands at the elbows and tied with a line of buckles, with the first starting at the right side of his chest and going down across his body at a diagonal.

After this he belted his swords scabbard around his waist so it hung down at the ready for him to pull free and terrify locals with. Once this was in place, he began strapping on his plated amour, starting with his shoulder pieces that were made up of overlapping silver scales. His chest piece matched the rest and I started to ring my hands in the silk of my dress as I watched him gear up, until I could take it no more. He had just finished twisting his body to buckle his armour at his sides and was now sitting on a chair, putting on his boots.

"Are we under attack?" I asked, making him finally look up at me. He then released a heavy sigh and slapped his hands to his knees before standing so as to make his way over to me.

"Don't fret, sweetheart, in all honesty, it is most likely my Lord is simply airing on the side of caution." I looked back towards the window where the glow in the distance was getting closer, knowing now that Marcus had obviously caused a riot in the village and riled up the locals enough to make their way up here. As for Lucius, I felt his fingers come to my chin before turning me away from the sight.

"Wait here and do not leave, do you understand?" he asked making my eyes go wide and my breath catch. The panic he saw now was real, if not for a very different reason than what he no doubt assumed.

"But I don't understand, what is the threat?"

"It seems as if foolish rumours have spread amongst the village as they ascended towards the castle with a mob greater than three and fifty." I frowned at this and asked the obvious question,

"Wait, how do you know that…? You could not have possibly counted them from this far away." He tensed at this before releasing a sigh and telling me,

"It matters not how I know, what does is that I must go." He made his way to the door and opened it, making me take a step forward as the last thing I wanted was to get locked in here. Because even though Sophia or Pip would no doubt come and get me, I knew it would only take time we couldn't afford to lose.

"But if it is a mob, they bring torches with them… do they intend to burn the castle down?!" At this he saw my panic and closed the door for a moment before reaching me and drawing me into his arms.

"Do not be scared, for I will protect you, of this you have my word… *always*… but you must remain here in this room." I started shaking my head, telling him,

"I can't be alone, please don't leave me here." I must have

made this damsel in distress act real enough as he frowned before exhaling heavily.

"Damn these beautiful eyes and how they entrap me... all right, my sweet little maid, come with me." He took my hand after making a decision that he couldn't say no to me, or the fact that he didn't want to leave me here seemingly frightened by myself. We then walked to where my father's bedchamber was and where he was obviously keeping my mother in her lavish prison.

Lucius knocked once before hearing my father's stern voice telling him to enter. So, we walked inside, and I had only seconds to take in the royal opulence of the room before my eyes settled on my mother, who like I was, was still wearing her restricting dress. As for my father, he was also dressed and ready for the potential fight, just like Lucius. Although he was wearing darker armour than his second in command, making the pair look as menacing and foreboding as you could get.

"It seems I am in need of your persuasive talents, Lucius... but what is this, you bring your own frightened doe with you... is she...?" My father let this question trail off, clearly finishing the sentence mentally and it was one I knew with Lucius's answer was my father asking if I could be trusted.

"Yes, and if not, I will gladly bear punishment in her place if foolish enough to do anything reckless." This was a warning if ever I heard one and I had to say, I felt guilty about the trust I was about to shatter the moment they both stepped foot out of this door. A trust I had no choice to break.

I almost wish I had a moment alone with him just to say my goodbyes, knowing that if all went well, this would be the last time I would see him in this time period. The thought almost brought tears to my eyes, just as it had done when I made love to Lucius before embarking on this dangerous journey to begin with. One I now knew he inevitably had discovered back in my own time.

Gods, he was going to be furious.

Just like he would be as soon as he discovered me gone from this room.

"Very well, my dear Catherine… I won't be gone long, and it seems you have more than one lady to keep you company." At this Sophia opened the door and glided in just at the right moment when my father explained,

"For my sister here is very capable at keeping guard and watch over the two of you." I swallowed hard at this and experienced another, *'if only you knew'* moment.

"Sister, I leave my most precious gift in your hands, do not fail me." At this Sophia bowed her head to her brother, and told him,

"I vow now and forever to always protect what you hold dear in your heart." Then Sophia looked to my mother before her eyes also slid to me in a discreet way. Because I knew what she was saying. Something I felt to my core, as my auntie Sophia would now and forever, always protect what my father would hold most dear to his heart.

His family.

Which, right now, included getting us out of here.

However, Lucius did not seem to miss this added look from Sophia, making me wonder what he thought about it, especially when his gaze narrowed slightly. Well, whatever it was, it didn't stop the inevitable, for as soon as my father's hand fell to Lucius's shoulder and grasped it, he thankfully drew his attention elsewhere and back on the problem at hand.

"Then let us be quick, old friend, for we have precious hearts to get back to." My father bowed his head to me the once, showing me the same respect he had done in the dining room earlier. But as for Lucius, he stepped up to me, just as my father was doing the same to my mother. I didn't hear what my he said to her as my whole focus in that moment was solely on Lucius, knowing this was where we parted ways.

"I won't be long, beautiful." I nodded, before raising up on my tiptoes so I could place a hand at his cheek and whisper,

"Be safe... *always.*" It was the most I could give him because the other million ways I would have said goodbye couldn't be voiced. He leaned into my hand and whispered back,

"Always." After this, they both left the room and I swear that my mother and I were both holding our breaths. A breath that was only freed once the door closed behind them. I felt my mum's hand wrap around my own now giving it a squeeze, granting me the strength I needed to let him go.

To let the second time I had fallen in love with this man... go.

I took a deep breath and shook off my pain before turning to my aunt.

"Okay so that's phase one out the way, what's next?" I asked Sophia, who walked towards us and said simply,

"Now it's time to strip."

"Thank god!" my mum said making me laugh and I had to say, I felt the same way. After this we helped each other out of the huge dresses, before a knock on the door had all three of us freezing. Which would have been a sight to see as I was crouched low in nothing but my corset, panties and stockings. Oh, and I was currently trying to untie the sides of Sophia's skirt while she was pulling at my mum's corset ties like a frustrated cat clawing at the living room furniture.

"Housekeeping," Pip said before walking in the room with her arms full of our original clothes. Of course, as soon as she saw this comical little scene, she burst out laughing at the same time kicking the door closed behind her.

"You look like the worst circus act in history." Sophia groaned and said,

"I forgot how hard it is to get out of all this shit."

"I for one am never moaning about wearing a bra ever again!" my mum exclaimed and I raised up a hand to high five her on this. Thankfully, with our joint effort at all undressing each other, it was a far quicker process than what it had taken getting us into them. It was a good job too or the men would come back and find the oddest family scene in the history of all getaways.

Soon enough, we were all changed and back to comfort level one hundred, as I swear, I was almost tempted to start doing jumping jacks just because I could. However, more importantly was our escape so with this in mind, we soon made our way out the door and down a servant's staircase. Oh, and this was where we found the first unconscious person making all three of us all look to the most obvious culprit.

"What did you do?" my mum asked beating me and Sophia to it.

"Oh them…? Don't worry, some free wine and they were anybody's and when I say anybody's, what I mean to say is mine for the taking, mawhaaa," Pip said ending this with a comical evil genius laugh.

"Okay, so what's the actual answer, this time without the evil laugh?" Sophia asked.

"Oh, nothing really, just a special brew of alcohol, a bit of opium along with a sprinkle of cannabis and maybe some valerian… but don't worry, they will all wake up soon enough, just not until the birds have forever flown this shiny nest… now make haste, Boobateers!" Pip said, thrusting her arm up in the air like she was leading an army and making my mum and Sophia groan.

"I thought we made her promise not to call us that?" my mum complained behind me.

"Oh, you mean just like the time we made her promise not to slip cannabis into your cookies for the PTA meeting." I spluttered a cough when hearing this, at the same time Pip said,

"What? They were all a bunch of tight ass lips pansies that needed to loosen up and poo freely."

"Loosen up, Karen took off her bra and lassoed the principal with it!" my mum complained.

"Yeah and?" Pip argued.

"She was the head of the PTA whose husband was county sheriff," my mum countered, making me giggle but then again, I agreed with Pip, Karen was a bit of a stickler for the rules and most definitely needed to lighten up. For starters, her son, poor Henry wasn't even allowed to go near the barest hint of sugar without her acting like the kid was going to start snorting the stuff like cocaine!

"Well, it looks like Marcus certainly pulled through," I said as soon as we made it outside and I could see down the valley. The angry mob that was still making their way up the hill towards the castle could have rivalled any mob from the Simpsons. I even found myself feeling guilty as it looked like my father and Lucius had taken a small army down to meet them.

"You don't think they will hurt them, do you?" my mother asked before I could voice the same concerns.

"No, they will not hurt innocents, which is why Dom needed Lucius, so that he could influence their minds and tell them to go back to their homes without any bloodshed," Sophia replied calmly.

"Well let's just hope that it takes a while for him to connect to all those minds or this is going to be a very short getaway," I said as we kept to the darkness of the walls that led us back towards the stables.

"I hate to be the fly in the much needed gin and tonic here, but if stealing horses is your plan, then I should point out now that Amelia and I are not exactly the best on horseback."

I laughed, as wasn't that the truth.

"It's fine, two horses are all we need as we can ride in doubles. Trust me, Pip and I have had enough experience, as we've been riding on them longer than in any cars," my aunt Sophia reminded me making Pip agree,

"Yeah, and I have been riding Adam every day since we exchanged hooves for wheels, so trust me, these hips are ready to go." We each held the same expression to this, which was the 'way too much information, Pip,' face.

We continued to make our way up the slight incline until we passed under the archway into the stable yard. Two horses were already saddled and ready to go waiting for us, which I gathered was another part of the 'Pip plan'. I took one look at the horse and then down at my trousers and boots, knowing this was going to be a lot easier than the last time I was forced on a horse.

"Toots, you're with me," Pip said before giving her a hand to get on the back of the saddle. Sophia did the same for me so that seconds later and we were both now left clinging on to our riders. This before we left galloping with haste as our horses flew out of the stables. Thankfully with the commotion at the front of the castle, we were able to freely make our escape. And I had to admit as uncomfortable as being on a horse was, it was far easier than running in mud which would have been our only other option.

Although I had to say, this feeling of good fortune and luck soon ran out pretty quickly, as about twenty minutes later and we soon discovered we were no longer traveling this road alone. Because the moment I heard the pounding of hooves slapping against the wet ground behind us, I turned my head at the same time praying not to see the one face I usually always longed to see.

But just as the moon came out from behind the clouds, there was no getting away from the fact that our escape had been discovered and we were now being…

Pursued.

CHAPTER 22
ESCAPING FATE
LUCIUS

"Whoa," I said, pulling on Sleipnir's reins to slow from its gallop into a trot until stopping next to my King's horse.

"Well, this is an inconvenience," I commented dryly insight of the angry mob that had formed, now all sprouting nonsense about witches living in the castle.

"Indeed, for something has the village folk riled making me wonder what could be the cause, for last I checked, we were far beyond the time for hunting witches," Dominic said in as bored as tone as I had just expressed.

"Little do the mortals realise, that the witch hunts were actually a way for us to contain the Demon outbreak, meaning that this little standoff of theirs would no doubt be quite different if they actually knew what they were up against."

"They didn't then, and they will not now, and as always, what little mortals know of us, the better." After this he nodded my way, giving me the go ahead to take possession of their minds and send them back to their homes. This along with taking away their memories of foolishness until they got there. But entering a mortal's mind was easy and nothing more than child's play. However, it had to be said that a large group like this did take a slight effort on my part.

Yet this time, it was not the effort that vexed me but the time which it took in doing so. Time that was taken away from spending with my little maid. A girl I was taking great pains and effort to restrain myself around, for I wanted her claimed in every way possible. I wanted this as soon as I set my eyes on her. Although, I also knew that I had to draw upon what little patience I had around her, as little did she know, that such patience was a gift not many were lucky enough to receive from me.

To be honest, I had never had to woo anyone in my whole life and in truth, it was a novel experience not to have a woman throw herself at me. In fact, I had to confess that I quite enjoyed the cat and mouse game we played, as she was worth every ounce of the attention I was bestowing on her. It was an enjoyment I had never before known the likes of, for trying to corrupt my innocent little maid had quickly become my new favourite pastime. I also found myself looking forward to the future immensely, already questioning how far away from here I was able to take my soon-to-be bride.

She had been vague about her history, until this evening that was. However, I was thankfully assured that no family would be an issue in her upcoming disappearance. This despite the slight ache it brought me in my chest when hearing how she had been left orphaned by those she clearly loved. Especially when she had spoken so highly of her father. But this feeling of empathy, had been an unusual experience for me, for I could not remember the last time I had felt such sentiments as this for another.

Yet despite the pains she had suffered, there was no getting away from the fact that her situation in life served my purpose greatly, for it meant there was nobody left to challenge me. Not that it would have done them any good if they had, but still, it did mean keeping in her good graces now that I wasn't forced to kill anyone she cared for.

Because I would soon take her from this place and situate her so fully in my life, she would not even have realized that she would have been a prisoner to it. Many would have called me a high-handed bastard, but as the son of the Devil, those who knew me would not expect anything less, *my King included*.

But then again, one look at the same expression on my friend's face and I knew I was not the only one feeling possessive and eager to return to the gift the Fates had bestowed on us. This being said, I still couldn't shake the unease I felt when it came to my delicious little maid. There was still so much left for me to discover, and what I had so far had left a sour taste in my mouth, for I knew that if she was not outright lying to me, then she was telling me half-truths.

So, what was it that she was really hiding I wondered? I had expressed as much with Dominic tonight as he too had his own concerns about his Electus. Instances shared together that neither of us could put our fingers on, but it did not negate the fact that doubts existed.

Of course, these doubts we spoke of had nothing to do with the certainty we felt down to the roots of our souls who our Fated ones were to us. No, in this we were as certain as we ever could be. But it was the stories they told and the lies they spun that made us both question the origins surrounding their discovery. In fact, we both agreed that they seemed far too familiar with each other and had Sophia not been there to keep watch over them, I doubted Dominic would have allowed them to be locked in the same room together.

As a result of our discussion, we both agreed that tonight would be the time for us to gain our answers by any manipulating means necessary. Of course, we would never lay a finger on our Fated Ones in anger, nor would we ever hurt them. This being that we would much rather rip of our own limbs than use them to cause pain and suffering to our Chosen Ones. Yet even with this being said, neither of us was without our own means in getting the answers that we wanted. For we each had a bad feeling in our guts that their reasons for them both appearing here was not a simple story of coincidence.

And soon we would find out the truth.

"It is done," I informed him, and proof was clear when the village folk shook their heads and turned like mindless dead souls that wandered a realm called the Harrowing, where they spend an eternity searching for a pointless way home.

"Good, for like you, I am eager to return," Dominic exclaimed after expelling a sigh of frustration.

"Indeed," I said as we both turned our horses to face the castle and my thoughts as I did so, travelled back to the conversation we shared earlier in the drawing room…

"The maid?" Dominic said the moment we were alone after first opting for brandy instead of coffee.

"Lia." I said her name with a grit of my teeth, telling him all he needed to know. His smirk was a reliable enough source to tell me he understood my meaning.

"It is a pretty name," he commented.

"It is and it shall forever be the only name that slips from my lips as I bury myself inside her," I said feeling possessive.

"So, she is truly to you what my Catherine is to me, for we have both found our Chosen Ones."

"It would certainly seem so," I replied, slipping up in my reply.

"You do not know for sure, have you not bedded her yet?" I tensed at the surprise in his tone.

"I'm taking it slow with her," I admitted, now being the cause of shock to take over his features.

"Not too slow I hope, for she is your Chosen One, is she not?" he asked extracting a frustrated sigh from me.

"Lucius?" he said my name in question when I did not answer him quick enough.

"She is, for there is no doubt there, I can promise you this."

"But still there is doubt somewhere?" he asked picking up on my wording.

"There is just something about her, something she holds back from me... *her true self,*" I admitted almost painfully.

"Why not simply take it and enter her mind? It is unlike you to be so patient in getting what you want." I granted him a look that made him chuckle.

"I will admit I know this from experience, for I have little patience when it comes to something I want or in this case, *someone*... but you know this of me, for it has not been so great a secret in all our years spent together. But this is how I know the same goes for you, as I have no doubt the same can be said for most Kings, of this, I am sure," Dominic said causing me to sigh once more before admitting,

"I cannot access her mind, one I must confess intrigues me so, for it is..." I paused before going further, something he quickly prompted me to do.

"What?"

"It is like she is not part of this time, or perhaps it is that she is simply not of this place, for one moment she speaks our tongue and then the next, I hear phrases from her lips that I have never heard before and, as you know, we are old enough for that to be surprising." He granted me a thoughtful expression before admitting the same.

"I must confess feeling the same way about my own, as like you, I too have no access to her mind. But what concerns me more is that you think it means something." I gave him a knowing look.

"As ever I hate to feed your ego, old friend, but I fear I must in this instance for I have rarely ever known you to be wrong." I would have grinned at this forced compliment coming from his lips had this been spoken under different circumstances.

"Did you notice how they looked at one another, as if they were being reacquainted?" I asked wondering if he too had noticed it, wishing in truth I was simply searching for something that wasn't there to be found.

"You think they came here together?" he asked, and I had to confess that the thought had already crossed my mind, for he knew me all too well and the fact that I did not believe in mere coincidences. No, we had fought too many wars and faced too many enemies together to be allowed such luxury as to not question the reasons behind everything that others do.

"The men you sent, didn't they say there were two in the house, a man they claimed to have knocked down and the woman who turned out to be your Chosen?" I asked causing Dominic to grant me a thoughtful look.

"Now I feel foolish for only capturing my Catherine, for you think they lied?"

"Perhaps," I answered thinking more about it.

"It is possible they lied to keep a vulnerable woman to themselves and intended to go back there to…"

"I suggest you not finish that line of thought unless you

do not care for your furnishing, for I will destroy something if even the thought of what could have happened to my Lia is brought to light." Dominic bowed his head once in understanding, as he would have been just as furious with the idea had it been his own Chosen One we were speaking of.

"In truth, I do not know why, only that not even a full day passed before my Fated was shown to me after your own was delivered to you by your order. For was it not Marcus who foresaw your Chosen One's arrival and after whispers of a commoner seeing a strange woman in his cottage?" He nodded telling me it was.

"And shortly after, it seemed as if my little maid knew exactly what she was getting into by entering into the castle and making herself known to me… for I could have sworn I noted recognition in her gaze when seeing me for the first time," I said starting to have a bad feeling about this but not only that, there was another sight that hadn't settled well with me. However, it was not one that I was willing to risk speaking of in front of the King. Not as of yet, not when the delicate matter included his sister.

"Then perhaps we had best go ask our betrothals this evening, for they seem to have some explaining to do," Dominic agreed, forcing me to question his own doubts,

"I take it you did not trust the story of origins from your own Electus?"

"She has of yet refused to give me any explanation of where and how she came to be in my lands, no matter how hard I have tried to extract this information from her." I raised a brow at this but didn't dare ask, as I could only imagine it being similar to what I had in mind when trying to gain my own answers with Lia.

"That in itself does not bode well for what we may discover," I pointed out causing Dominic to sigh.

"It matters little."

"How so?"

"They are now in our clutches, and neither are going anywhere. That is all that matters for now. As for you, I suggest bedding her while feeding from her life's blood, for only those two things will truly give you the answers you seek."

"She is mine, I know it down to my core," I replied with the grit of teeth at the very thought that she may be taken from me.

"Then there is nothing to fear, and no doubt is to play a part in your future, especially not when your King orders you to do the deed. For what you tell me, proof is not for yourself but simply for others of our kind." I understood the inner meaning of his words for it was a clear order from my King. As I may be assured of the fact that she was mine, but he was not, not until I claimed her. After all, it was his own rule made that stated one of our kind could not take a mortal as a mate and for good reason. Not unless it was deemed Fated by the God of time.

However, what my King did not know, was that despite all possible outcomes, I was keeping her regardless of if she was granted to me from the Fates or not. For one of the advantages I held over the King was his assumption of being more powerful than I was. The years past had made him forget the time when we first met, for the only way for me to prove my worth to him had been to demonstrate my power over his mind. Something at the time I was arrogant and cocky enough to be quick to oblige myself in. Despite it almost costing me my head.

He also did not know the true extent of my own Kingdom that was quickly gaining in strength and power. Most of which was admittedly, not in this realm but the one not occupied by mortal life. Meaning that if I chose to do so, I could take my little mortal prisoner back to my realm in Hell where he would never have the chance at taking her from me.

Yet despite this comfort, the truth was that Dominic was my friend and I was loyal enough to him not to want us to go to war over this. Besides, he had his own Chosen One to consider and there was that age-old saying, keeping your friends close but your enemies even closer. No truer words spoken than when referring to supernatural Kings, as at our core we would always have our own loyalty served first towards our own people.

And after all, first and foremost I was…
The Vampire King.

After this conversation had ended, I had returned back to my Fated, fully intent on gaining all the information out of her that I could, in hopes that she would trust me enough to open her mind to me. Of course, that had been before the villagers had picked up their pitchforks and lit their torches.

Which brought me back to my continued task at hand as I was eager to get back to my little maid once more. And clearly, I was not the only one, as we both commanded our horses to gallop back up the hill towards the castle. However, the moment we made it inside, I couldn't help but snarl,

"Something is wrong." Dominic clearly felt it too as he growled, caring little for who was around as we both made our way up the stairs with unnatural speed. We then came to a sudden stop the moment we encountered the first servant unconscious and slumped on the floor. However, the heartbeat was still steady enough to know that whatever poison had been administered, it was not of the lethal kind.

"It was a diversion!" Dominic snarled as my own heart started to pound within my chest, now fearing the worst. Then with the same speed, we continued on until Dominic was seconds later, ripping his chamber door from its hinges and making me sidestep, so as I missed being hit by the projectile as it smashed into the wall behind me. He was inside another heartbeat later, quickly resembling a growling beast as he roared in anger before he snarled a single name,

"*Sophia.*" I gritted my teeth and restrained myself from showing the same furious emotion before voicing what Dominic could not.

"It seems as if your sister has betrayed you."

"I will take my men to the west, you take the east road and find her, find them all and bring them back to me! Go and do what it is you do best... *hunt them down!*" I curled my gloved hands in to fists making the leather groan as I snarled my reply...

"With pleasure."

CHAPTER 23
HORSE RACE
AMELIA

I don't know what was harder, gripping on for dear life as my aunt Sophia rode the horse like we were at the racetrack, or every time I tried to look back, I thought I would fall straight off. Because I tried to keep sight of the men who were gaining on us. They must have seen us stealing the horses and acted, as I couldn't see Lucius or my father with them. I also doubted that they would have trusted their men to come after us alone.

"What are we going to do?!" I shouted over the sound of the horses' hoofs pounding on the ground with the wind whipping at our faces as it blew my cloak over the horse's back.

"Over there, by the river… Pip, you know what to do!" Sophia shouted, knowing that Pip would hear her despite being a way off in front of us.

"ON IT!" she bellowed back before coming to a halt at the edge of the river, one I could only just about see glittering under the moonlight. Seconds later I was once again awarded with the rare sight of Pip's impressive power as she raised her hands and started to part the water. Then I gaped in awe as she made the sides of the riverbank shudder as if there was a living entity traveling under the ground. It then started to move, rolling over the sides of the riverbank before gathering in the middle to where she had spilt the water apart. It was like a dark carpet, moving along the ground and creating a road of earth. It soon made me realize that she was doing this so we didn't get bogged down in the sludge of the riverbed as we crossed.

"Just call me Moses!" Pip shouted, laughing happily before urging her horse forward and I was thankful that the sides weren't too steep so the horses didn't have a hard a time doing what was asked of them. Then as soon as it was safe to do so, we galloped across and safely made it to the other side. I couldn't help but sigh in relief as Pip allowed the water to come gushing back together, preventing the riders following us from continuing in their pursuit.

"That should slow them down," my mother said seeing now they had started shouting from the other side, no doubt asking themselves how the Hell we had managed to get across when they would not dare chance it.

"It might have slowed them down, but it won't prevent them from riding back to the castle and telling my brother where they saw us last. Which means we have to carry on at speed." I practically heard my mother groan from here, as she felt the same way I did, ass numb and thighs burning.

Yet despite the discomfort, we continued on without complaint as my aunt Sophia was right, I knew we were far from being out of the woods yet. My father would stop at nothing to get my mother back and as for Lucius, no doubt he was already planning his own quest in recapturing me.

This meant that the journey was far from easy, and it only managed to get harder the longer we travelled. I didn't know how much time had passed but my best guess was it must have been hours, despite it still being dark. In fact, if it hadn't been for the clear night sky, then I wouldn't have been able to see a thing without the comforting glow of the moonlight. I was also concerned when I saw my mother's silhouette starting to sag against Pip, this was enough of an indication that us mortals were hitting our limit. Sophia noticed this too, as she didn't even question it the moment Pip slowed down the horse.

"We're going to have to find somewhere to stop, before Toots becomes Tipper Toots," Pip said,

"If I remember right, there is some Roman ruins near here, a little more than crumbling walls but at least it's something," Sophia said, giving me little confidence we were in for a comfortable rest. Which was why I made the comment,

"I think we're gonna need more than that, but let's keep going and pray for an inn before we get there."

We continued on, trying our best to keep off the road but eventually we had no choice, as the Roman ruins were too hard to get to from this point. Thankfully, it looked like an inn was our best bet after all. And even better, the glow of light coming from the windows was like a beacon of hope calling us forward, telling us there was life awake inside. It was a good job too as my mother did not look to be faring well at all.

It was clear that out of the four of us, coming back to the past was taking its biggest toll on my mother. But then again, she had spent nearly thirty years being a supernatural being and now being stripped of that side of her, had clearly affected her. She had undoubtably forgotten what life had been like as a mortal. As for me, well I had only had a little over three months, so as strange as this was to me, it was nowhere near as bad as what it was for my mother.

We urged our horses up to the inn, slowing them down and trotting around the side towards the stables. Sophia had to help me from the horse before rushing over to help Pip take my mother, who looked close to passing out. I too tried to rush over to her, willing my legs to work and the feeling to come back to them.

"Is she okay?" I asked as they each took an arm.

"She'll be fine as soon as we can lay her down somewhere warm and give her something to drink," Sophia said as they both helped her inside the inn, whereas I followed after first giving instructions to the stable hand to house our horses for the night.

Inside was as you would expect from an inn mainly used by travellers needing a bed for the night. This, and a warm hearty meal to refuel weary bones being jarred from a long journey on horseback. The beamed ceilings were low, the walls panelled, and the roaring fire created a comforting feel with worn wooden tables and chairs dotted throughout the room. A few lanterns were lit, as well as wooden blocks with iron spikes holding wax dripped candles in place. They were a cheap but effective candle holder. The scent of ale and burning wood filled my nostrils and I looked to my right to find my mum slumped in a chair with Pip holding a cup of water to her lips.

As for my aunt, she was speaking with a man standing behind a bar, no doubt trying to secure us a room for the night. Which meant it was only moments later that we were making our way up a narrow staircase, helping my mum to stay on her feet long enough to get us to our room.

As soon as we made it inside Sophia told us both to get our rest, as we would need it. And well, the promise of doing another journey like that and I didn't doubt her. It already seemed like we had been travelling most of the night. The slight glow of early morning peeked on the horizon, telling me it would soon be daybreak.

The room was as basic as they came with only one thing important enough to really take in, and that was the single bed with its lumpy looking straw mattress. But the sheets looked clean enough and that was all I really cared about.

I got into bed with my mum after removing my own boots as well as my mother's, someone who was already fast asleep by the time I slipped in next to her fully clothed. It was amazing what exhaustion did to a person, as this horrible lumpy bed felt like heaven, and I was just happy to be in a horizontal position.

I felt my aunt Sophia kneel down next to the bed, so she could whisper to me,

"I will wake you shortly, as I'm afraid we can't stay here long." I understood the concern in my aunt Sophia's eyes so I simply nodded, agreeing with her. She then patted my shoulder before smoothing the hair from my forehead as she stood.

As for me…

I was asleep before she even closed the door.

∾

In what seemed like no time at all, Sophia was back with her hand once more to my shoulder and this time, trying to gently shake me awake.

"How long have we been asleep?" I asked, feeling groggy and only barely responsive.

"A few hours, I'm afraid we cannot chance any more than that."

"Okay, I'll wake up Mum and we'll be downstairs in a minute," I replied making her grant me a small smile.

"I will have food waiting for us on the table," she said before leaving me to try and wake my mum, which was not an easy task.

"Come on, Mum, I know you're tired, but we have to get ready and go, Sophia mentioned about food being ready for us." Thankfully that did it, as my mum sat up and said,

"Food?" This made me chuckle before answering,

"I wouldn't get too excited, not if the quality of the bed is anything to go by." She laughed at that.

"Right about now I would eat some of the chicken feet your dad keeps ready as a treat for Ava." I snorted a laugh as I remembered this well growing up. As he would often let me throw them for her off the side of the balcony. Ava was my father's pet bird, who was a cross between a Raven and an American bald eagle in size. She also hated children, despite her liking me well enough.

"Eww," I said pulling a face, making her scoff a laugh.

"Are you sure you're okay?" I asked after we'd both used the chamber pot and were now putting on our boots.

"I'm okay… I guess I'm just not used to being mortal again, you know," she said, confirming what I already believed to be the reason for her fatigue after such a ride.

"I understand, it can't be easy." She took my hand and said,

"None of this can be easy for you, either." I knew what she meant by this… *Lucius.*

"Well lucky for me, I'm made of good, strong stuff and it's like Dad always said, a Draven never stays down." At this she winked at me and said,

"Damn right, we don't… now let's go conquer the past, kid."

We walked from the room hand in hand and made our way down the crooked staircase and into the panelled room.

There we found Pip and Sophia at a table closest to the fireplace, no doubt for our benefits as we both felt the bite of cold this morning. Four bowls of steaming stew and a loaf of bread sat in the middle waiting for us, along with a jug of water. I looked around to see a few other tables occupied, making me wonder if these too were travellers getting some rest ready for the journey ahead.

"We have gained some distance, and hopefully in the opposite direction they believed we would go. But right now, I'm afraid it's all left to chance," my aunt Sophia said, reminding us that we were far from being in the clear yet.

"I think the biggest question of all is going to be how we're going to get to Fort Julien," I said, mentioning a place they all knew was in Egypt thanks to gaining a brief history lesson from me back in the library before we left our own time.

"I thought you said it would be in Sais?" my mum asked, pausing her spoon and holding it suspended.

"It was but that was when I thought the Gate would take us back to 1202, a date before it was moved. But by what Lucius and Dad were talking about when mentioning the Quasi-War, I would gather we are in the year 1799, which means come this July, one Colonel d'Hautpoul is going to give the order to strengthen the defences at Fort Julien and they will find the Rosetta Stone before we do," I told them, making Sophia agree,

"She's right, given that I was in Italy at this point, the date sounds right. So, we're going to have to find our way to the nearest port where we can acquire safe passage on a ship."

"Yeah, that's not going to be easy, not with the Lord of Muncaster putting the bounty on our heads," Pip said as if forgetting herself, making Sophia hush her before looking around to see if anyone was listening. Her response to this was the usual one we had all heard a million times before,

"My bad."

Of course, hearing this also made my mum release a heavy sigh, as she knew just as well as I did that by us running, Lucius and my father were going to stop at nothing in trying to get us back.

"Let's eat up and get going… *I don't trust the locals,"* Sophia said in a quiet voice. Meaning we all decided that this was an excellent idea and finished our bowls in record time. I don't think each mouthful hit the sides on the way down as at the end, both me and my mother picked up our bowls and drank back the broth. Sophia and Pip grinned at each other, clearly thinking 'like mother like daughter'.

Feeling rejuvenated and more positive about the day to come, we were soon back on the horses. And this time, we had no choice but to use the roads. With all the hills and mountains surrounding us, we knew going any other way would no doubt lead to nowhere or worse… *us getting lost.*

But as the day dragged on, we knew we could only keep up our pace for so long, and come midday, we had no choice but to stop. This was to give both the horses and ourselves a much-deserved break. Thankfully, Pip had raided the larder at the castle, so the horses had bags of food tied to their saddles and leather flasks of water to help keep us hydrated. But this latest stop meant refilling the water, which my mother and I opted to do while Pip and Sophia kept a look out.

"Okay but stay close," Sophia warned as soon as we pointed out the stream we could hear was close by. We nodded before making our way through the trees and down the bank, quickly using the water to quench our thirst and also splash the dirt from our faces. Thankfully, unlike the days before, the weather had made a turn for the better and we were not doing this journey with a downpour of rain soaking us to the bone.

"And you wondered why we never took you camping as a kid."

"Because we suck at it?" I asked, giggling when making my mother smirk after she made this comment.

"Although what I wouldn't give for a camping stove and a kettle right about now." I laughed and with a shake of my head replied,

"You and your tea addiction."

"So, what…? You're telling me you wouldn't sell your soul right now for a donut with a sprinkling of maple syrup bacon on top?" I groaned at this and while pointing the end of the flask at her, said,

"Now that's just mean." She snorted back a laugh, which was always funny to hear coming from my mother.

"Come on, we'd better get back before Sophia wonders where we are," my mother suggested as I wiped my wet hands on my cloak.

"Yeah, she's surprisingly good at all of this," I said, to which my mother made the point,

"I suppose it's more natural for them, like they said, they were riding horses for a lot longer than they were riding in cars. Our modern world compared to the ones that they have lived in means that technology has only been a blip in the ocean for them, so coming back here is just like slipping back into your memories I guess."

"Makes sense, and maybe when we're finally on the ship on the way out of here, she'll be able to relax a bit more."

"We all will. But then, she definitely seems to know what Lucius and your father are capable of, a lot more than we do," she replied making me suppress a shiver at the idea of them currently hunting us.

"That's what worries me, it's strange to see Sophia so anxious."

"And for good reason no doubt," she said before we both turned around and gasped, making me utter,

"I think we just found another reason to add to it."

For naturally…

We had just been found.

CHAPTER 24
DISAPPEARING ACT

"*Looks like trouble just found us,*" my mum muttered next to me.

"Yeah," I said in response to the three men we could see drawing their weapons and coming closer towards us. I soon recognized the faces of the men that had been occupying one of the tables back at the inn and realised what must have happened. Something they confirmed when the guy in the middle said,

"Now we don't want to hurt you, we just want you for the bounty." In reaction to this, I took a step in front of my mother, curling my arm back to make sure she was safely tucked behind me.

"*We need to call out, Fae,*" my mum whispered, making me shake my head.

"If we do that, then we could chance people hearing us… say, certain somebodies with enhanced hearing." She nodded to this, understanding that we couldn't risk it.

"Besides, I've got this," I assured her. I may just be a mortal and without my powers, but that didn't mean I was without all my skills when it came to fighting.

"I'm not sure about this, Fae," my mother warned, but she needed to trust me. I could handle these guys.

"Now come quietly, girly, and you and your friend there won't get hurt."

"Nice to know I still don't look old enough to be your mother," my mum mused making me groan,

"Really? That's what you wanna focus on right now?"

"Wait 'til you are my age, trust me, it will count," my mother replied, making me roll my eyes before deciding the best way to deal with this was using the element of surprise, starting with the fearful damsel act.

"Trust me, okay?" I whispered to my mother before turning back toward the closest guy, one who looked to have a yellow overbite and terrible oral hygiene. As for the other two, they weren't much better in the looks department. Not when one had wild hair like he had made a toupee from a rat's ass, and the other had a monobrow the likes of Frida Kahlo would be envious of. Man, but what did he shelf on that thing, spare pencils?

"No please, please don't do this, I promise you, we have no money," I said, starting to play the victim and luring Mr Gurn-a-lot into a false sense of security, enough for him to lower his dagger slightly. Then as soon as he was within reach, I grabbed his wrist, held it out and hammered my other arm up, forcing the bone a way it really didn't want to go. The dagger also dropped from his hand at the same the guy started howling in pain, now clutching his broken arm to his chest. To which I then kneed him in the nuts making him drop to his knees, giving him a whole new thing to howl about.

"Now you guys have a choice, you can either count yourselves lucky that I am going to give you one chance to run, or you can be left broken in pieces just like your friend here," I said, dropping the frightened act and going straight for bad ass.

"Nice," my mum muttered making me smirk. The two men looked first at each other and then back to their friend who was still very much in pain. And from the looks of things, undecided on which part of his anatomy he wanted to cradle first... *like this would help.*

"So, what's it going to be, fellas?" I asked with my hand against my hip and admittedly being cocky.

"That is our brother, Bitch!" Mr monobrow said, and he was lucky that he wasn't keeping a pencil rested above the slugs over his eyes, as the last time I fought with one in my hand, the guy didn't fair too well.

"Then I feel sorry for your mother, as she will be looking after three assholes instead of one if you two don't make the right choice and leave."

"Our mother is not an asshole!" The rat-head said, raising a small belt axe up at me and one that looked so rusted, I was surprised the metal hadn't fallen from its handle.

"That's not what I... *oh well,"* I said the second they charged at me, making me swipe my leg out and force bigbrows to fall to the ground, before kicking him to the face, knocking him out. This was so I could block the guy with the axe coming straight at me because, well, I didn't fancy dying of tetanus anytime soon.

I dodged the swipe, jumping back, before ducking when he swung his arm out wide, clearly having no idea how to fight with a weapon in his hand. I spun on my foot, putting my position behind him and giving me the chance to kick out his back leg, forcing my foot into the back of his knee. He dropped down and staggered forward, losing his axe as it flew from his hand the moment he decided to use them both to save his face from hitting the ground.

I rolled towards it, grabbed it, and leapt back to my feet just as he was back on his, now charging at me.

"Fae, look out!" my mum shouted in fear that I wouldn't make it out of reach in time, and she was right. The guy with roadkill for hair took me off the ground when I had focused on my mum. However, I grabbed his leather doublet and forced him into a roll so I was on top. Then I quickly maneuvered myself so my arm was across his throat as I bore my weight down onto his neck, cutting off the air flow. His arms flayed around trying to hit out at me, so I moved my leg up to pin it down, now lying my body lengthways across him.

"Just… go… to… fucking… sleep!" I groaned but then froze the second I heard a very real threat being made,

"Stop or I'll slit her throat!"

The sound chilled my bones as I turned to face the mistake I made. Mr slug brows, who I thought I had put down, was now back up on his feet.

Oh, and he now held a knife to my mother's throat.

I realised then that I had been wrong not calling out for Pip and Sophia like my mother suggested. The sound of the small rapids in the stream no doubt drowning out any sounds of the fight and making me realise I should have been screaming this whole time. But in my cockiness at thinking I was able to handle these three, I had now put my mother in danger. I gritted my teeth and looked back over my shoulder. My mother soon got the hint as she suddenly started screaming,

"HELP US!"

"Shut up, bitch!" he threatened, grabbing her hair and holding the blade so close to her throat that I could see blood drip from a single point as she hissed in pain. I quickly held up my hands in surrender.

"Don't hurt her!" I shouted in panic, making him sneer,

"You should have come with us when you had the chance! Now move away from my brother!"

I started nodding before moving further away from his brother who was now coughing and gasp for breath on the floor. Then the second I heard Pip and Sophia finally make their way down to us, I breathed in my first sigh of relief knowing that Sophia was sure to access his mind and make him pass out.

"Nobody move, or she dies!" he shouted the second he saw them approach. However, before any of us could do anything, something unbelievable happened.

Something none of us could explain.

Meaning I was forced to watch in utter horror as my mother suddenly…

Disappeared.

CHAPTER 25
THE HUNT CONTINUES

"NOOOO!" I screamed as I watched in horror as my mum simply disappeared. The man who had seconds ago been holding her hostage was just as shocked as I was. However, he was not prepared for the rage I unleashed his way, as I threw my body into him, taking him off his feet. I then started punching his face over and over again, until the point where Sophia and Pip both had to drag me off him. I knew he hadn't been the cause for my mother disappearing suddenly, but the memory of the knife he had held to her throat was too fresh in my mind to let go of.

"Easy, Amelia… calm down," Sophia said as she fought against me when I was trying to get back to him.

"Calm down! How the fuck can I calm down?! My mother has just disappeared!" I shouted, breathing heavily as hot, angry tears streamed down my face.

"Yes, but that cretin there didn't do it," Sophia pointed out, making me argue back,

"He held a knife to her throat! He could have killed her, damn it! Gods but by her just being here… I… I could have taken them... I should have been alone... *I did this*... I never should have let her come... *I never should have let any of you come... I should have done this on my own!*" I sobbed into my aunts' arms as they both held me tight, comforting me as I cried. I felt so responsible for this. Everything that I felt now was burying me alive, as if I was being crushed under so much guilt!

This had been all my fault.

I don't know how long this self-loathing continued for but the moment I finally calmed, I realised I was on my knees still being cradled in my aunt Pip's arms. I then watched as Sophia left us and walked up to where my mother had once been. This was what pulled me back to my senses enough to ask,

"Any... anything?"

"I don't sense any magic used... it was like... almost as if..." Sophia trailed off, making me sniff back a fresh set of tears and ask,

"As if what?"

"Like this time didn't want her anymore," she answered making me gasp. Pip started to rub little circles on my back trying to keep me calm.

"Do you think she was sent back home, because the Fates knew she was in danger?" I asked, astonished and hoping... no... no, more like *praying to any God out there that would listen,* that this had been the cause.

"I don't know but wherever she is, she's Fated to be there. And we have to believe that she's safe wherever that is," Sophia said, making me rub my face on my sleeve to dry my eyes and nose before asking the painful question,

"But how can we..."

Sophia quickly cut me off, "We have to carry on, we have to keep moving, there is nothing we can do, and you still

QUEST OF STONE

have a reason to be here, Amelia. But our window of opportunity to escape is closing quickly the longer we remain."

I knew what my aunt Sophia said made sense, it was just hard to think beyond the ache in my heart knowing that my mother was gone from this time. I had no idea what had happened, but she was right, I had to live on in hope that wherever my mother was now, she was there for a reason and most of all...

She was safe.

"Do you think this is the prophecy the Oracle of Light spoke of, that it did in fact include my mother?" I asked after Sophia had checked to see that I hadn't killed any of the men, despite their injuries. Of course, the one that I had nearly choked to death, she made pass out, along with the one who had become my first victim with the broken arm.

As for the one I had beaten to a pulp, as his face was barely recognisable anymore, this guy had been out for the count long before I stopped hitting him. Not that I felt bad, not considering these men had been quite happy to take us and use us for ransom. It was also clear they were most likely highwaymen, and Sophia was right, they deserved no pity. And well, the Gods only knew how many people they had killed in their time in order to take what was not theirs.

"Come on, little bean, time to wash the blood off your hands," Pip said helping me to my feet and making me look down at my fingers to see that she was right, they were soaked in blood. I walked over to the stream, and washed my hands, feeling the sting for the first time as I saw that my knuckles were all split from my rage attack.

After this I grabbed my cloak, putting it back over my shoulders from where I had taken it off to wash my face and have a drink without getting it wet. Then I finally allowed my aunts to lead me back to the horses before we all once again were charging across the countryside.

I couldn't help one last look back, hoping like never before, that I would see my mother reappear just in time. However, when this didn't happen, I was forced to give up hope and tried not to let my guilt eat me alive. But then this wasn't exactly easy, not when the journey only made the worries in my mind fester. As every time I looked to Pip's horse and found the lack of another rider, it was like a dagger to my chest. I looked out over the rolling hills of the Lake District, and asked the land out loud,

"Where are you, Mum?" my aunt Sophia heard this and squeezed my hand that was around her waist. But other than that, she didn't say anything as she was no doubt thinking the same thing. Because Sophia loved my mother like a sister and always had done. Meaning that both her and Pip would be feeling the same pain I was. Although, granted, theirs wouldn't have come with the same bucketload of guilt that mine did. There was only one person to blame here and that was me.

But it was like Sophia said, I had to believe that wherever she was, she was safe and that it was Fated to be this way.

The next time we stopped, the sun was starting to set and, thankfully, we found an abandoned house with only its walls still standing strong. There was most definitely no danger of its owner coming back, that was for sure, the structure didn't even have a roof. No, if anything, it looked more like it had been claimed by the forest long ago. Yet despite this, it at the very least provided some shelter against the wind and was enough to be able to get a fire going. My aunts obviously didn't feel the cold like I did, so clearly this was only for my benefit. Just like when Sophia took off her cloak and lay it down on the mossy ground for me.

"Here, try and get some rest. We still have a long way to go."

I did as she suggested and laid down, thinking again of my mother and wiping away the tears that slipped free. I didn't want to give way to anymore tears than this because I knew if I started again, I wouldn't stop.

Memories quickly merged into nightmares of when my mother had been standing there one minute and then gone the next, thoughts that kept me tossing and turning. Until these nightmares were soon consumed by the past, and sights of my mother writhing around in agony gripped me. Visions of her pain being used against me as a way to manipulate me into doing Matthias's bidding back when faced with an impossible choice in Hell. I couldn't help the guilt I felt eating away at me knowing that whatever her Fate now, I had been the cause of it by bringing her with me.

Just like I had been the cause back then.

I wanted to be optimistic, but this sense was overshadowed by my fears that she was hurt or worse, meaning that a deep sleep evaded me. This also meant that the second I heard the snapping of twigs, my eyes quickly flashed open.

My gaze shot to the dark just in time to see a shadowed figure with a long cloak lowering a still body to the ground. I sucked in a quick breath as I realised it was my aunt Sophia who was now in danger.

I shot up to sitting quickly before scrambling back when I saw that hooded figure snap his gaze my way. He'd had his hand on her forehead, as if this was the connection he had needed to make her pass out.

Crimson eyes started to glow from the shadow of his hood, like pools of Hell's fire responding to their prey. However, movement flashed to the side of him but before Pip could land on him from above, like she intended, he caught her in his grasp. My heart caught in my throat as he held her by the neck, making her struggle and squirm against his hand.

"NO!" I screamed before pleading with him,

"Don't hurt her!" he turned his curious gaze to me before back to the struggling Imp at the end of his arm. Her face was covered by her hood, one that she had used to mask her appearance. Then without a word, he placed a hand over her face, and soon her body went limp in his hold. I screamed again, praying he had only made her unconscious and fearing anything but this. Although, he didn't just drop her like I had expected him to, but simply placed her gently on the floor like he had done with Sophia. Surely if she had been dead, he would have simply tossed her aside like garbage?

This sparked a hope inside of me because I could not stand to lose any more of my family today, as my heart would not survive it! However, the moment he stood, I realised what I had to do. So, I too stood quickly and the moment he started to reach for me, something unbelievable happened. A blinding light came from within me, shocking him enough to stop him in his tracks as he threw up an arm to shield his eyes. I didn't know what just happened, but I wasn't wasting the opportunity, now using it as my chance to escape.

I heard the vicious growl behind me, before the sound of Lucius's furious orders came quick and fast.

"What do you wish us to do with the women?"

"Take Sophia back to her brother, for she will have to answer for her crimes. Now make haste, for the King needs to be informed that his Chosen One is gone and the hunt continues!" Lucius replied sternly.

"And this one?"

They must have been talking about Pip, as I could only

barely hear their conversation echoing through the trees as I ran.

"Leave that one to me, for she will sleep until I allow her to wake. I will need someone to interrogate and grant me the answers that I seek. Now go…" he growled, and I couldn't help but shiver the moment he finished this order with a promise of his own…

"…For I have a Chosen One to hunt."

CHAPTER 26
RUNAWAY HEART
LUCIUS

The hunt.

Without a doubt, the most important one of my long life so far.

But for the first time in that life, the hunt no longer gave me a thrill, one that I usually lived for. Because this time the prize was something far greater and not just someone I intended to torture and eventually kill when I found my prey.

I was furious that Lia had run from me. But not only that, as it was clear now that my festering concerns that she was not who she said she was, were warranted, *for she had lied.* She had lied and like a fool, I had allowed her to get away with it. Meaning that for the first time since my rebirth, someone had gotten the better of me.

Hence the problem I was now faced with and the result of what happened when I was not granted access to a mind I wanted to possess. It was very rare indeed that anyone got away with being deceitful around me. For my power to manipulate the mind was superior and above all others that could class themselves as beyond par. As even where others of our kind were skilled enough to prevent their thoughts from being read, there was no one that held such power around me, for I could force anyone to give up their mind.

It was why I knew that I was so useful to the King of Kings. Why I was so good when it came to hunting fugitives in all my years spent as the King's Assassin. Because even when faced with the most powerful beings, it was still a guaranteed result when extracting information needed from them. But to know that I was being bested by a little mortal maid, well let's just say that the irony was not lost on me.

There was very little to quell my building anger, forcing my men to ride faster and harder than they ever had before. In fact, the only reason I hadn't erupted into my Demon form and was still managing to keep it under tight rein, was knowing that I would find her. It was also all of the punishing thoughts of what I would do to her for disobeying me that eased my Demon's rage.

How I would tie her to my bed and make her beg me for hours to let her find her sexual release. How I would make her beg for my cock, enslaving her sexually until she realised just who her Master was. In all honesty, all that stopped me from snapping the leather of my reins was the thought of building her a pretty gold cage, and sitting her naked inside it upon a crimson bed of cushions. A sight that I would enjoy immensely, for her beauty often rendered me near speechless. And this made even more so when first seeing her as she entered the dining room this last night gone.

Yet despite how exquisite she looked dressed up in her gown and dripping in finery, I found her just as beautiful dressed as a simple maid. But I also found that the effect she had over me was disarming and dangerous, for I found it near impossible to say no to her. I wanted to give her the world and more. And now, knowing how she had abused my trust and relied on sentiments for her to make her escape, angered me more than anything else.

Of course, this vexation was not helped by the knowledge that a powerful supernatural was aiding their escape and I knew by its very essence that it wasn't just Sophia. No this was the power of an elemental being, now as for who they were, remained a mystery, for they were masking their scent, making them harder to track. I found myself near murderous when I realised that we had spent half a day travelling in the wrong direction, which I gathered was their plan all along.

But then I could not find myself surprised considering what the King's men had told us about them cutting across the river, something that should have been impossible for anyone but an Elemental. I had to confess that this complicated things, but it did not dissuade me from the hunt. Because there were only a few directions for them to travel in and now I knew for certain which road I would find them on.

Which meant that as soon as we came to the first inn, I ordered my men to stop. This offered two things, for it let my men tend to the horses, giving them a short reprieve, and it gave me chance to discover if they had stopped here like I believed they would.

I didn't have the patience to ask questions but merely plucked them from the inn keeper's mind the moment I walked through the door. I had to say, the utter relief I felt when seeing my little maid in his memories rocked me to my core, for I had never felt this type of emotion before.

It also granted me confidence that I would be finding my prey soon enough. But the memory of them helping a blonde woman, who was undoubtedly the King's Chosen One, walk towards the staircase, told me that fatigue was most definitely setting in. This meant that the journey ahead of them would be far harder with two mortals slowing the Supernaturals' down. Which naturally gave me the advantage and eased my mind somewhat with knowing that their time was limited, for I would soon find them.

After I had released the innkeeper from my control, I next found myself in one of the rooms, now staring down at the small bed where both women had clearly slept. I then found myself reaching for the covers, snarling when raising the material to my nose and inhaling the scent of my woman.

So many emotions hit me all at once, and one of them was relief that I did not scent any blood in the fabric. As for her own emotions and the ones I could detect from her scent were feelings of being anxious, exhausted and troubled. She had slept in her clothes, meaning she was drained enough not to care about undressing.

I took the sheet with me, wanting to leave no trace of my woman behind. Even her scent was mine and I would have no one else claim it for even a moment. So, I left the room and made my way back to the stables, tossing a coin to the innkeeper for care of the horses, even if had only been for no more than twenty minutes. It was at the very least enough to supply them with water and some substance.

"Their horses were here, My Lord, they left a few hours after sunrise," one of my men informed me, making me grip the sheet tighter in my fist before stuffing it into the saddle bag.

"Good, then it means we are not far behind," I said mounting Sleipnir and commanding him forward at greater speed. My time seemed consumed by my constant thoughts of her, with my concern overriding almost all else. Yes, I was angry at her, furious even, but this was overshadowed by the desperate need clawing at me to have her safely back in my arms.

I started to slow as soon as I heard the lapping water of a

stream nearby, knowing this was a likely spot they could have stopped. Because they had two mortals with them that would cause them to take more care than Supernatural life. I dismounted, handing the reins to one of my men before walking a few more steps, when suddenly, I stopped in my tracks.

That was when I scented blood.

My moment of blind panic evaporated the instant I realised it did not belong to my mortal. A sudden heavy weight in my chest lifted the second I realised this, shocking me enough to stop me in my tracks.

Then I heard groans of pain, which quickly had me moving once more, upon of which where I would make an astonishing discovery. But first, I found one man that had clearly dragged himself towards a rotting stump, clutching what looked like a broken arm to his chest.

Good, someone to rape of his memories.

The man shot fearful eyes to me but when seeing a knight in his armour and one as furious as I looked, then it wasn't a surprising reaction. And as for the looks of him, it also seemed as if this bad day of his was about to get worse.

But for now, I left him to his mumbling prayers to God and spared but a glance to one that remained bloody and unconscious on the floor. Then I continued on before finding another, and one who seemed to have fared slightly better than the other two. Although he was not completely unscathed, as there were red marks around his neck and a painful looking bruise at the side of his face. But like the other man resting at the stump, he was conscious, if not a little dazed in his countenance.

I stopped beside him and soon snarled when I discovered the addictive scent I picked up on him.

My woman.

She had been here.

But not just that, for her scent was getting stronger as I lowered my frame next to the now whimpering man, one seemingly desperate to get away from me. This was made even more so when I growled like a wild beast the moment I knew he had touched her. I grabbed him by his leather doublet and lifted him up into the air, making him cry out in agony from his wounds as it seemed his leg had also been twisted, no doubt in the fight. I brought him closer to my face and snarled inches from his quivering features.

"You dare touch my woman?" I thundered, allowing my Demonic side to peek through.

"No, no... it was her, she attacked me and my brothers." I scoffed at this, and the unbelievable story that flowed from his lying mouth. For I knew my Chosen had skills enough to defend herself, but this... no, this was nothing short of a brutal attack.

I looked around at the other two, one that was broken and the other beaten bloody, that was still unconscious. He also looked as if he had been beaten so badly, that his face would be barely recognisable to those who knew him. In fact, I would have thought him dead had I not heard his heart beating for myself.

"You expect me to believe a woman barely reaching the height of my chest and of such slight of frame, did this to the three of you!?" I roared, making him squirm once more in my hold.

"It is true, your lordship! We heard them speaking of a bounty on their heads back at the inn... we... we wanted the ransom... we weren't going to hurt them... But then the dark haired one, she... she attacked us all and the blonde... she... she..." He sputtered in fear.

"She what?! Speak!"

"She disappeared… vanished like air itself took her… like God had claimed her!" If he had been able to, he would have crossed himself, making me growl further.

"I will see this for myself!" I snapped, no longer being able to listen to his lies and opting to enter his mind as I rid him of his memories. However, the moment I saw the replay of what had happened, I dropped him in my shock, making him groan before curling up on himself in a foetal position. As if this would aid him in his Fate or that his tears would have the power to cleanse his soul of all his wrong doings.

I cared little for these men and was tempted to kill them myself. Yet I confess that knowing that they had received such a beating from a small woman was enough as of punishment. But I could barely believe what I had seen. My Chosen One, my sweet little maid, who had first been so fearful of me that she flinched whenever I touched her. Yet she had beaten these men bloody and one near to death. She had been as formidable as any of my warriors and I was utterly astounded for I had never been so shocked in all of my life.

My little maid was not what she seemed at all.

I also knew I should have been focusing on the fact that the King's Chosen One had suddenly disappeared, seemingly vanished like some Supernatural force had taken her from this realm. But I confess, I found this hard to do when visions of my own Chosen One fighting, flickered like pages from a book in my mind.

But whether she could fight or not, the fact remained that if the King ever got hold of her, her skills would be rendered useless, for he would not stop until he found his Electus. Which meant I suddenly feared for my little maid's life, despite it being clear from the memories I had seen, that Lia had been devastated by the blonde girl's disappearance. It also confirmed what I already suspected after seeing their first encounter with one another for the first time...

They had known each other.

But it wasn't only that, as it was clear now that their friendship went far beyond simple acquaintances. They cared for one another, that much was obvious. Now in what capacity, I did not know, as the man's memories were warped by his own sense of understanding. But there had been no mistaking her pain, not when witnessing the way my little maid had reacted after the King's Electus was taken from this land. A troubling mystery in itself, for I had no idea where she could be or what could have taken her. In fact, had there been even the barest hint of light seen behind her, I would have believed a portal had been made right before she was pulled into it.

But there had been nothing.

A fact I doubted would matter to the King, as he would demand someone's head for this. Meaning I knew my own Electus was now in even greater danger. Because if the King managed to get hold of her before I did, then there was the potential that he would try and torture the truth from her. Hurting her until he received the answers, ones he needed to aid him in getting his woman back. And when he couldn't, then he would hold Lia responsible for the disappearance of his Chosen One and no one would survive his wrath...

Lia especially.

I left the bloody scene with haste, knowing now there was even greater a risk to my Chosen One than there was before. I couldn't afford to let anyone get their hands on her before I did. And the proof of my concern was one I walked away from now. As like those men that she had attacked, they had obviously heard of the bounty the King has issued on them being found and returned. And next time, she may find herself faced with men more skilled than just a handful of clumsy thieves.

I remounted my horse with purpose, knowing that by nightfall I would have her in my grasp once more. I could afford nothing less. Which was why I ordered for my men to make haste as the hunt was nearing its end. I could just feel it...

We were getting close.

In fact, it was just as night was falling that I was then signalling for my men to slow their horses as we came across their tracks, which would soon lead me to an abandoned building.

I quickly dismounted with my men following my lead so as we could sneak up on them by foot. I could mask the sounds of my men well enough and therefore Sophia would not notice my presence until it was too late. As for who else may be with them, then that was still one question left unanswered...

But not for long.

However, this did mean that Sophia would be the first I would need to take out, as considering who her kin was, it meant that her mind was incredibly strong. Therefore I would need to make a physical connection to render her unconscious. It was why after I considered my men to be close enough, I made sure that they held back, leaving me free to creep silently through the trees, intent on dealing with her alone. I soon came across the crumbling ruin that they had decided to use as a shelter for the night.

Thankfully the wind was high, and therefore dissuading any wildlife from giving away the fact I was stalking them. I continued on, creeping along the stone wall and listening out for the heartbeats of three. I easily managed to pinpoint my Chosen One, already more acquainted with her heartbeat than

I was with even that of my own. Her blood sang to me, just as the scent of it made me take pause for a single moment so as I could relish in the fact that she was here.

That I had found her.

Now I just had to get rid of the other two.

Sophia was first for me to deal with and before she could react to my presence, I had my hand on her forehead making her sleep. This meant taking away her ability to function beyond a dreamful mind, one that would stay this way until her brother could snap her out of it. He would need somebody to blame for all of this, and I would give it to him, before he thought to come looking for my Chosen One.

For I would have to make my men believe that Lia had been taken against her own free will or the King would stop at nothing before hunting her down himself. For he would demand his answers from someone and if his sister did not give them up, then he would come for the next best soul…

My Fated soul.

Of course, I would fight to the death before I let him take her. Yet despite this, it was an outcome I hoped to avoid at all costs, especially considering I wanted to be alive when I made Lia mine for all eternity.

I closed my eyes for a second after laying Sophia gently down on the ground. This was as the second heartbeat I was still yet to discover who it belonged to, was trying in vain to sneak up on me from above. I allowed this foolish being to believe for a moment that this would work. Although to what end, I didn't know, for I was curious what their plan was to be, as it was not as if I could be defeated. I could feel the elemental being, a female if correct, and her thundering heartbeat before she made her move.

And then I made my own.

However, what I did not expect was the overwhelming

feeling of familiarity hitting me in the chest, and suddenly the one squirming at the end of my arm controlled by my hand was a scent I knew.

And one I knew well.

As for my Chosen, it was clear she feared for her friend, as she quickly shouted for me to spare her. Something I would have done no matter what considering the nature of our relationship. Which was why, just as I did with Sophia, I covered her face with my hand. Then I calmed her mind and gently lay her down, knowing that I would not allow my men to take her.

Not when she was one of my most trusted friends.

Something that confused me more than anything else, as I could not scent Adam nearby, and they were never seen apart. In fact, currently they were on a mission by my orders, and should have been overseas, for they had been gone for months now. He was also my second in command, so it made no sense as to why she would betray me like this… *unless she was protecting what she knew was mine?*

I almost growled in frustration, but at that moment didn't want to scare my little maid any more than she already looked to be. After all, I would get to the bottom of this but first, I had my Fated One to reclaim and teach a lesson as to why she should never run from me ever again.

Although, the moment I took my first steps towards her, something happened. Something I had been hoping to experience and had questioned why I hadn't yet. Well, it was happening now, and at the most inconvenient moment at that. A blinding white light, making her look like a blazing Angel fallen from the Heavens, momentarily blinded me, forcing me to shield my eyes against the intensity of its blaze.

It was the sign from the Fates for what my heart already

knew to be true. A confirmation I no longer needed to discover by claiming her body or her blood.

It was the truth of our souls.

I had found my Electus.

And once again…

She was running.

Amelia

CHAPTER 27
FOOTPRINTS IN THE SAND

He had found me.

But of course, I knew he was chasing me, as he hadn't come all this way to lose me now. Half of me wondered why I even bothered still running. I guess it was my flight or fight response kicking in, because I knew I was out of all other options. But I wasn't ready to just give up, despite knowing I was now facing this alone. At least I could be assured that Pip and Sophia were okay, as now the more I thought about it, the more it looked like he had simply made them fall asleep.

I just hoped that they would be okay. I felt guilty for just leaving them. Although what I could have done, I didn't know. No, the only chance I had left of getting us all out of this mess was to escape and somehow make it to Egypt alone. Then I could call on the Rosetta stone, open some magically locked portal into a forgotten Realm, free myself some Wraiths and hey presto job done, vow complete, prophecy fulfilled.

Piece of impossible cake right there.

So, with this in mind, I ran as fast as I could. The

branches whipped back against me, scratching my clothes as I travelled past, using what little light there was left in the sky to guide me.

However, the moment I knew he was gaining on me, I decided my best chance now was to hide. So, before he came into view, I stopped behind the biggest tree I could find, hoping I could at least take him by surprise. If I could just knock him down, maybe it would give me enough time to run again.

Yeah, wishful thinking that, Fae.

Because I knew deep down that it was all pointless, he would catch me regardless. But I guess my pride wouldn't allow me to go down without a fight. I wanted him to know how serious I was about getting away from him. I wanted him to know that I wasn't the weak little mortal he believed me to be. I wanted him to know who he was dealing with.

"I can feel you close by, little maid." His voice echoed through the trees making me flinch and grip on to the bark until my fingers ached, the cuts on my knuckles stinging.

"I can feel your heart beating, and now you know why, for you can no longer feign ignorance of my world!" he shouted sounding furious.

"Did you really think you could escape me? Did you really think I would not hunt you down? Did I not warn you what would happen if you ran from me?" The sound of his anger was getting closer and closer, making me close my eyes as the weight of it bore down on me.

"Give up your pointless hiding place and make this easier on yourself, for I promise you, you have not a chance at keeping yourself from me… not when I have the pounding of your heart to follow like a Siren's call."

I swallowed hard as I knew every word he said was true. But he was underestimating me if he thought I was simply going to step from behind this tree, hold up my hands and shout, 'you win'.

I could hear him getting closer still and I swear I actually heard him chuckle. As if he could hear my heart pounding faster and faster with every step he took that bridged the gap between us. The cocky bastard knew how much he affected me.

"Tell me what is it you fear, for I promise you that will make this easier on yourself, for your punishment will be less severe if you willingly give yourself to me."

I almost laughed at this, because he certainly did not know me in this time, if he thought that was going to convince me to give up so easily.

"Come out, little Lia, for heed my warning, girl, *my patience is at an end,*" he warned and the second his foot came in line with the tree I made my move, shouting as I took him from behind,

"So is mine!" Then I launched myself at him and grabbed his leg with both hands, keeping my fingers interlocked behind his knee. Then I positioned my leg in between his own and hooked it around the back, before pushing into him with my shoulder so he had no choice but to fall to the floor. A move that he himself had taught me when taking down a bigger opponent and, well... *he certainly classified.*

I could tell the attack surprised him, as he slowly stood up, unbuckling his cloak from his shoulders and then releasing his armour so he could move more freely. It was as if he was readying himself for the fight. I had to admit, that seeing this sent an excited thrill down my spine, just as it always did when we trained together.

"Alright, little maid, let's see what you've got," he said as he unbuckled his belt that sheathed his sword, motioning for me to come forward once his gear was on the ground.

"You're going to regret that," I said in an overly cocky tone, before taking my stance. He lunged first, just like I knew he would, making me spin out of the way, before kicking him in his back and propelling him a few steps forward. Anyone else and it would have knocked them to the ground. But then again, Lucius was far from being just anybody.

He didn't say anything to this, but simply chuckled as he rolled his shoulder as he walked forward before facing me once more. After this, he became more cautious. Now dodging from side to side and trying to take me off guard by making me question which direction he would come at me from. However, I ended up ducking under his arm, putting me at his back. I then jumped up and put him in a choke hold, holding my own wrist to keep the lock tight around his neck.

However, he simply reached up after twisting his big body, and grabbed me by my clothes, so as to give himself the grip he needed to throw me over his back and dropped me to the floor. Before I could do anything else, he grabbed my wrists and pinned them to the ground, now stranding my waist with his knees either side of my hips.

"Now you will yield!" he demanded, just like he had done many times before when I had taken sparring together too far in my pursuit to win. And winning was admittedly, something that never happened. But as for right now, well I had two things going for me, surprise and experience. As there was a lot left for Lucius still to learn in the next few hundred years. And it was time for his first lesson…

Never underestimate a Chosen One.

I lifted my hips suddenly, bridging them until my body was held at an angle, forcing his body to fly up and forward. This meant that he had no choice but to let go of my wrists to save his face from hitting the ground over my head. My natural reflex kicked in, making me turn my head to the side just in case he landed on me.

Which thankfully, he didn't do as my hips were fast enough to thrust him forwards. Then I moved my arms swiftly down, like I was doing a snow angel, so I was in the right position for what move came next. I raised myself up and wrapped my arms tight around his waist, tucking my head against his stomach, making me feel like a damn monkey holding on for dear life to a tree.

But as funny as it would have looked to someone watching this, it gave me the chance to reach up, grab his arm with one hand and with the other, move it around his back. This was so I could push with my bent knee and gain enough momentum to quickly flip him on his back with me now on top.

I then placed him in another choke hold and winked at him before commenting,

"You were saying, handsome?"

At this his eyes widened in shock before narrowing. Then he wrapped his legs around my waist, gripped my elbow with one hand and my wrist with the other, before shifting his leg so he could use them to throw me to the side. I rolled away and sprung back to my feet as he did the same. Both of us now took deep breaths as we stared at one another, each of us working out what our next move would be.

"I will not fight you any longer," he declared as I could tell he didn't want to hurt me and was worried that continuing to do so would end badly. But again, my stubbornness naturally wouldn't allow me to yield just yet.

"Then I will make this quick as I drop you to the floor, and for a third time!" I shouted continuing to fight him, and you could tell he still had a lot to learn, as he did not know how to fend off all my attacks the way he did when we sparred on the mats. I could see his frustration growing and suddenly I found myself pushed up against the tree with his hand up my neck.

"Don't make me hurt you!" he snarled down at me, before granting me a warning,

"Now yield!"

"Not a chance!" I snapped back before breaking his hold, and in doing so he soon found his arm held behind his back. I then used this hold on him to force his own body to the tree, quickly turning the tables on him before letting him go as I had no intention of trying to break anything. His hands came up just in time to prevent his face from smacking into the bark before he turned to snarl at me over his shoulder. I couldn't help but wink at him, grinning now in what I liked to think was a bad ass, cocky way.

"You seriously underestimate me if you think I will make this easy for you," I told him and he turned around slowly.

"Well, if I had been in any doubts of what happened to those men being caused by your hand, I confess that doubt no longer holds any weight." This was as close to a compliment as I was going to get, as it was clear he had found the mess I had made by the stream before my mother had disappeared.

"And nor should it, given who I am," I said in my haste, stopping myself before revealing much more than I should… *Like who my father was.*

"And who is that exactly? For I am not to be so foolish as to believe a single word that has passed through your lips." Ouch, okay that hurt, despite it being justified.

"I didn't want to lie to you, but I had no choice." At this he raised a brow, intrigued by what I was saying.

"If that be the truth, then tell me who sent you?" he asked as we slowly started to circle each other, keeping a distance between us. And I knew enough about Lucius's style of fighting to know he was waiting for his opportunity to lunge when I least expected it. Lucky for me I always knew to expect it.

"No one sent me, I came by my own choice," I told him firmly.

"Were you looking for me?" he asked, and I knew he wasn't going to like the answer.

"No, my quest was not supposed to include you," I replied, having no reason to lie about this. His features tensed a moment as I knew my words had stung.

"But you do know of me… you knew who I was to you, it's why your gaze fixated on me across the ballroom, it is why you were wounded by what I was doing with another woman. I had wondered at the time of the jealousy I saw in your eyes… but if this is true, then why, Lia…? Why did you not expect me to be where you found me?" I swallowed hard and pleaded in a strained voice,

"Do not ask me this."

"Oh, but I am, and will continue to do so until I get the answers that I seek," he warned making me sigh.

"Then you will force me to lie, and considering I know how you cannot enter my mind, I fail to see how you will be able to detect truth from a lie even with your hand held up at my throat!" I snapped, hating that he was backing me into this proverbial corner. It was at this point that my words once more ignited his anger enough for him to lunge at me. Thankfully I was ready for it as I counteracted the move.

I grabbed the left side of his padded gambeson with my right hand, before using my left arm to tuck under his while twisting my body side on by taking a step back with one foot. Then I turned my body fully so my back was to his chest, and I was facing the woods. Then I dragged him over my back and rolled into the throw, tossing him once more to the ground.

He growled in frustration, hammering a fist to the ground at the same time he shouted,

"ENOUGH!" Then he jumped back to his feet and this time, when he came at me, it was fast, and it was hard. In fact, it nearly managed to wind me, as I was gasping for breath with my back to the floor. But before I could do the same move as before, he held both my wrists in one hand above my head and this time, he pulled a dagger from a hidden sheath at his back. A dagger that was now…

Held dangerously at my throat.

Thunder in my heart, that was what this felt like. Yet even as I thought it, I still knew deep down that it was so much more than that. It felt as if I was running along the wet sand and trying to catch up with the footsteps ahead of me. Trying to catch up with them before they sank away to the memories that no longer had the power to hold them to this world. As if someone had already made this journey once before and I was merely the unseen shadow that lagged behind.

Because I knew in that moment that I wasn't the first to experience this deep-rooted fear. The fear of that threat against my neck. The fear of who's hand now held my life tightly in their grasp.

The fear of the love I knew he might no longer feel for me, not after I had broken his trust. For I may have been the Keeper of his heart in my future, but right now, I was his prey.

And he was my hunter in my…

Quest of Stone.

These thoughts all assaulted me at once, and I felt my own mother's past prophecy roll through me until suddenly that fear vanished. Because I knew Lucius, better than anyone in the world, and right now, this was simply about... *control.*

So, I decided to prove it with words.

"You won't hurt me," I challenged as he had me pinned dangerously to the floor, still with the dagger held at my throat to keep me in place. However, I knew this was to stop me from trying anything more and no doubt thought it his only way to stop the fight before getting his answers. I knew that when I raised my head up slightly, putting my skin closer to the blade. One he quickly pulled back after snarling down at me and allowing his fangs to grow to try and frighten me.

"No? How can you be so sure, are you really that foolish!?"

"You don't frighten me, and neither do those," I said nodding to his fangs and making him growl menacingly.

"Then you are more foolish than I thought!" he snapped.

"Not foolish, just well informed, for I am your Chosen One and I know that this means that the Fates forbid any harm to come to me by your hand... so do us both a favour and drop the dagger." His eyes flashed crimson at hearing me admit this, telling me instantly that it meant something to him.

However, something started to change further in his eyes, a sort of cunning realisation, before he suddenly stabbed the dagger into the ground next to me, making me flinch.

"You're right, I cannot hurt you and I refuse to do so, even if I could. Which means you have left me no other choice." As soon as he said this, a chill rippled through my body, especially as seconds after, he simply let me go. A blink of an eye was all it took for him to suddenly be standing above me.

"What... what do you mean?" He stared down at me for another few seconds before he started to walk away, shocking me. I scrambled to my feet, shaking my head, now trying to figure out what he meant by this.

"Lucius!" I shouted his name, making him pause, yet he remained with his back to me. Then finally he looked over his shoulder and told me in a sinister tone,

"I may not be able to hurt you, but there is one I *can* hurt and if I am not to get the truth from you, then I will certainly get the truth from her!"

I gasped in horror.

"No!" this pitiful sound escaped my lips the second I realised that he meant Pip, as this was confirmed when he started to walk back towards the ruins. I knew I couldn't allow this to happen! So many people had already been lost because of this journey, and I couldn't add one more to my guilty soul. Which meant against all the advice I had been given, against all the rules set against this time travel, I made the decision that I knew in my heart was right.

So, I ran towards him, I saw his back tense as he felt it coming. I leapt on his back, using my weight to swing him to the ground taking him so completely off guard that I soon found myself straddling his stomach. I then held my hands to his shoulders before telling him the truth,

"Please don't do this. I will… *I will tell you everything."*

His furious gaze seared into my own, as if his look alone had the power to brand this moment to my heart for all eternity. His hand came to my neck and soon I found myself flipped onto my back with an angry vampire once more held above me.

"I want to feel your lies for myself," he snarled down at me, but I would soon astonish him with what he would hear coming from my lips.

It would be the truth.

"Who are you and where do you come from?" I

swallowed hard at his first question, something even more difficult with the near bruising grip he held at my throat. Like a verbal knife edge held to my flesh and the future of this prophecy held in his hands. I knew now in this moment I had been following footsteps in the sand. My mother had been faced with this same turning point in her own journey to the past, but I had to believe that I was making the right decision.

I had to trust that the Vampire above me would take this information and bury it deep… deep enough to protect it for the small drop of time that was needed.

So, I took a deep breath and told him what I had wanted to say since the very first moment we met back in that ballroom.

The truth of where I was from.

But most of all, the truth of who I was to him.

"I come from the future and in it…"

"I am your wife."

CHAPTER 28
FAMILY AFFAIR

As soon as the words were out of my mouth, one second Lucius was above me and the next… *he was gone.* I actually gasped and for a few horrifying seconds, I actually thought he had disappeared too. As it turned out, he had just moved off me with supernatural speed, something he obviously now felt free to do.

I sat up slowly, seeing him pacing between the gaps in the trees, obviously trying to process what I had just told him.

"I know it's a lot," I said making him scoff.

"What you claim as being a lot, I name as being absurd!" I released a sigh as I got to my feet and muttered,

"And you wonder why I hide things." He snapped his head back to me and barked,

"You lied from the very first moment your lips opened to speak."

"Excuse me, but I wasn't the one who demanded I become your little maid! I am here to do a job… I made a vow and you're pissed because that reason doesn't include you!" This was the wrong thing to say, as he was now storming over to me and making me back up.

"Do you see any piss on me! For trust me, as capable as you are at fighting combined with the lashing of your tongue, your words do not incite such fear in me!" I felt like rolling my eyes at this point but held back.

"For starters, pissed in my time means angry or drunk, and is rarely used to describe actually pissing yourself because… eww. And as for believing me, well if you doubt me because of the lies I had no choice to tell you, why not ask me to prove it," I challenged.

"And how would you do that exactly?"

"You're my husband, Lucius." I stated like this was obvious, making him scoff,

"So you say."

"Then ask me anything," I said crossing my arms over my chest and finding it hard not to let his distrust get to me the way it did. Because despite knowing it was warranted on his side, it still hurt. He raised his brow at this, making me continue.

"I know you better than any other, trust me, there isn't a question I won't be able to answer," I said with my confidence dripping from every word.

"Is that so?" he asked folding his own arms over his plated chest. So, I sighed, letting my arms drop, along with my attitude and told him,

"You are the King of Vampires and born from the Devil's own blood." At this he shrugged his shoulders and told me,

"This is not uncommon knowledge with my people."

"But I am mortal," I pointed out, making him jerk his head slightly as he shrugged his shoulders.

"Yes, and even mortals have eyes and ears a plenty."

"Fine, you want more, then here it is…" I took a deep breath and gave him the proof he would by angry to hear. A secret he believed kept from everyone. But before I could open that family can of painful worms, I tried the name I knew would affect him.

"Many may know your name to be Lucius Septimus, assassin to Dominic Draven, once Roman Emperor. But how many know the man you were before… the mortal name of Judas Iscariot?" At this he flinched, and I watched as his fists clenched at his sides in reaction. His jaw tensed before he forced it to relax enough to answer,

"It is true, that this name is not commonly associated with me, but my past is known to few and so far, this is all information you could have gathered by nefarious means." I rolled my eyes at this before hitting him with the big stuff, having no choice to do so.

"Alright, ask yourself how many people know this, you have a brother named Dariush, a being who can create portals and who currently sits on the throne as your second in the Kingdom of Death ruling in your place." At this his features finally twisted into anger, now stepping closer and arguing,

"Who the fuck are you?! No one is supposed to know of my…" I quickly held out my hand and decided to hit home even further.

"I know because I am your fucking wife! Just like I know about your daughter…" I paused the moment he started shaking his head.

"No, no it is not possible! I would never…"

"What, not even your wife?! Lucius, please listen to me… please believe me."

"No!"

"You named her Kala, after your mother's favourite flower, she used to call you her little Kalanit, a field full of poppies." He continued shaking his head, as I continued taking,

"I am so sorry, I know of your heartbreak, I know how she di…"

"Don't say it!" he shouted suddenly, now panting heavily making me sigh as I finally stopped, knowing I didn't need to say anymore. Not when I saw how his shoulders dropped and he dragged a hand down his face before he started shaking his head again. I instantly felt guilty the moment he closed his eyes in pain, before he stammered,

"I… have never… no one… *not a soul.*" I swallowed hard before whispering,

"Not until you found your Chosen One."

He reacted to this first by suddenly erupting into his other form as if trying to frighten me and judge my reaction to him. Meaning that the second his Demonic wings stretched out behind him, this time without a feather in sight, I didn't even flinch. I didn't give him a single reaction he expected, even as his gambeson shredded as Demonic armour tore its way through it, shredding it and leaving a Hellish warrior in its place. Not a single reaction as deadly black spikes grew from his shoulder plates and sinister scales rippled down his arms until his hands became weapons. Razor tipped claws glinting in the twilight, making him look more like the devil than that of a fallen angel.

But my lack of fear continued even when fangs grew, and horns emerged. Even when branches of darkness marred the flawless pale skin I was used to seeing on his handsome face. And most of all, not even when the crimson blaze grew in his eyes. Not a single part of it frightened me.

"You really think that's going to frighten me, handsome?" I questioned in a calm tone, before walking straight up to him and after gaining height on my tip toes, I reached up with my hand. Then I took hold of one of his horns on his head and used it to yank his lips down to me, before growling over them,

"...*Not when I have fucked you in this form!*" Then I crushed my lips to his, making him freeze in shock. Then he snapped out of it when I bit his lip and sucked on his blood, making him growl low in his throat. It was also enough to make him a react the way I wanted. Which was when he wrapped his Demonic arms around me, making me moan into his kiss as he dominated the rest of it. Meaning I was left breathless and craving more... *much, much more.* Which was why the moment I felt my body being pushed up against a tree, I jumped up and wrapped my legs around his waist, moaning,

"*Yes... oh yes... Lucius!*"

He growled in response as his hands went to my ass and lifted me further up allowing me to feel the hard length pressing into me. Something that made me wish that I was naked so he could slip inside and claim me. I didn't care that he was a Demon, I wanted him with a fever that could only be sated by this dark force within him. Which was why I broke the connection and kissed my way along his jawline all the way to his ear, before practically begging him,

"*Fuck me... claim me, my Demon.*" He snarled in response to this before I felt his claws at my hips, tearing into my trousers, and panties so the material fell away from the lower half of my body. This was before I felt him lift me up and hold the head of his bulbous cock at my dripping core, he pulled back and said in his Demon voice,

"*YOU ARE FORVER MINE!*"

"Yes... YEEESSSS!" I roared the second he impaled himself up inside me, making me cry out at the intrusion, a sound that was drowned out by his own roar of pleasure. Because for Lucius this was not only his first time claiming me, but was also his Demon's first time claiming anyone. Yet even being in this form, it did not distract him from his concern, as he held himself seated inside of me, giving me time to adjust to his size.

"FUCK... So tight, little one," he rasped making me whisper back,

"But made for you." At this he grunted his agreement before he started to move, making my head fall back against the bark and moan up at the sky. However, the moment he started to thrust into me at greater speed, I felt him transfer one hand to the back of my head to prevent me from banging myself against the tree as I went crazy in my pleasure.

"Yes, yes, yes, yes!" I cried over and over, and I could feel my orgasm building in strength as I gripped onto his horns and used them to meet him thrust for thrust.

"Fuck, woman!" he growled making me smile.

"Shut up, Demon, and make me come!" I shouted riding him as I rotated my hips on each downward motion, ignoring the burn in my arms from pull ups as I chased my pleasure. He snarled at this before tightening his hold on me, and his wings shot forwards, the largest horns that connected them now turning so they framed each side of the large tree. Then I looked up over my head to see the claws at the tips of his wings suddenly stab into the bark. They had latched on and now cocooned our connected bodies completely, hiding us from the rest of the natural world.

"You want more, little maid?" his dark voice rumbled.

"I want it all, Demon!" I answered and he grinned Demonically before he warned,

"Then hold on, little maid, whilst I really fucking claim you!" I did as he advised I do, now locking my hands at the back of his neck just before he started to hammer into me at such speed, I knew the powerful thrusts were aided by his wings that were anchored to the tree as he used it as leverage. The edges of his wings started to snake behind my body, putting boned fingers and rippling leathery skin at my back, offering me protection from his brutal thrusts that would have bruised my back. However, with him using his wings, it meant that he could pull my body into his with every trust.

Not surprisingly, I was screaming my release seconds later, making my channel grip his cock and ripple around its length as I gushed my arousal around him.

"YEEESSS AHHHH FUUCCCCKKK!" I screamed shuddering around him, feeling it like a never-ending wave I almost feared had the force to rip me apart. My entire body lit up and not just metaphorically as the same light that bloomed from within me earlier suddenly erupted, making Lucius close his eyes against it. Yet this didn't slow him down in any way, as he was too close himself. Meaning he just pulled me in tighter, using his wings to curl under my ass in place of his hands. This was so he could suddenly hammer his claws into the tree either side of my head, digging into the wood as he roared his release. It was as if knowing his Demon needed to hold on and fearing if it would be my flesh that would take the injury, he chose the tree instead.

"RRRRAAAAHHHH!" His bellowed roar of release even shook the trees around us along with the ground. It thundered to the point that I could feel it vibrate up his legs, making my own legs shake that were still wrapped around him. This meant that when we finally came down from our intense sexual pleasure together, it was also the moment he placed his forehead to mine and I knew that realisation was setting in deep within him. This was confirmed when he softly made the claim,

"My Chosen One."

I nodded breathlessly, now cupping his cheek and telling

him silently that I was and always would be. But then the beauty of his next words came, and I melted into him even further.

"My wife."

"Yes... *yes, my husband.*"

However, this moment was then shattered as suddenly wood exploded all around his head and he groaned when he was knocked from me just as I heard a violent scream,

"GET OFF MY LITTLE BEAN!"

Oh shit.

Lucius was knocked even further to the side as he was hit again by a flying branch and before he could react, roots from the forest floor suddenly grabbed him, dragging him backwards. My head snapped to the cause and my mouth dropped open in utter shock as there was Pip, now standing there glowing like some forest goddess. Her green hair was flowing around her like she was captured underwater, and she held her hands out to her sides as the green light poured from her palms, mirroring the same green glow in her eyes.

"PIP, NO!" I screamed, now dragging up the fallen material of my trousers that were still hooked around my ankles as I ran to her. Doing so with one hand fisting what was left of them, holding them to my waist.

"Pip, listen to me, he wasn't hurting me!" I shouted now trying to shake her from this rage. Her eyes finally flickered to me when hearing this, as if my words were starting to penetrate conscious thought.

"He wasn't?" she questioned half in a daze.

"No, we... we were having sex okay!"

"Oh... *Ohhh.* Oops... my ba..." She never got to finish this famous catchphrase of hers, as Lucius's Demonic rage hit. He burst from the roots that had entwined around him, causing an explosion of wood to splinter around us. Pip protected me, shielding me with her body, crouching over me until the last of the raining wood fell. I quickly looked around Pip to see Lucius's Demon form now striding angrily towards us, making me dodge around her before running straight for him.

"No, no, wait! She didn't know… she thought you were hurting me, she thought you were attacking… she was only trying to protect me!" I argued trying to get him to stop and calm down. But when he didn't slow down, I muttered,

"Oh fuck it!" then I dropped the hold I had on my ripped pants and jumped at him, now clinging on butt naked to the front of him. I tried not to think of how this looked, me with my ass out, clinging onto Lucius as this big bad ass Demon was on a mission. Which was why I had to put my face in his line of vision and keep his attention on me.

"My love… please, she didn't know… she didn't know you were finally claiming me." Thankfully these words worked as he finally stopped and after releasing a sigh, his eyes fixated on my own before he wrapped his arms around me.

"She is your guardian?" he asked and I nodded before telling him,

"And Sophia." He released another sigh, this one heavier than the last before he nodded, setting me down. Then when he looked down the length of me, and quickly noted my naked bottom half. One that was also showing evidence of his seed leaking from me and soon being the cause of why his eyes heated.

"I will fix these but as for my seed, you will keep it where it is, for I want to know it coats your thighs, as this will be your punishment for lying to me and keeping what was always mine to claim from me for far too long." I swallowed hard and decided not to argue. Because I also knew that scenting himself on me and knowing his claim was still inside of me, would only help in keeping him calm. Especially when there was a lot more for us left to discuss.

And speaking of things to discuss…

"Hey boss man, sorry about the branchy freak out, thought you had lost your blood-soaked marbles and was attacking her," Pip said making him frown down at her as she approached. Then he simply said,

"Your hair is green." At this she laughed as he lowered to help me back into my trousers, now fixing the damage he had made to my clothes. Which also included my underwear, a pair that was still caught in the leg of my trousers, so I wasn't doing the rest of this quest bare assed naked.

"And your dick is still out… you know, if we are pointing out the obvious and all that," Pip replied, making me cough a laugh as Lucius unapologetically continued to walk towards his gear, and with every step he took, his human form returned.

"Where is Adam?" he asked as he started to arm himself once more with his sword and his armour. Pip grimaced before telling him,

"Erh, this trip was more of a girly thing." He looked back at us both over his shoulder and narrowed his gaze.

"Both of you, you used the Janus Gate?" We both nodded like naughty schoolgirls skipping class.

"Yeah, Sophia and Toots too."

"Toots?" he questioned as he walked back towards us, stopping a few feet away and crossing his arms over his chest.

"Yeah, you know, blonde chick, just did a disappearing act on us, the King's Electus and Little Bean's mother… oh, wait, was that too much?" Pip said when I elbowed her side even after it was way too late.

"Your mother?!" Lucius asked in astonishment, making me sigh, especially when he started shaking his head and started to mutter,

"But if she is the King's Chosen One, then that means…" I swallowed hard and finished for him,

"…The King is my father."

CHAPTER 29
TALES TO BE TOLD

"So that went well," Pip commented, making me give her a wry side look as we waited for Lucius who was off giving the remainder of his men orders. Because after we had dropped this royal bombshell on him, we had to explain how we had used the Janus Gate and that it was all part of some Fated Prophecy. Naturally we hadn't gone into too much detail, as well, it became obvious that there was just too much to tell when it wasn't yet safe to do so. Not when Lucius had his orders left to give and he knew his men would only wait for him for so long before they came searching for him.

Hence why we were back at the ruins and after igniting a fire with the click of his fingers, he told me to wait for him, telling me he wouldn't be long. As for his men, some of them had waited with the horses as the other half had already left, taking Sophia with them. Naturally, this part worried me the most as we were left standing here waiting, hoping and praying that he was able to bring her back in time.

"What part exactly, the moment you had the forest try and kill him or when we basically blurted out that I'm the King's daughter, making him look like he was close to passing out?" I commented in response to Pip's 'that went well'.

"Man, that would have been cool… what? I have never seen Luc pass out before and it would have made for an even better 'dun, dun, dun, duh!' moment," she said making me groan.

"Yeah, well so much for all the time traveling rules, as I would say we just burned the damn handbook," I commented dryly.

"Oh yeah we shredded that baby, but hey, at least no heads exploded, and the world didn't end, so I would say it's still a win-win for team Boobateers." I shot her an incredulous look.

"A team that is dwindling fast, may I point out," I said making her sigh sadly.

"Yeah, I miss Toots, wherever she may be." I would have said more but Lucius was making his way back towards us looking grim.

"Any news on Sophia? Will your men catch up to them in time?" I asked the moment he was close enough.

"I did not give the order," he admitted making me gasp.

"But why!?" Lucius sighed before telling me,

"Because the King will need someone to blame and while he is doing that, he is not blaming you, nor is he hunting you." I shook my head a little as if I couldn't believe what I was hearing.

"I can't let that happen!" I shouted before storming off in the direction of the horses, having no idea what I could do but knowing I had to try something. I felt my arm being grabbed from behind stopping me in my tracks, expecting it to be Lucius.

But I was wrong.

It was Pip.

"Little Bean, stop." I frowned in question before she too sighed just like Lucius had. Then she told me,

"Luc is right."

"What?!" I shouted making her wince.

"Just listen, okay? Right now we need the King focused on someone to blame and if he is directing that at his own sister, a being he will not hurt, no matter how angry, then he is not hunting you, and sweetie, you're the only one who can put an end to all of this, but not if you are in a jail cell being tortured for information." I sucked in a quick breath at this.

"That would never happen!" Lucius growled making me argue,

"He wouldn't... he's my..." Pip shook her head and cut me off,

"He is your King and nothing more. He doesn't know you, Little Bean, because in this time you're not his daughter and more than that... *he is not your father."* I flinch back at this, hating that she was right. Because right now, I was nothing more than an angry King's enemy.

"I know it's painful... Gods, it's heartbreaking, baby face, but we have to face facts," Pip said biting her lip, one that was usually so colourful with mad lipstick and some smiley faced lip piercing.

"But what about Sophia? We can't just leave her, Pip!" I argued making her close her eyes for a moment as if she felt the same pain I did.

"I know, that's why I am going to go and break her out," she stated making me shake my head, before grabbing her hand and holding it to my chest.

"No... you can't... I... *I can't lose you too,"* I whispered in a wounded way that made her expression soften.

"You will never lose me, baby Toots. Not when I am right in here," she said placing our joint hands over my heart making tears fill my eyes. Then I grabbed her to me and hugged her tight.

"Please don't leave me," I pleaded in my weakness making her hold me tighter.

"You won't be alone, I promise you," she said, nodding over my shoulder to where Lucius stood watching this touching scene play out. I nodded once knowing that she was right. She was the only one that had a chance at saving Sophia, as no one else knew that she was part of our time traveling team other than now Lucius.

"Please be careful," I whispered as tears fell, making her cradle my head to her. Then after a tender moment passed between us, she pulled back before nodding to Lucius.

"My Lord, take care of her, just as you always have done." I looked back at him as he nodded, before stepping up to Pip. Then he placed a hand at her shoulder and told her,

"As you know my word is my vow, she will be safe. No go and take care of your own, little Imp. As always, you have made me proud." She beamed up at him before giving him a hug and making him chuckle while patting the top of her head. Then she released him, wiped a stray tear away before hugging me one last time.

"Be strong, Amelia." I bobbed my head, trying to hold back the tears. Then while holding my arms around myself, I watched her walk away, disappearing into the dark of night. I felt Lucius's arms envelope me from behind and after a time, he turned my face to his so I was looking up at him. Then he said softly,

"Hello, my Amelia." I smiled as he knew that by speaking my true name, this would help lighten the heavy weight on my heart.

"Come, we must leave before the king's men come this

way and it has all been in vain," he said leading me towards his horse and helping me mount Sleipnir.

"Where are we going?" I asked, at the same time holding back the added question, 'and will my ass hurt by the time we get there?'.

"Far from here," he answered after mounting behind and taking the reins in front of me. After this, we didn't speak again as despite there still being so much that needed to be said between us, right now, it seemed as if none of us had the words.

But what we did have…

Was the will to run.

∽

Many hours later and I must have fallen asleep as it was the gentle sound of my name being called that roused me from my dreams. I woke to find myself slumped against Lucius, with my body sitting sideways on his horse and wrapped under his cloak with my head resting on his chest.

"We are here," he said softly, and I rubbed my eyes before straightening up, seeing that we were at another inn and clearly one that Lucius intended for us to take shelter in. At least for the rest of the night.

"Is it safe to stop?" I asked as he directed the horse into the stable yard, and I had to say that this place looked far better than the first one we had stopped at. Like the difference between staying in a hostel and the Four Seasons.

"It will not matter, for I have a plan," he told me, making me frown in question but before I could ask, he was dismounting his horse and reaching up for my waist to help me down. Then I waited next to the stunning creature, stoking Sleipnir's head when he nudged me.

"Well, I hope you trust that he knows what he is doing," I said to him, making Lucius's horse nudge its velvety nose against my cheek this time making me giggle. But then I stopped when I overheard Lucius speaking with the stable hand, telling him he would be paying to keep his horse for a few weeks. I watched as he handed over what must have been more than enough coin, as the man's eyes widened at his palm full.

"Be good, Sleipnir," Lucius said coming up behind me and stoking his own hand down his horse, as if saying goodbye. The horse made an unimpressed sound making Lucius chuckle before nodding to the man waiting. Then he took my hand and led me into the inn, making me ask,

"Are we continuing on foot?" Lucius glanced down at me and shook his head, refusing to explain further. I decided not to argue or push him until we were in a room and had some privacy. As for the inn, it was mostly empty apart from one table of men drinking ale and a lone cloaked figure in the corner dipping bread into a bowl of something. The cloaked figure raised their head to look our way and for some reason I felt something strange tug at my soul the moment they did.

Almost like... *I knew them.*

In fact, I found myself taking a step towards them only to be held back when Lucius refused to let go of my hand, jarring me out of my actions. I looked back to Lucius, who had been conversing with the inn keeper.

"Stay close," he warned before he went back to asking the man for his best room.

"Got only one room, as not many have the coin in these parts to pay it," I heard him say as Lucius was once more handing over his money, which again seemed to be more than enough if the inn keeper's reaction was to go by. I then half listened as he gave him directions to the room and handed over the key. But as for me I couldn't seem to take my eyes off the mysterious figure sitting alone eating. Although just as they were raising their head, about to show me their face, Lucius stepped in my line of sight.

"Come, Amelia," he said before leading me towards a staircase but the moment he stepped away, I noticed that the figure was gone. I frowned in confusion, now wondering if I had imagined it all because even the table was clear.

As if no one had ever been there.

Moments later and we were in a modestly furnished room that even had tapestries on the wall and a large canopy bed with four spindled wood posts. Thick tasselled curtains were pulled back, and no doubt used for warding off the chill more than for decoration they were used for back in my own time.

"Now we have much to discuss," Lucius said after locking the door.

"Yeah, just about a few hundred years at least," I said wryly making him smirk.

"Let's start with the facts, as I have gathered by now that this quest of yours is of the most importance or you would not have risked the Janus Gate to begin with." I sighed at that and deflated back, sitting on the bed.

"Gods but I don't even know where to begin," I confessed.

"Then I will start, do I even know that you are here?" he asked making me tense.

"You mean the future you…? No, you do not," I admitted knowing there was little point in lying about it, as it would achieve nothing.

"I surmised as much," he admitted making me raise a brow at him, prompting him to add,

"I would not have changed as much as to let you freely undertake this journey alone, even if it is a few hundred years more I have yet to live through." Well, I couldn't argue there but there was one important fact that he was missing out.

"I was not alone," I reminded him in a small voice as it was a painful reality to remind myself of all I had lost.

"Ah, your mother," he said making me bite my lip to hold back getting upset.

"I know this is a lot to take in, finding out that the King of Kings is my father," I said, and at this Lucius released a sigh and took a seat opposite the side of the bed that was positioned next to a small table.

"I confess, it was not expected but strangely, it makes more sense than you would think."

"How so?" I asked him.

"The fighting for one, as I do not believe the King would have allowed his daughter to grow up without being capable of defending herself, despite you being of mortal blood, which is also a mystery to me," he said making me tense because that was most definitely one part of history I didn't want to explain. So, I shrugged my shoulders and agreed,

"Yeah, there is that."

"But it is also your strength and your courage in which I speak." I raised my head at this, surprised.

"It takes bravery to undertake such a journey, despite being furious on my older self's behalf." I chuckled at that part.

"Don't suppose you could write him a letter telling him that you have forgiven me, could you?" He laughed at this.

"Which brings me on to the main question… why are you really here, Amelia?" I released a deep sigh before telling him,

"It's a long story, Lucius, do you really think you're ready for it?"

"I am ready for whatever you have to tell me,

sweetheart," he replied making me hope this was true. But then there was only one way to find out, and I knew it started not at the beginning of the story...

But what I was hoping would be the end...

"I am here to kill a Wraith King."

CHAPTER 30
KNOCK ON WOOD

By the time I had finished my story, it was hours later, and the evidence was a table full of empty cups and plates, along with the yawn that escaped me. As for Lucius, he was clearly in shock, as he had scrubbed a hand down his face at least six times during all I had to tell him. Of course, he'd had a lot of questions. Most of which I had tried to be vague about when giving my answers. Because Lucius and I had a lot of history together, despite only really getting together as a couple not too long ago. But a lot had happened in that time and with the Wraiths needing to be my main focus in all of this, that was where I naturally lead my story.

Of course, I had spared him the painful knowledge that he had lost me once and I had essentially died in his arms. Because I didn't want to put him through that. Not when it didn't matter or change the outcome to the end of what happened. But I hadn't wanted to lie either, so told him I was attacked by the Wraith King without going into too much detail what the outcome of that had truly been.

No, instead I told him that I became connected to the

Wraiths and for a time, a piece of me had been trapped inside his lost realm. Of course, this piece of the past was easier to tell from the point where Lucius had saved me.

He had questioned why then my need for this quest, making me explain my dreams and the connection I still had to the Wraiths. I had also explained the war we fought, making him question how as a mortal I had accomplished all that I had. This in itself had opened up another can of worms, one I had avoided by giving only half truths. Quickly telling him that I had started to change when I was in Hell. He accepted my reasons, being that it was our time together that caused him to unlock this other side of me, along with the help of consuming his blood.

In conclusion to this story telling, he was convinced enough to agree to help me get to Egypt and find the Rosetta stone. But he had also asked what I planned to do once my quest was complete as he did not believe that time would simply reset itself and I would wake to find myself back in the world I knew. In fact, it was only when he was assured that this was my thought process, did he seemed more eager to help me. As if he was satisfied that once I had severed my connection to the Wraith King, that I would be going nowhere. I had tried to mention the Janus Temple I knew lay beneath the grounds of Witley Court, but he simply said sternly,

"This is impossible." And would say no more about it, even after I asked. This obviously made me fear that Lucius therefore had his own plans and in them, it included stealing me away and keeping me as far from my Father's English manor house as he could get. Oh, and doing so for the foreseeable future... *no pun intended.*

So, with this all being said, I knew at some point if this all went to plan that I would have another problem to face when the time came in trying to get home. But for now, I was just happy that he was willing to help me because I knew there was no way I was going to accomplish this task alone.

"So, what is the plan from here?" I asked as he rose to his feet and walked over to the window.

"For now, it is time you get some rest."

"Just me?" I asked surprised that he wouldn't be joining me.

"I will have to leave you for a short time."

"Wait, you're leaving me?!" I asked almost in panic this time, making him grant me a soft smile, as if he liked me being needy for him.

"Do not worry, I will not be gone long. I just have to enlist the help of another so as we may get to Egypt."

"Oh, please tell me you have a friend who has a bloody big boat." He laughed at this, walked over to me and tipped my chin back so I was left looking up at him,

"Try a brother who has the ability to make portals." I blew out a relieved breath and said,

"Oh thanks the Gods." He raised a brow at this, making me confess,

"I get the worst sea sickness." He chuckled once and said in a soft smouldering voice,

"Well, we can't have that, can we?" Then he leaned down and still with his hand at my chin, he kissed me.

"I won't be long... *my little maid,"* he whispered against my lips making me sigh.

"You know you can stop calling me that now, technically, I wasn't ever really your maid." He paused at the door and turned back to give me one of his bad boy grins that I had missed so much. Then he told me,

"Yes, Amelia... *yes, you were.*" Then he left, chuckling to himself when I muttered,

"Cocky royal ass."

After this I got up just so I could take off my clothes and release my hair from its tight pinned braids. This was before slipping back under the sheets, instantly feeling better knowing that I wouldn't be spending yet another night sleeping in my clothes. I also didn't know how long it was before Lucius came back but I knew it was long enough for me to be in a deep sleep. This was because I woke with a start when I felt a hand running up my leg.

"You are naked." I heard his voice and instantly felt better, knowing he was back.

"Yeah," I breathed as his hand travelled further up my body under the covers and I couldn't help myself when I arched into his touch when he grazed my bare mound with the back of his fingers.

"Mmm, are you ready for me, little one?" he asked in the dark making me sit up and reach for him. Then I grabbed his shirt in my fist and yanked him hard to me.

"What do you think?!" I practically growled before I crushed my lips to his, making him moan his approval as his tongue duelled with my own. I realised then, that he must have taken off his gear leaving him just his shirt and breaches. I was grateful for this as it meant getting him naked easier and quicker, starting with maneuvering my body so I was the one now straddling him.

"I am always ready for you," I told him after breaking the kiss so I could drag his shirt over his head, before pushing him down so he was lying flat beneath me.

"Looks like the Gods favour me indeed, for they gifted me with not only beauty that rivals any Goddess, but the appetite of an insatiable wife." I chuckled at this and said,

"Yes, well you can blame your future self for that one, as I can assure you, I was a virgin before you claimed me and made me this way." He growled happily before fisting my hair and pulling me down for a deeper, more sensual kiss, and one that had the power to curl my toes.

"Fuck yeah I did!" he snarled before going back for more and making me grind myself against him, wishing he was free from the rest of his clothes.

"You… need to… be… naked," I said between breathless kisses and soon I felt myself come into contact with his skin as he made his breachers disappear.

"And that right there, is the best type of magic." He howled with laughter at this before bringing me back down so he could continue kissing me. But as for me, well I had another type of kissing in mind. So, I sat back and pushed at his chest when he tried to reach for me.

"Now lie back, handsome, and get ready to discover something else your wife is good at." Then I winked at him before I started to kiss my way down his chest and making his eyes glow in the darkness. But before I could utter my wish for light, the candles in the room suddenly ignited. I grinned to myself knowing that he wanted to watch this as much as I wanted him to.

I even licked my lips against his tight abs, making him shiver at the first feel of my tongue against his skin. Then as I shimmied even further down his body until I was directly above the part of his anatomy I was most interested in. He watched as I licked my lips as if looking down at the treat I would soon consume.

"You tease me, woman," he growled making me grin up at him before purposely biting my bottom lip. Then after flicking my hair back, I told him,

"Oh, you have no idea, handsome." Then I blew him a

kiss and before he could reach for me, I suddenly took his straining, hard cock in my mouth. Then I sucked him down deep, making him throw his head back to the pillow and groan in pleasure, before hissing,

"Fuck!" I then moaned around his cock, making the sound vibrated all the way down his shaft as I slid my lips even lower, coating his length with my tongue.

"Gods, woman!" He shouted once more, making me grin. This was before stretching my mouth around his girth even further, as I moved my lips back up and down him again and again. Also keeping the suction tight and sucking in a way I knew would drive him wild.

"Fuck, Amelia!" I loved the reactions I was getting, pushing for more and more. Then I let him go completely, now using my tongue to drive him just as crazy as I dragged the length of it up from the base to the tip. And once there, I decided to pay close attention to the top, swirling the tip of my tongue around his opening, lapping up the beads of pre cum I tasted there. I moaned as the flavour of him burst across my tongue, making me pump his shaft with my hand to try and gain more of the salty drops. Meanwhile he was gripping onto the sheets as if trying to keep his hands locked there on purpose and prevent himself from taking control.

Of course, I wanted to make him snap, enjoying watching the inner turmoil raging within him, knowing I could push him over the edge quite easily. So, with this in mind, and the dripping arousal I could feel between my legs, I let my dirty obsession for this man take over. His eyes widened in shock when he watched as I rose above him, leaving his cock for the moment so as to give him a show. I then lifted a finger to my mouth and purposely sucked it in deep, getting it soaked. Then I purposely let him watch as I pulled it from my mouth before I snaked it down to my awaiting pussy. I spread my legs and while keeping my gaze locked to his own, I plunged it inside, fingering myself and gasping the moment it entered me.

He growled in desire and the moment he looked as if he was trying to reach for me, I quickly took his cock in my mouth once more. The feeling of pleasure I forced upon him made him drop back to the bed, as I started to suck him harder and faster than before. Then to add to the sensation I cupped his balls and rolled them in my palm, squeezing slightly every time I sucked him deep. At this he started to shred the bedding as his grip became brutal.

"Fuck... fuck... FUCK! Gods, woman, I am going to... going to..." I grinned knowing he was close, and the fact brought me closer in return as I raised my head and commanded quickly,

"Come and let me drink you down, my King!" Then I sucked him deep and bobbed my head up and down taking him so deep I gagged around the impressive size. At the same time, I fingered my pussy faster and harder, bring myself to orgasm the same moment I brought him to his, making him lose the fight within himself.

"FUCK! AHH RAAHHH!" He roared just as his hand came to my hair, fisted it and held me down over his cock as he pumped his release down my throat, making me choke around him. Something that just managed to turn me on even more as I came screaming around his length. This made me lose some of his cum, causing it to spill from my lips as I was unable to swallow it all down.

Soon his fingers flexed before loosening in my hair so he could begin stroking it back down my head, as I lovingly lapped up the mess I had made. He simply watched me with his red gaze as I licked up the length of his dripping wet, still hard cock like it was candy.

"Gods, that was… *fuck.*" I looked up at him as his thumb came to my lips to wipe some of his release from my mouth.

"Good?" I asked before he pressed his thumb in between my lips making me suck the small amount from his skin.

"Unlike anything I have ever experienced before," he admitted making me grin around the digit before pulling back so I could kiss the pad. Then I started to make my way up his body but before I got there, he had his hands under my arms and was pulling me up the rest of the way. Then he rolled me to my back and ordered,

"Spread yourself for me." My eyelids hooded at this, knowing he was far from done with me yet. Which was why I happily complied letting my legs fall open as he seated his hips against mine.

"I don't know what I ever did to deserve such perfection in my dark life, but I could not be more thankful for the light you bring my soul… now light up for me once more, my Amelia, as I claim your beauty for my own." I sucked in a breath at his beautiful, tender words, a breath that was quickly stolen as he thrust up inside of me, making me cry out his name,

"Yes, Lucius!" He then shackled my wrists and pinned them above my head as he continued to move inside me, driving me crazy with his game of revenge. Because that was the only way to describe it. As he would hammer into me at speed, building my orgasm quickly, only before it could tip over, he would purposely slow to gentle drags of his cock stroking my nerves and making me arch up into him. I dragged my nails down his back and begged,

"Please… Lucius" he hummed against my neck before nipping down my throat, until his lips were at my breast.

"I must confess how I do love the sound of my name coming from your lips as you beg me for your release," he said and just as I started to complain, he finally acted in my favour.

"Please just let me…"

"Come, Amelia!" he demanded before sucking my nipple into his mouth, biting around the nipple at the same time he thrust into me deeper, making me cry out as my orgasm hit.

"AHHH YEESSS!" I vibrated around him as his lips left my breast so he could pinned me harder to the bed and pound into me with greater need. His cock drove inside over and over, hitting all the right places until I was screaming in my next release, as one orgasm barely had chance to end before I was rolling right into the next. This made even more so as his bloody fangs still dripping from my breast suddenly buried themselves in my neck. Which was when I found my third release. This time I came harder than those before it, making me gasp and writhe beneath him as he continued to feed from me. He drank me down and with every drag of my blood he took, it kept my orgasm from ending, meaning I was soon gasping for breath.

"Now bite me and take what is yours, my wife, my Electus… my Love!" he said reaching up and making a slice at his neck before cupping the back of my head and holding my lips to his dripping skin. I instantly latched on and at the first pull of my own mouth, he thrust only a few more times before he too was tipping over the edge of his pleasure.

"YES, YES… DRINK… CLAIM ME! AHHHHH FUCK!" he roared as he burst inside me, filling me up with his seed until I could feel it leaking out around his still thrusting cock. This made me wrap my legs around his waist to hold on and keep him inside me for longer. Then once he started to come down from his sexual high, he placed his forehead to mine and told me the sweetest words I would ever hear in any time period.

"I love you, Amelia." I smiled big, feeling my heart near burst and told him,

"I love you too, Lucius."

A little time later and morning light was filtering in through the curtains of the bed. We had made love many times and thanks to Lucius's blood, I didn't feel sore or tender.

"I think we might have angered some neighbours last night," I commented as Lucius's hand ran lazy circles along my back from where I was still tucked against his side, with my head resting on his chest.

"Jealously is no doubt what caused the pounding of annoyance from next door and one that only spurred me on to make you scream ever louder." I had to chuckle at this.

"Well, it looks like you finally got me into bed and without needing to marry me again," I said teasing him, which was when he admitted,

"Oh, don't worry, little maid… *I still locked the door,*" He whispered making me burst out laughing in his arms.

Shortly after this we got up and got ready to leave. And because I didn't really want to use the chamber pot in front of him, because well… that was a sexual mood killer and there was still chance of sex on the road to look forward to… I told him I would meet him downstairs.

Then once I was done, back to being dressed and with my hair braided to the side in a plait, I stepped out into the hallway, just as someone was doing the same. In fact, I turned and bumped straight into them, making me instantly start apologizing.

However, the moment I looked up and saw who it was, I couldn't help but let the name slip from my lips. One that was said in excitement and aimed straight at the person I not only knew.

But knew as family.

"Aunty Ari?!"

CHAPTER 31
TALL ORDERS

"I'm sorry but do I know you?" Ari said making me feel like slapping a hand to my forehead in my stupidity. Of course she wouldn't know who I was, but it did explain a few things. As now I knew that she had been the cloaked figure I had seen downstairs last night. The one I had been drawn to like family.

Ari was beautiful, with very naturally light blonde hair, with streaks so pale they could often look white. Although right now most of it was hidden away under a bonnet that matched the navy-blue cloak she wore around her shoulders. And speaking of blue, this managed to bring out the intense blue in her eyes, making them almost as startling as my uncle Vincent's.

But then it was at this point that I also noticed what room she had just walked out of and couldn't help but blush knowing that she had been the one forced to listen to us most of the night. I looked back at my door, and she soon knew the root of my shame.

"I... erm, so sorry, I am mistaken," I said causing her to release a sigh, and as if wanting to ease my fears, she told me,

"Be not ill at ease, I was here to attend the sick in the next village and well, was weary last night from my day. So please, do not think of it, after all, love is the most pure and natural sentiment and the expression of such is just as important with the body as it is with the mind. I apologise if I interrupted as such." I shook my head and smiled.

"You don't know what it means to me to hear you say so. For we all deserved to be loved." She sighed at this and admitted,

"Yes, I believe we do, although I must confess I have yet to find such a blessing for myself." Hearing this and I couldn't help but take her hand, give it a squeeze and tell her,

"And I believe with all my heart that one day it will find you, so never give up hope." She smiled at this, making her dimples appear at her cheeks before she thanked me. Then after wishing me a good day and safe travels, she left. Something that also made me wonder what she would have said had I told her where I was planning on going. As I think I would have needed something a little stronger than a simple 'safe travels'.

I continued my way downstairs to find Lucius waiting and just like I had moments ago, he had with him family of his own. In fact, as soon as I saw Dariush I very nearly lost my senses and ran to him ready to give him a hug. Thankfully, I held back and stopped myself before making a second blunder of the day.

Lucius held out his hand for me to take, making me quicken in my steps to get to him. After this he presented me to his brother and he did this by saying,

"Dariush, this is the girl I was telling you about, for I have found my Chosen." His olive-green eyes danced with mirth as he looked me up and down, obviously amused at seeing a girl dress in clothes that were in this time period only seen on men. I knew that I must have looked a bit strange, as everything about me screamed *not from around here*. Luckily, I still had my contact lenses, or I would have looked even weirder in my glasses.

Dariush held out his hand for me as a gesture and once I placed my own in his, he raised it to his lips, bowing his head so he could kiss the back of my palm. Then his almond-shaped green eyes met mine, as he said,

"I am honored, Miss Draven." He whispered this part, obviously conscious we weren't alone in the inn, one that now had a lot more people in than late last night.

"The pleasure is all mine," I replied making him grin down at me. However, Lucius grew frustrated at this exchange and clearly didn't like that someone else was monopolizing my time and attention, despite it being his brother. I knew this as he took my hand from his brother's and snapped,

"Yes, yes, that's quite enough of that, now let us leave before we are noticed further." This gave me cause to smirk as I lowered my head in sight of his jealously, something Dariush didn't miss, as he too looked amused by his brother's possessive reaction.

After this we left the inn and instead of walking in the direction of the stables, we started on foot down the road.

"Where are we going?" I asked trying to keep up with Lucius's long legs.

"There is a wooded area near here where we will not be seen as my brother creates a portal," he told me making me nod, trusting in him. As clearly, he knew what he was doing. It also made me wonder how he had connected with his brother so fast. Although, seeing him here so soon wasn't surprising, not when he could practically create a portal to anywhere with the click of his fingers.

Which was why the moment we stopped in a secluded part of the woods, I asked,

"If he can create portals, can he not just create one to Hyperborea?" At this it was Dariush that answered, coming up behind us.

"I am afraid that I cannot, as that place has been forbidden for a long time and remains a dormient realm, for the only life there has one foot on the side of life and the other on the side of death. It is the only reason the realm remains at all, for it is life that powers a realm." I swallowed hard before asking,

"Then how will the Rosetta stone work?"

"I do not know that it will, only that if it is still connected somehow, then it stands to reason that it is the last link to the realm." I nodded at this, hoping that he was right, and this was all prophesised to be this way.

"You know the exact location?" Dariush asked, and I looked to Lucius who gestured for me to tell him.

"Fort Julien, which is a fort located on the west bank of the Nile and north-west of Rashid or known as Rosetta, which is on the north coast of Egypt." Lucius gave me a look of shock as all this information came out, and I shrugged my shoulders before telling him,

"I work at a museum and specialise in Egyptian archaeology, so basically I'm what you would call a bit of a scholar." Dariush chuckled before nudging his brother and said teasingly,

"So, she is more intelligent than you, brother... I dare say, I like you immensely well, Miss Draven." I blushed at this and added the smile when Lucius rumbled a slight growl.

"Do you think you can work with the information I have given you?" I asked making him bow his head.

"We have been to this place before, not long after it was

built by the Mamluk Sultan, Qait Bey," Dariush answered making Lucius remark,

"He also built the Citadel of Qaitbay in Alexandria." Then when he caught me gaping up at him in surprise, he smirked in return and commented,

"You are not the only one educated, my little scholar." I chuckled at this, wondering whether or not I should tell him that he often called me this back in my own time. In end I didn't have time because Dariush was creating the portal, now tossing his long cloak back over his shoulders. He too was also dressed similar to Lucius, only without all the armour, although he wasn't lacking in weaponry.

The same style of sword I had seen him favour in Hell was hanging from his waist. It was called a shamshir and known as the 'Lion's fang' in the Persian language. He wore the same padded style jacket that was typically worn under armour, only Dariush's was slightly longer, ending in sections at his knees.

As for the portal, he was working his hands out in front of him as light erupted like a firework pinwheel before the centre started to distort the view of the forest, morphing it into something else. Then by the time the portal settled, it cleared enough that it was as if someone had suddenly dropped a live painting down from above that showed golden sands beyond.

"Are you ready?" Lucius asked me, making me nod and prompting him to take my hand.

"Shalom aleichem, Brother," Lucius said after turning to Dariush, who clapped a hand at his shoulder and said the same in return. Then he looked to me and said as way of goodbye,

"Miss Draven, it has been interesting."

"Call me, Amelia..." I paused and without taking my eyes from Lucius, I finished my claim by saying,

"Amelia Septimus." Lucius's eyes heated and this time, it was in a more tender way and not the lust or anger I usually associated his crimson eyes with. A grin tugged at his lips before we turned to face the portal. Then, as we clasped our hands together, entwining our fingers tight, we gave each other one last look before...

We walked through.

Thankfully Dariush's portal had put us right inside the abandoned fort. And well, seeing as Napoleon's forces only took possession of the dilapidated fort on 19 July 1799, only a few days before the Battle of Abukir, it meant that right now, it was fortunately *empty.*

They had also embarked on a hasty rebuilding, just before this battle took place. It was during this point that Lieutenant Pierre-François Bouchard spotted the slab with inscriptions on one side that the soldiers had uncovered.

As for us, it meant we would have to find it first. As for the fort's construction, it was a low, squat, rectangular structure with a central blockhouse that I knew would overlook the final few kilometres of the Nile before it joined the Mediterranean Sea.

"I don't suppose in those scholar days of yours, you discovered the exact location within the fort where we may find this Rosetta Stone of yours, do you?" I winked at him and said,

"Lucky for me, I had access to my father's library and in it contained a written document by a friend of the Lieutenant who discovered it with his men. Apparently, this Lieutenant Pierre-François Bouchard wrote to him and explained of their exciting discovery. He spoke of the stone's unearthing being when they were fixing the worst of the walls defences... and I don't know about you, but that part over there looks in pretty bad shape to me," I said, pointing to an area of crumbling pale yellow wall. Lucius nodded before we both started walking towards the area, making me thankful that I was here before July. Because this would have been a lot harder to accomplish had this place been teeming with French soldiers.

"What you said to your brother back there, it was Hebrew wasn't it?" I asked, making Lucius look down side-on at me and with a single brow raised, it was an expression I knew well.

"I guess I should not be surprised you are proficient in many languages, not given your birth-right," he replied evenly.

"I know basic Hebrew, but not enough to be classed as proficient," I said making him grin.

"I take it then that this line of enquiring is you asking me what it was I said to him?" I smirked, nudged his shoulder and teased,

"Now who is being the smarty pants?" He laughed at this, telling me,

"That is not a saying I am acquainted with but no doubt one I will hear often from Pipper in the future." I chuckled at that and muttered,

"Oh, that and many, many, many more." He kept his grin in place when he heard this before telling me,

"Peace be upon you… That is what it means."

"Well as nice a sentiment as that is, I don't think we will find much peace where we are going… look, is that what I think it is?" I said after we had approached the crumbling section of the wall. I was now pointing to a dark piece of black granodiorite that looked as if it had been used as part of the foundations at one point.

"Stand back," Lucius said, and waited until he thought I

was a good enough distance away before he used his mind to start clearing the remaining pale stone around it. I gasped the moment I saw it and unlike in all of the descriptions and written text about this discovery, it was not damaged like they all said.

No, it was... *whole.*

"It's... it's..." I stammered after Lucius had used his power to raise it up so as it was standing upright. And with its extra piece, it was now as big as a large door and had easily doubled in height.

"Amelia?" Lucius asked in concern.

"I don't understand. When they found the Rosetta stone, it was broken, and they said no other pieces were found. But if it was whole, then why...?" I let my question trail off as my confusion grew.

"I think you should be asking yourself *who,* as I don't believe the French were the first to find it after all," Lucius replied and it made sense. But just seeing it this way, in one piece, was incredible.

In fact, it actually brought tears to my eyes, as after all my years of studying it, knowing of the endless discoveries made because of it, this was like a dream seeing it intact this way. The Rosetta stone was the reason historians were able to crack the code of Ancient Egyptian hieroglyphs. It held three blocks of text, two of which they did not know, including Egyptian Demotic script. But thanks to the ancient Greek that was sectioned at the bottom part of the stone, this was something that scholars did know. Therefore, they were able to translate the rest. However, on this stone, unbeknown to the historical world beyond this point, there wasn't three texts at all...

There was actually four.

"Is that... Hyperborean text?" I asked in utter

astonishment when seeing the domed top part of the stone tablet that held carvings of a mountain range and elaborate curled script in symbols and letters I had never seen before.

"I have no knowledge of this," Lucius admitted, making me do the same.

"Me neither, I wouldn't have the first idea how to even read it, let alone understand it even if it is." I released a frustrated sigh, feeling like I had come so far and now to be faced with this puzzle was like a punch in the gut.

"Gods but what if it was all for nothing!" I complained making Lucius sigh.

"There must be a way, do not give up now, Amelia," he encouraged as I slumped down on one of the broken blocks of stone.

"I feel like I am missing something," I said half to myself as I shook my head.

"You said you are connected to the Wraiths, correct?" Lucius asked making me raise my head to look at him.

"Yeah."

"Then that also means you should be connected to the Realm," he surmised, making a good enough point, but it still meant nothing if I couldn't understand the bloody thing. Which is why I told him,

"But what good is it to be connected to the thing if I can't summon the portal, if I can't even make the door open by reading the text?"

"And how many doors do you walk through have text in order for them to open?" I frowned a moment as I processed what he was saying. I got to my feet and asked,

"You think it will recognise me as being worthy or something?"

"What I am saying is not all portals need words spoken, or keys to unlock them, sometimes all it takes is a simple touch and the acceptance of the right soul." My eyes widened at this before I launched myself at him. I then clung to his neck, kissed his cheek and said,

"You're a genius!" He grinned down at me mischievously and said,

"I will remind you of that when your lips are sparring with me in annoyance." I winked before kissing him again. Then I turned back to face the Rosetta Stone and took a deep breath.

"Well, here goes nothing," I said before raising my hand and slapping it to the stone.

Then I waited.

And waited.

And then waited some more… and still… *nothing.*

"Argh! Gods but what has a girl gotta do around here?!" I complained, stomping my foot and walking away.

"Amelia," Lucius admonished gently.

"No! I swear that unless you're some, Supernatural big ass King in this world, then you don't get… wait… oh Gods, that's it!" I shouted in excitement, now rushing back and before Lucius could ask me what the Hell was going on, I said,

"Lift me up."

"What?" he asked making me wave a hand at him, gesturing for him to do as I asked.

"Just trust me, lift me higher." Lucius shrugged his shoulders and gripped me around the waist so I could reach the top part of the tablet. Then I placed my hand at the centre of the Hyperborean text and the second I did, the mountains started to glow blood red.

"You did it," Lucius said, making me smirk back up at him.

"The Hyperborean were said to be taller." He chuckled at this and patted me on the head in a teasing way.

"My clever little scholar," he commented, giving me that warm feeling inside my chest as it reminded me of the Lucius I had left at home. As for the stone, the lines of the mountains were joined to a lined frame around the edges, and that same red glow started to travel down its sides until it was all the way around. The moment this happened the whole thing turned into a shimmering red portal and the second it did, Lucius took my hand in his just like last time.

Then he asked once more,

"Ready?"

"Born ready," I replied, making him grin before we took our first step inside...

A Forbidden lost realm.

CHAPTER 32
LIGHT IN THE ETERNAL DARKNESS

S tepping through into the lost Realm of Hyperborea was exactly how I expected it to be. It was a barren wasteland that looked exactly how it did in both my dreams and my memories. Dark, jagged mountains surrounded the edges of the vast open plane, making me wonder if they ever held any beauty before the Realm's demise. Had green lush life ever flourished on the now harsh dead lands we walked upon? Had the ocean of black sand ever once known clear blue waters, fields of flowers, or mountains of trees? As just like in my visions, not a single blade of grass swayed gently in the breeze, nor did the sounds of birds fill the empty grey sky above.

As for the portal, it thankfully brought us close to the castle and as soon as I felt the familiar rumbling beneath my feet, along with the thundering clashing sound of steal, I knew what it would be. The second Lucius heard it too, he pulled his sword free of its scabbard as if readying himself for the fight. I placed my hand atop of his at the hilt and told him,

"You won't need that, not yet."

"But I can hear the army in the distance," he disputed making me shake my head.

"They are made to fight, as if on a constant loop to be lived through and tortured with the horrors of what occurred that day. Trust me, they won't notice us as none of this is real, not to us anyway," I told him, yet despite this new knowledge, he kept his sword in his hand regardless.

We walked closer to the castle, one that at one time would have no doubt looked magnificent in all its towering glory. But right now, its regal splendour was long gone and only showed the aftermath of how brutal battle could be. This made even more so, as like before, there was a group of ghostly soldiers tearing down a metal statue of the King.

These had once been his brother's men, believing they had won the war against him. Which meant I knew what part of the past we were currently in and more importantly, where the King of Wraiths would be.

Selling his soul for the price of his victory.

I had already explained to Lucius what had happened here and how he had freed me. The grim and gruesome way he had no choice but to fool me enough to endure. That I'd had to eat his heart, while he made my mind believe it was nothing but a tender piece of steak. I had also explained about how he made it through to reach me in the first place.

Which meant I didn't know whether to be surprised or not that Lucius still had his powers. As the last time he had managed to infiltrate the connection the Wraith master had over me, he had been forced to do so as a mortal man. This had only changed when I had allowed him into my own mind, as before it had been the Wraith's mind he had been forced to try and access me through.

But I had to keep reminding myself that where we were now was real and no longer just some warped version of it.

But then, with that being said, it seemed as if the whole land was under the same spell the Wraiths were cursed with. Meaning the castle would change just as it did when I had witnessed it whole and just as when I had seen it crumbling.

As for its current state, well it was in the midst of being attacked, meaning this brought us some luck as we were able to easily slip inside. Especially considering there was an SUV-sized hole at the entrance, with twisted iron gates barely recognisable as ever once being functional enough to hold enemies at bay.

I could feel the tension coming from Lucius in waves as he was at the ready for anything. I could also tell his main concern was my safety, just as it usually was back in my own time. Although since I had kicked ass on the battlefield he'd had no choice but to trust in my abilities after that point. However, as for right now, there was no getting away from the root of his fears, because here I was mortal, and it was a fact neither one of us could ignore. Especially as I didn't fancy dying in this forgotten realm any time soon.

But Lucius wasn't the only one who was feeling apprehensive, because in all honesty, the Wraith Master scared the shit out of me. Not something I wanted to admit out loud but seeing as he had been controlling my dreams and giving me nightmares for the last three months, that fear had only grown in strength. Although I was curious as to why I hadn't yet experienced any of those nightmares since being back in the past. Was it because I was already on my quest?

"This place, it feels…"

"Wrong," I finished for Lucius as we crept across the broken tiles of the entrance hall, and when he started to make his way up one of the double staircases, I pulled him back.

"He won't be in there," I told him with a grim expression on my face, especially considering what we would soon find when entering the banqueting hall. The room was just as I remembered it, making me shiver at the first sight of the doors opening. Everything from the glossy diamond pattern floor in black and red stone, to the dark panelled walls and high vaulted ceilings. All those dead, bodyless creatures on the wall, their heads hung there like Demonic trophies for all to see. Weapons fanned out like lethal pieces of art and red up-lighting gave the room its hellish ambiance.

But like last time, the elements of the room were overshadowed by the horror displayed like some sickening feast for some blood thirsty beast. A long table dominated the room and its long blood-red tablecloth did nothing to disguise the contents of the silver platters laid out before the mad Wraith King.

"Gods," I heard Lucius utter under his breath and he wasn't wrong in his reaction. Although it was pretty clear to us both that any Gods of Hyperborea had long ago forsaken this land, as well as the cursed souls that had been forced to remain.

As for the reason of this Realm's downfall, he was currently sitting at the head of the table as I knew he would be, playing out the gruesome and despicable act of eating the hearts of those he was supposed to love the most. A sacrifice made and in return, an unbeatable army of Wraiths to command for eternity.

Until today.

"I thought you would never come," the King said, making me freeze in my tracks and as I did, Lucius came to stand in front of me protectively. The King scoffed at this and said,

"I have no intention of killing your woman, Vampire." I frowned at this and stepped around Lucius's towering frame… or at least I tried to before Lucius held me back.

"I don't trust him," he snarled in his direction, despite this being said to me.

"Neither do I, but something is different." Lucius growled at this before nodding and at the very least, lowering his hand enough to let me stand next to him.

"You know why we are here," Lucius said, his voice stern and unwavering in its authority.

"I do, just as I welcome your blade," he said making me frown.

"I don't understand, you wanted us to come?" I asked after shaking my head and trying to make sense of this. At this the King stood up, making Lucius react by holding out his sword and placing his free arm across me. As for the King's own reaction, he simply rested both his blood hands on the table either side of the heart he had been about to consume. Then he told us,

"I was counting on it." After this he raised his head and his soulless eyes burrowed into us, a gaze that looked void of any reason left for living.

"Very well, if you want my blade, *then you shall have it!*" Lucius replied in a dark and dangerous tone, as he was now taking long steps towards him. Something he continued to do until he was within striking distance. I held my breath prisoner after first gasping, holding myself frozen in place as Lucius raised up his sword and with a swift and brutal twist of his body, he sliced straight through the King.

A King who was now laughing like the mad man he was.

"I am a Wraith, boy, a blade by your hand will not touch me," he told him as Lucius narrowed his gaze in confusion. Then he looked back at me and said,

"I thought you said we were here to kill him?" That was when I shook my head as realisation hit me.

"Not you…" I said making the King laugh once more,

only this time the madness I heard there turned to a choked sob of pain. I then looked to the rest of the room, seeing the reason for his agony spread out in front of him, every day being forced to relive the horror of his sacrifice. Hi wife's body, slumped over the seat next to his own. The tragic sight of two smaller hearts each with a platter of their own and ones that his wife looked to have been reaching for when her own heart stopped beating. It was as sickening as it was dreadful. The most heinous of all acts committed when creating a life you should only ever vow to protect.

I remembered thanking the Gods that those little bodies had not been there to join her, no doubt their lives taken in their sleep, if mercy ever played a part in this nightmare. I looked over at it all with nothing but sadness, wondering how the Wraith King could even stand it. But that was when I realised that he had no choice. Because he may have had his victory, but all he gained in return was a prison of his own making.

This wasn't just his curse.

It was his eternal punishment.

That's when the last of the puzzle pieces started to slot into place, creating only the very picture of sadness.

"You lured me here... you used our connection to create my nightmares, to torture me with them," I said, making him cease his mad laughter and his silent sobbing enough to answer me.

"I knew if I could haunt you enough that you would come. That you would not forget your vow, that you would return to finish what... *what you started.*"

By the time he said this, Lucius had already made his way back to me, flinching the moment the doors suddenly opened and his Wraith army all started to file in. Lucius held up his sword, curling himself around me, and I could feel he was seconds away from bursting into his other form. Not that this would have done him any good, as Wraiths could not be killed.

But it didn't matter in the end.

Because these Wraiths would not hurt me. Not when they were mine to command. But I knew that's not why they were here now. No, there here to watch.

To watch... *and to wait.*

"It's okay, Lucius, they won't hurt us."

"How can you be so sure?" he asked, and I allowed myself a small grin when I saw my Wraith friend Trevor standing there at the front of them all. As if he was waiting for me to make my move. Just like they all were.

The King included.

So, knowing this, I looked up at Lucius, placed my hand at his cheek and looked deep into his steel blue eyes. Then I asked him,

"Do you trust me?" He swallowed hard, and I knew he forced himself to say,

"Yes."

"Then you must let me do this," I said, now wrapping my hand around the grip of his sword before pulling it free from his grasp.

"Amelia, wait!" he said as I started to walk away towards the King, making me look down at his fingers now curled around the top of my arm. I turned back to face him, and seeing the pained expression there made my heart ache.

"You can't trust him, we don't know what he will try and do," he argued making me release a sigh.

"Look around you, he has nothing left. It's why he lured me here."

"I don't understand," Lucius confessed with a shake of his head.

"He knows I am his last chance."

"His last chance at what?!" he asked, his voice strained as worry coated his words with frustration.

"To be set free," I said looking back at the King who had his head lowered, now holding something I couldn't see in both hands. Lucius's shoulders lowered as his resigned himself to the fact that this was why I was here. It was why we all were. So, I reached up and kissed him on his cheek, telling him,

"The Fates chose me for you but, Lucius... *they also chose me for this."* He nodded once before his hand fell from my arm, now letting me go and trusting me to do what was needed. Then I took a deep breath, straightened my spine and walked down the length of the room, each step taking me closer to that very Fate.

As soon as I was standing in front of him, I was left astonished as the King started to lower to his knees before me. I then looked back over the table of death and that of his wife's body, a gruesome reminder of all he had taken from his world. Then I looked back down to the one responsible for it all and asked,

"Do you atone for your sins?" He raised his head, and black tears began falling down his face. It was then that he told me,

"My sins may have been bred from my madness, but it was my own jealousy that was the only seed he needed for me to make a trade in death for that of my soul." I narrowed my eyes and asked,

"Who owns your soul?" He swallowed hard and with a grimace of twisted lips, he told me,

"Thanatos." The second he had hissed this name, it caused me to suck air through my teeth, knowing that Thanatos was the God of death in Greek Mythology. In fact,

he was the very personification of death and despite being only a minor figure in Greek mythology, he was often referred to, even if rarely appearing in person. Thanatos has no father, but was the son of Nyx, the Goddess of night, and his twin brother was Hypnos, the personification of sleep.

Now exactly what Thanatos wanted with King Theron's soul, I did not know, as he was usually the commander of Death, not the actual dealer of souls. Yet despite these questions running through my mind, right now was the not the time.

I was here to complete my vow.

"And the souls of your men?" Theron looked around the room, too many warriors to fit all in the once grand space. I knew they must have been spread out within the castle, since I had set them free of their glass cells months ago. That had been the very least I had managed to do.

"Their curse dies with me, for where I go, they will not follow," he told me, and I could barely believe how different he was now than that of the monster I had only ever known. But now, he looked like a broken man, barely a shell of frightening figure that had once hunted me. That had once stalked me through this phantom realm before then haunting my dreams as the last part of me he could reach.

And all of it had been just so I would be connected enough that I could put a right to his wrong. That I may cleanse the souls of his men and set them free of his sins. Sins that were never their own to pay for.

"Any last words?" I asked before I sentenced this king to an eternity in Hell, one he seemed to have already been living in. One of his own making. He looked back at his wife, the black tears falling once more, before he raised up a hand and I finally saw what he had been holding onto…

It was the necklace.

One I had seen before, and one I now knew belonged to his wife. It was a glittering blue stone as big as my palm, held suspended by a silver hand. As if someone was holding a chunk of jagged ice, for it wasn't flat or cut smooth by any machine. It was as if a single piece had cracked right a much bigger crystal, its finder leaving its raw beauty as it was. As it should be.

"Take it, for it was stolen long ago and doesn't belong in this realm. It deserves better… *just like she did,*" he added with sadness and self-loathing. And as her murderer, he deserved far worse than just the guilt he felt, this was true. But what if his madness had been Thanatos's doing? What if he had watered that seed of jealousy until nothing of the man he once was remained?

I couldn't think of that now.

I couldn't let the weight of that question bury me under a mountain of 'what ifs?'. Not when I was on the cusp of becoming this King's executioner. I just had to get this done. So, I reached for the necklace and wrapped its chain around my wrist before taking hold of the sword with both hands. Then while keeping his ink filled eyes on his dead wife's cold, lifeless face, he told me,

"I loved her, she was the rising sun, and I was the night."

"Then eternal darkness will be your punishment, King Theron… *Master of Wraiths, no more,*" I said before closing my eyes and plunging the sword straight through his heart, hearing the echoing cry of the Wraiths roaring all at once.

Then the world around us…

Crumbled.

CHAPTER 33
LOVE IS SACRIFICE

"AMELIA!" Lucius shouted across the room, seconds before I felt his arms coming around me, taking me clean off my feet and out of the way of a piece of the ceiling as it crashed to the floor. I shook my head from the jarring motion and found myself on the floor with Lucius on top of me.

Seconds after he had just saved me from getting crushed.

"We have to get out of here and back to the portal!" he shouted quickly.

I nodded in grave understanding as the world continued to shake around us, grabbing his hand as he pulled me to his feet after first getting to his own. I looked around the room, seeing all the Wraiths one by one starting to disappear, evaporating into thin air. All of them, with a fist to their hearts in silent salute. Each bowing their heads to me as one by one, their bodies were taken away, floating as if a breeze from the Heavens was sweeping in and finally free to take their souls from this horrific place.

"Come on!" Lucius urged, making me start running with

him as he navigated our way around the rubble, pulling me quicker as the castle started to crumble around us.

"Watch out!" I screamed as we made it to the entrance hall, and a piece of the staircase the size of table broke away and fell in front of us. This was when Lucius had enough of chancing me getting through this unscathed. Meaning he turned suddenly and scooped me up into his arms, now running with me across to the hole in the wall we had first entered through.

"Shit!" I shouted the moment the hole suddenly filled with broken stone from above, now completely blocking our escape.

"Follow me, I can get you out!" A new voice suddenly spoke and the moment I saw who it was, my mouth dropped in utter shock, making me shout in astonishment,

"Trevor?!" The man bowed his head to me, before gesturing for us to follow, something Lucius didn't hesitate to do. His face had been that of a human man, dressed now as the warrior he once was. His hazel eyes warm like honey, despite the deep frown and creases in his forehead that showed his concern for our escape. He was much taller than he had been as Wraith, with wide shoulders adding bulk to his frame. His long hair bellowing behind him as he ran with surprising speed for his size.

Lucius followed close behind, with me still in his arms, as we raced across the entrance hall and followed him through a rattling door frame at the other side. Both of us making it through just in time before it became another blocked door. And in sight of the roof caving in above it, it made me tighten my grip on Lucius just as his wings erupted to fly us over a falling pillar as it was crashing to the marble floor. I also watched as Trevor dropped to his thighs, skidding under the thing just in time, moving like a lithe cat before springing back up on the other side.

After this narrow escape, we then made it through what looked like a ballroom lined with scalloped marble pillars. All of which, were now falling down either side of us like dominos. We then burst into a drawing room, just as the panelled walls started exploding into splinters around us. It was as if they were being ignited from the room behind, making me scream as this wood-chipped shrapnel flew in every direction. This made Lucius use a wing to shield us from most of it as he continued to run, leap and jump over the destruction in our path.

But then, right in front of us was a large double, arched doorway that must have led back outside as another grand entrance. Oh and it was also one that looked like our last chance at making it out of here without being buried alive.

However, in these last few harrowing seconds, the whole castle shook more than it had done before and I soon knew why. This became obvious when I looked up as some movement above caught my eye. A section of the roof was missing and therefore I could now watch in horror as one of the castles turrets started pulling away from the rest of the building. But more than that, it was also falling down in front of the opening we were heading towards.

"Oh shit! We won't make it!" I screamed as I saw Trevor running for it and just making it through in time.

"We will!" Lucius roared back, now gripping me tighter and flying straight at it.

"No, we won't… no, we won't… NO… WE… WON'T… AHHHHH!" I screamed as I looked up to see the tower falling directly on top of us just as time seemed to slow down. Even as we both burst from the human sized hole that was left, doing so only milliseconds from being filled by the tower of stone, I still doubted that we had made it. The sounds of my own screams of terror drowned my ears as we made it through with not a single moment to spare!

Lucius tucked himself around me as we spiralled along the ground, landing hard with his wings taking most of the brunt of our fall.

"We... we made... it," I panted inside his arms as we were now finally free of the castle, feeling it thundering behind us. Lucius had his forehead to mine as we took the seconds needed to realise that we were both still alive.

"Amelia." He uttered my name as if he needed it to remind himself that I was still here, making me grip on to him tighter. Then after this grateful moment passed between us, he unfolded his wing so he could help me to my feet. After that, we looked back at the castle, seeing it had now started to completely cave in on itself. The black sand bellowing up in huge dust clouds all around it like some giant phantom was trying to consume it whole.

"The portal, we have to go!" Lucius said and I turned to see Trevor, the last Wraith standing. Only he was no longer a Wraith but that of a man. I pulled away from Lucius and walked closer to him.

He bowed his head to me, making me say,

"Oh sod it!" Then I ran into his arms, holding him to me, gripping him tight.

"Thank you, my friend," I whispered but before I could say more, he whispered back,

"I am sorry."

I pulled back, looking up into his bright hazel eyes, shaking my head as if I didn't understand. That was until he looked over my head to Lucius and then told me in a pained whisper,

"The portal is too weak... it only has enough strength to

send one of you back." I gasped at this as tears instantly filled my eyes.

"No... no, it can't be."

"You must go, my Queen... *go and save your heart,"* he said just as he too started to fade away just like the others.

"I... Trevor..."

"Aelian... my name is... Ael..." He never got to speak it again as his face was the last part of him to fade into nothing.

"We have to go!" Lucius said in panic as he looked towards the portal that I could now see was cracking. As if the piece of Hyperborea was about to shatter from the Rosetta stone. I grabbed his hand, Aelian's words playing in my head like a painful melody of sadness. Because if he was right, then I knew what that meant.

What it could only ever mean.

This was goodbye.

We ran towards the glowing red doorway, just as the first piece of the portal started to cave in on itself, getting sucked back through the way we had entered it. And I knew then that what Aelian had told me was true. It would only have the power to send one of us through.

And there was only one of us it could be.

So, knowing this within the depths of my soul, I took his hand, pulled him back and grabbed his face to me. Then I told him with tears falling down my cheeks in a never-ending flow that felt as if I would never have the power to stop them,

"I love you, Lucius, more than you will ever know. *More than this time has given us."*

"Amelia...?" he said my name in question, but I stopped him from saying anything more. I just needed to kiss him...

One.
Last.
Time.

Then I told him,

"Live for me, Lucius and… please… *forgive me,"* I said before I suddenly pushed with all my might at his chest. The action meaning that the last word I heard from his lips was my name being roared. A sound to match the pain on his face as he realised.

In this realm of pain and suffering, the very last act committed was not one of hate, or jealously.

Not of greed or selfishness.

No. It was one last act made by the heart.

As I…

Sacrificed myself for love.

CHAPTER 34
QUEST OF STONE

He was gone.
This was the end.
I fell to my knees and cried out in my grief as the rest of the portal broke away piece by piece, doing so a single heartbeat after Lucius had disappeared. The only solace in my soul was that I knew he would live on. Because I knew in that moment that I would never chance risking his life for my own. I would not do that, *not ever*. Because being stuck in this realm, where time had mirrored that of my own, meant that even if I made it home, there would have been no guarantee that Lucius would have been there waiting for me. That time would have reset itself like the past week had never happened.

Lucius had so much future left to live for. So many lives were left to rely on him… *so many more to come*. No, I couldn't take that from the world. But most of all, I didn't want to live in a world he wasn't a part of.

I did want to ever live without him.

So, as I sank down to the black sand, I cried not only for

my pain and my loss, I cried for the heartbreak I knew my actions had caused.

I wouldn't be coming home.

Not this time.

I could only hope that Sophia, Pip, Ella and my mother all made it back regardless of my Quest. I just hoped the Fates kind enough to grant me this one last thing. The only hope I had left, for I did not want my sacrifice to be in vain if others only suffered from it.

I raised my head up just as the mountains in the distance boomed as they too started to fall. Meaning that I knew then that I didn't have long before I would fall with them. The ground beneath me continued to shake as the end of this realm started to break away like the very cosmos were dying.

This was my end of days.

And what did they say…

"It was better to have loved and lost than… *never… loved at… all."* My voice broke at this as great sobs of agony gripped me, making me fist the clothes at my chest as I felt the part of me that loved the most, loved the hardest, loved the strongest, started to crack along with the world around me.

What I would give for just a few more words.

A few more I love you's.

A few more seconds so I could hold his gaze. His hand. His cheek. *His heart.*

Just.

A.

Few.

Seconds.

More.

Did I not deserve that!? Did I not deserve more than being

ripped apart like this?! *Did I not deserve more from the fucking Fates?!*

I suddenly stood on the shaking ground and screamed, throwing my hands back,

"GODS WHY!?" I heard something fall to the ground behind me, as I felt the chain slip from my wrist. Which was when I realised that it had been the necklace. I turned my head and saw it there, smeared in the sand like the last beautiful thing this world had to hold onto.

Well, it didn't fucking deserve its beauty!

Just like I didn't deserve its pain!

Its hatred!

Its fucking heartbreak!

Which was why I snatched it back up from the ground and just as the land around me began to crack and open up into great, mighty chasms, I screamed up at the sky,

"YOU CAN'T HAVE IT!" Then I threw it so hard to the ground that the crystal stone shattered into five pieces. The silver hand being the only part that remained, with the glittering stone lying in pieces, as if it had always meant to break. Then as I knew I only had minutes left, I fell hopelessly to my knees, lowered my head into my hands and cried Lucius's name over and over again. For I wanted the sound of my love for him to be the last thing from my lips. The last thing heard in this world.

"I love you, Lucius… I love you… my Lucius, my Vampire King… I love you… until the end of time and beyond," I whispered and just when I thought I would feel myself falling back into an abyss opening up behind me, I felt something that shouldn't have been possible. I felt something pull me forward, *not backwards.*

"No… it… it… can't be… possible," I uttered in

bewilderment as I looked up to see a glowing blue light right in front of me.

It was the light of a portal!

One that was created by the five pieces of stone that had shattered. They were now held suspended in the air, circling around in a large oval shape, keeping some kind of magical connection between them. A shimmering space between them, calling me forward like a beacon of hope. What lay beyond it, I didn't know but I wasn't going to wait here long enough to doubt it would be no better than dying here alone.

So, I quickly got up to my feet and as the land behind me started to fall away, I jumped, leaping for the portal just in time. I started to fall through it, reaching with my hands and saying goodbye to the death of a realm in my wake.

But it wasn't like any portal I had ever been through before, as instead of instantly stepping into another world, another place, another time, this one held me suspended. I looked back at the closing hole I had just stepped through to see the destruction I was gladly leaving behind.

I then watched wide eyed, as the pieces of stone that had created the portal all got sucked through with me. These pieces all then started spinning around, like some out-of-control spiralling vortex. They travelled as I did, backwards, as I was sucked further down into this seemingly never-ending rabbit hole.

Then one by one, they flew off in different directions, as if no longer being able to keep the connection they once had. They quickly disappeared beyond the portal walls until the last one went out of sight.

And the second they did.

I fell before I landed.

Landed…

. . .

Into a Vampire's arms.

CHAPTER 35
ENDING WITH PERFECTION

L ooking at myself in the mirror now as I waited for the others to arrive, I couldn't help but feel blessed at how far we had come. Or should I say…

What we had overcome.

Three months ago, when I had fallen into Lucius's arms, I had felt as if I had died and woken up in Heaven. I had felt his arms around me and instantly started sobbing. I felt as if I had been broken into a thousand pieces and the second I made it back to him, he instantly pieced me back together.

"You're here! You're… really… here…" I sobbed, gripping onto him so hard, it was as if I was holding on for fear that some other portal would appear only to rip us apart again.

"I'm here, Amelia… as I always was *and always will be,*" he told me, making fresh new tears fall.

"I thought… I thought I had lost you… I thought…" I couldn't finish that sentence before heart-wrenching sobs burst free and I buried myself in his neck, soaking it with my tears.

"Oh, Sweetheart." He had whispered against my hair as

he held my head to his chest and kept me in his arms. And right then, I knew there would be a time for facing his anger, his disappointment, his feeling of betrayal. I knew I had all of these things to come but right now, this was all I needed.

He was all I needed.
And he knew it.

But this wasn't all I had to cry about, as the utter relief I felt in my heart when I peeked over his shoulder and saw the sight I did stole my breath. For there was Pip held in Adam's embrace. There was Sophia wrapped up in Zagan's arms. And there was my mother, gripping onto my father, crying with relief just as I was. But my heart broke as I saw Ella running to my parents, crying out in sorrow and when I looked around for another and didn't see him… I knew why. Because when I saw her there alone, I knew then that her tears were not shed like ours were. They weren't in relief and happiness like we experienced.

It was in grief.

As there was no Jared there waiting for her.

I knew I should have gotten up at this point. I knew I should have run to my family. To grab each of them to me and hold them tight. To tell them how much I loved them. To tell them I was overjoyed with happiness that they were all safe.

But I couldn't move.

Because for those next few minutes, I remained exactly where I was and absorbed every last thing that was Lucius. I was selfish in my comfort. But after believing only moments ago that it was the end… *that it was our end…* and that I would die and never see Lucius's face again. Never feel his touch, or hear his voice…

I needed this.
So, I took it.

I took all he had to give me and because of it, I felt his love pouring from him with every breath I took. A love that, in the end, had the strength to save us all. And it was that same love that brought us to now and as I smoothed my hands down my white wedding dress, I took a deep breath when hearing a knock at the door.

"Come in," I said, my eyes softening when I saw the handsome man enter wearing a tux and looking like he was ready for the red carpet.

"Dad," I said blushing the moment he saw me and froze in his steps at the very sight of me. He even had to shake his head and clear his throat as if trying to refocus enough to think, making me grin. Then he walked closer to me, his long legs eating up the space between us in seconds.

"Oh Amelia, how beautiful you are, my daughter," he said making tears form as he took both my hands in his.

"I could not be a more proud father and you looking beautiful enough to envy the Gods, is only one reason of many."

"Dad, you're going to make me cry," I told him softly before biting my lower lip.

"Then as you hear my words and take them into your heart, I consider each tear a gift, for you, my girl, are the strongest of us all, for your heart and courage knows no bounds and I am only happy to give you to away today because Lucius knows it. He understands it, he is grateful for it, and he treasures it. Which means that I give you away today for love and as we both know, there is no nobler a cause. I love you, Amelia… *my little girl,"* he said pulling me into his arms just as I watched a single tear fall from his eye.

"Oh Dad! Thank you… thank you for always being there for me. I love you."

"As I love you... *always,*" he returned tenderly before pulling back. "I will meet you at the altar."

I nodded, unable to speak for fear of making my face blotchy with tears. He then ran the backs of his fingers down my cheek and smiled to himself before stepping away and leaving the room.

I turned back to the mirror and as I took in my reflection, I could barely believe I was at this point. Three months ago, I believed it was the end and now, well...

Now I knew it was only the beginning.

I looked down at myself and laughed at the irony of it all, feeling emotional and still trying to process all that had happened. Something I knew wouldn't be achieved until later today. So, with this in mind I rearranged the layers and layers of ruffle tulle around my legs, that fell in a waterfall style, adding volume to the skirt. It also had a dramatic train at the back. One that was added to by the gathered bodice that wrapped around me and ended in a bow at the base of my spine. The long lengths at the end of this bow added to the train as the same tulle material was crossed over my torso to create a V-shape neckline. Which also admittedly had a bit of a plunge to it to show some cleavage. An added detail I knew Lucius would appreciate.

In fact, I was just tucking an escaping loose spiral behind my ear from the cascades of curls pinned half back from my face, held there by simple pearls, when I heard a commotion. It happened right outside the door and adding to this banging sound, I heard muffled voices. So, I walked straight to the suite door and opened it to find Sophia, Pip, and my mum quickly stuffing something into what looked like a supply closet.

"Well at least I don't have to worry about any fingers this

time," I heard Pip say just as she was elbowed by Sophia hushing her. Then all three guilty faces turned to me.

"Do I want to know on my wedding day?" I asked as I took in the comical sight of three stunning ladies in their finest now all trying to look casual as they leaned against the door like they had all just stopped for a break.

"Nope."

"Probably not."

"I would say yes but I will get elbowed again… so no." All three of them spoke one after the other, making me sigh.

I had seen everyone as I was getting ready, along with my bridesmaids, crying when I finally saw Wendy for only the second time after such a long time. We had been at the hotel since last night, one where Lucius was not happy to conform to tradition by not spending the night with me before the wedding. However, his groomsmen had stolen him away, giving him a stag night, just like my bridesmaids had given me a Hen.

Although, when Lucius had dropped onto my balcony late last night, opened the door and started getting naked I can't say I was surprised. Nor was it unwelcome as I sat up just as he was taking off his clothes, making me think for a few seconds that I was having a sex dream. One that turned out even better as I got the sex part without the frustrating *it isn't real* dream.

He had snuck out earlier this morning after we had fallen asleep in each other's arms. Of course, we were already married, so neither of us thought 'the bad luck' stuff counted. But I had smiled when I woke up to find a single red rose on my bed and the letter written underneath it.

One that simply said,

Today you make me the happiest man
in the world for a second time...
Meet you at the altar,
My beautiful wife.
Lucius x

Which was why I grinned down at the letter I had purposely left on the table next to my bridal bouquet of stunning red roses.

"Yes, I will, handsome," I said before picking them up, turning to my time-traveling boobateers and said,

"Let's get this show on the road."

"Where we are going, there are no roads... only hearts... see what I did there?" Pip said, adding this extra part to the line and making me hug them each to me.

"There sure is, Pip... there sure is," I said, looking back at that letter before closing the door with a smile on my face.

~

"Well, I think that went well," Lucius said after we had finished our first dance as man and wife in the more traditional sense. Because I had been walked down the aisle with my hand nestled in my father's arm and given away to Lucius, who looked close to tearing up when first seeing me.

We had then said our vows and it had been utter perfection. However, it wasn't over yet. Not when I had one last surprise to bestow on my husband. Hence why I told him,

"It's not over yet... come on." I then took his hand, gathering up my skirt and giggling as I dragged him through the grounds of Witley Court where I had wanted to get married, just like my parents had. Because with it being so close to the Janus temple, I thought it was symbolic of how precious time really was…

Even to an immortal.

So, I pulled him though the grounds, making him growl when we approached the fountain.

"Please don't tell me this surprise of yours includes the 18th century?" he said dryly after he had obviously heard all from me of what had happened three months ago. I smiled wryly at him and teased,

"Maybe." At this he moaned making me grin.

"Come on, old man, time for my surprise," I said as I pulled him past the fountain and towards the stone pavilion with its domed roof. The lush green grounds of Witley Court were now graced by the golden touch of the sun setting. The vibrant flower beds, ornate terraces and magnificently landscaped gardens made for the perfect setting to tell the man I loved of how he had my heart for all eternity. But for what I wanted to tell him, I had another place in mind.

One more perfect than even this.

"Now this is more like it," he said as soon as he thought we were alone, pulling me into his arms and kissing me under the stone arch in between the pavilion's pillars. Kissing me breathless just like he had the ability to do in any time period. However, we weren't as alone as he would have hoped for.

"I would offer my congratulations, but I fear I might get punched for interrupting."

"Dariush?" Lucius asked the moment his brother stepped from behind one of the other pillars. Of course, he had been a part of Lucius's groomsmen and therefore had been at the ceremony. Which meant that him being here now, well it had been my idea and Lucius knew this the moment he looked back at me to find me nodding to his brother.

"What are you up to, wife of mine?" he asked, making me wink at him.

"You'll see… Dariush, if you please," I said giving him the go ahead to create a portal. Then I took Lucius by the hand and said to Dariush,

"Give us half an hour." Then laughed when Lucius said,

"I don't know where I am going but make it longer." Then I pulled him through the portal, holding my free hand against the bright sunshine as we stepped straight into our poppy field.

A fictional place that had been created for moments like this as I learned a while back that the field had been lost long ago to the evolution of time. However, the memory of it was never lost in his mind and it was a place that would always be special for us and today, I would make it even more so.

"Now this is the perfect ending to a perfect day… or it will be when I finally get you naked." I laughed at this as he pulled me into him and tipped my head back to kiss me. And this time, we weren't interrupted. Meaning I waited until after the kiss had finished before finally confessing my secret.

"I have a gift for you," I said when pulling from his lips, making him grin down at me.

"You are the only gift I need in my life," he told me making me want to melt into him.

But instead, I said,

"Are you sure about that?"

"Amelia?" he said my name in question before I took a deep breath, placed his hand to my belly, and with tears of happiness in my eyes, I looked up at him and told him the very last thing he ever expected to hear…

"Baby… I'm pregnant."

EPILOGUE
LUCIUS

SIX MONTHS LATER

erfection.

My life was utter perfection.

Because as I looked down at the sleeping bundle of beauty in my arms, I knew that everything in my thousands of years had led me to this point. All the sacrifices I had made, all the pain I had endured, simply vanished the moment Amelia finally came into my life. And since then, each day was the gift of life that kept giving. Each moment shared was like seeing the world with fresh new eyes and I blessed each day, finally having something to thank the Gods for.

For the Fates were finally on my side.

I knew that with every breath I took, breathing new life into these old bones that now felt reborn. Just like the beautiful little girl in my arms.

Our little Lia.

Named such, for she would have never been born had it

not been for my wife's courage and strength to make such a harrowing journey to the past.

Just like our son.

Zachary.

A name Amelia had picked, for it couldn't have been more apt in its Hebrew meaning,

'The Lord has remembered'

As soon as she told me this, moments after giving birth to the twins, I had tears in my eyes, unable to say more than tell her that it was perfect as I kissed her forehead. As for my daughter, I had picked her name to symbolise the past and what it now meant to both of us. To be blessed with children had been a joy I never believed I would have been lucky enough to experience ever again.

Which was why as I looked down at my sleeping daughter, I couldn't help but bite my lip in order to keep my tears of happiness at bay. They had been born only a few weeks earlier and naturally still looked tiny in my hands. Making them so precious, that I had feared my own strength when even holding them for the first time.

"Well, your son most definitely takes after you, as I swear his appetite never ends," Amelia said now joining me in the living space, sitting down next to me with my son in her arms and like his sister, fast asleep after his meal.

I smirked at her in response, especially when she warned,

"Don't say it." I laughed at this, knowing she spoke of my insatiable need for her that never wavered. Even when at her biggest, I found the primal thought of her carrying my children so fucking sexy I was a man obsessed. And thankfully for me, the uncomfortable task of carrying two babies for nine months hadn't tamed her own insatiable needs. Meaning some days consisted of little else than claiming her body in between bouts of eating a startling amount of junk food on her part.

But I had to say, the added curves motherhood had awarded her with only added to her beauty, for even now, I could barely keep my hands off her. Admittedly being thankful she was fully healed after the birth. And I wasn't the only one, for if she wasn't attending to our children, *she was attending to me.*

Or I her.

Gods but I fucking loved my wife!

Fucking perfection.

My life was now the very embodiment of flawless.

Who would have ever of thought such a thing possible? *Not I.*

"Okay, so I am thinking next time we strap you to that damn thing and just see if we can get anything… who knows, maybe male supernatural's can lactate after all." I couldn't help but laugh at this, making little Lia squirm in my arms and making me freeze my movements.

"I'm serious, I think you need to be the one who feels like the cow for once… don't worry, I have nipple cream if it helps convince you." Again, I laughed, and my daughter woke further.

"Can you stop making me laugh, you will wake her," I said in gentle reprimand, one she would never take seriously, for she was always making me laugh. But as I said this, I rubbed Lia's little full belly, feeling her tiny hand wrap around my large finger. Then something curious happened as she pull my finger and put it in her mouth. I decided in that moment to get my own back.

"Oww!" I said feigning the reaction.

"What… what is it?" Amelia asked falling for it. Then I shot her a look of astonishment and said,

"She just bit me." Amelia gasped and holding Zachary closer to her chest, she leaned in and uttered,

"Nooo... really?" That's when I winked at her and said,

"Like mother like daughter." At this she burst out laughing and said,

"Yeah, whatever, Vampy."

I growled playfully, making her lean over and kiss me. And once more my life was filled with love and laughter when she pulled back long enough to say,

"I'm sorry, handsome, what I meant to say was... yeah, whatever..."

"My Eternal Life Partner."

The End.

ACKNOWLEDGMENTS

Well first and foremost my love goes out to all the people who deserve the most thanks which is you the FANS!

Without you wonderful people in my life, I would most likely still be serving burgers and writing in my spare time like some dirty little secret, with no chance to share my stories with the world.

You enable me to continue living out my dreams every day and for that I will be eternally grateful to each and every one of you!

Your support is never ending. Your trust in me and the story is never failing. But more than that, your love for me and all who you consider your 'Afterlife family' is to be commended, treasured and admired. Thank you just doesn't seem enough, so one day I hope to meet you all and buy you all a drink! ;)

To my family…

To my crazy mother, who had believed in me since the beginning and doesn't think that some"thing great should be hidden from the world. I would like to thank you for all the hard work you put into my books and the endless hours spent caring about my words and making sure it is the best it can be for everyone to enjoy. You, along with the Hudson Indie Ink team make Afterlife shine.

To my crazy father who is and always has been my hero in life. Your strength astonishes me, even to this day! The love and care you hold for your family is a gift you give to the Hudson name.

To my lovely sister,

If Peter Pan had a female version, it would be you and Wendy combined. You have always been my big, little sister and another person in my life that has always believed me capable of doing great things. You were the one who gave Afterlife its first identity and I am honoured to say that you continue to do so even today. We always dreamed of being able to work together and I am thrilled that we made it happen when you agreed to work as a designer at Hudson Indie Ink.

To my children, my wonderful daughter"Ava...who yes, is named after a cool, kick-ass demonic "bird and my sons, Jack who is a little hero and Halen

And last but not least, to the man that I consider my soul mate. The man who taught me about real love and makes me not only want to be a better person but makes me feel I am too. The amount of support you have given me since we met has been incredible and the greatest feeling was finding out you wanted to spend the rest of your life with me when you asked me to marry you.

All my love to my dear husband and my own personal Draven... Mr Blake Hudson.

To My Team...

I am so fortunate enough to rightly state the claim that I have the best team in the world!

It is a rare thing indeed to say that not a single person that works for Hudson Indie Ink doesn't feel like family, but there you have it. We are a Family.

Sarah your editing is a stroke of genius and you, like others in my team, work incredibly hard to make the Afterlife world what it was always meant to be. But your personality is an utter joy to experience and getting to be a part of your crazy feels like a gift.

Sloane, it is an honour to call you friend and have you working for Hudson Indie Ink. Your formatting is flawless and makes the authors books look perfect.

Xen, your artwork is always a masterpiece that blows me away and again, I am lucky to have you not only a valued member of my team but also as another talented Author represented by Hudson Indie Ink.

Lisa, my social media butterfly and count down Queen! I was so happy when you accepted to work with us, as I knew you would fit in perfectly with our family! Please know you are a dear friend to me and are a such an asset to the team. Plus, your backward dancing is the stuff of legends!

Libby, as our newest member of the team but someone I consider one of my oldest and dearest friends, you came in like a whirlwind of ideas and totally blew me away with your level of energy! You fit in instantly and I honestly don't know what Hudson Indie Ink would do without you. What you have achieved in such a short time is utterly incredible and want you to know you are such "a short time is utterly incredible and want you to know you are such an asset to the team!

And last but by certainly not least is the wonderful Claire, my right-hand woman! I honestly have nightmares about waking one day "and finding you not working for Hudson Indie Ink. You are the backbone of the company and without you and all your dedicated, hard work, there would honestly be no Hudson Indie Ink!

You have stuck by me for years, starting as a fan and quickly becoming one of my best friends. You have supported me for years and without fail have had my back through thick and thin, the ups and the downs. I could quite honestly write a book on how much you do and how lost I would be without you in my life!

I love you honey x

Thanks to all of my team for the hard work and devotion to the saga and myself. And always going that extra mile, pushing Afterlife into the spotlight you think it deserves. Basically helping me achieve my secret goal of world domination one day…evil laugh time… Mwahaha! Joking of course ;)

Another personal thank you goes to my dear friend Caroline Fairbairn and her wonderful family that have embraced my brand of crazy into their lives and given it a hug when most needed.

For their friendship I will forever be eternally grateful.

As before, a big shout has to go to all my wonderful fans who make it their mission to spread the Afterlife word and always go the extra mile. Those that have remained my fans all these years and supported me, my Afterlife family, you also meant the world to me.

All my eternal love and gratitude,
Stephanie x

ABOUT THE AUTHOR

Stephanie Hudson has dreamed of being a writer ever since her obsession with reading books at an early age. What first became a quest to overcome the boundaries set against her in the form of dyslexia has turned into a life's dream. She first started writing in the form of poetry and soon found a taste for horror and romance. Afterlife is her first book in the series of twelve, with the story of Keira and Draven becoming ever more complicated in a world that sets them miles apart.

When not writing, Stephanie enjoys spending time with her loving family and friends, chatting for hours with her biggest fan, her sister Cathy who is utterly obsessed with one gorgeous Dominic Draven. And of course, spending as much time with her supportive partner and personal muse, Blake who is there for her no matter what.

Author's words.

My love and devotion is to all my wonderful fans that keep me going into the wee hours of the night but foremost to my wonderful daughter Ava...who yes, is named after a cool, kick-ass, Demonic bird and my sons, Jack, who is a little hero and Baby Halen, who yes, keeps me up at night but it's okay because he is named after a Guitar legend!

Keep updated with all new release news & more on my website
www.afterlifesaga.com
Never miss out, sign up to the
mailing list at the website.

Also, please feel free to join myself and other Dravenites on
my Facebook group
Afterlife Saga Official Fan
Interact with me and other fans. Can't wait to see you there!

- facebook.com/AfterlifeSaga
- twitter.com/afterlifesaga
- instagram.com/theafterlifesaga

ALSO BY STEPHANIE HUDSON

Afterlife Saga
Afterlife
The Two Kings
The Triple Goddess
The Quarter Moon
The Pentagram Child /Part 1
The Pentagram Child /Part 2
The Cult of the Hexad
Sacrifice of the Septimus /Part 1
Sacrifice of the Septimus /Part 2
Blood of the Infinity War
Happy Ever Afterlife /Part 1
Happy Ever Afterlife / Part 2
The Forbidden Chapters

*

Transfusion Saga
Transfusion
Venom of God
Blood of Kings
Rise of Ashes
Map of Sorrows
Tree of Souls
Kingdoms of Hell

Eyes of Crimson

Roots of Rage

Heart of Darkness

Wraith of Fire

Queen of Sins

Knights of Past

Quest of Stone

*

The HellBeast King Series

The Hellbeast King

The Hellbeast Fight

The Hellbeast's Mistake

The Hellbeast's Claim

The Hellbeast's Prisoner

The Hellbeast's Sacrifice

*

The Shadow Imp Series

Imp and the Beast

Beast and the Imp

*

King of Kings

Dravens Afterlife

Dravens Electus

*

Kings of Afterlife

Vincent's Immortal Curse

*

Afterlife Academy: (Young Adult Series)

The Glass Dagger

The Hells Ring

The Reapers Book

*

Stephanie Hudson and Blake Hudson

The Devil in Me

Ingram Content Group UK Ltd.
Milton Keynes UK
UKHW010831180723
425342UK00001B/19